"Is the spider dangerous?"

"I know our biology teacher pretty well. Fred would know if the spider is dangerous or not, but I don't think that it is."

"I'm not sure waiting to be bitten is the way to find that out," Hoyt said, his imagination already racing toward harm to Reese and the baby.

"Well, I wasn't bitten. And we have a few at the high school. I'd hardly think the school board would appreciate having poisonous animals around the kids."

The thought that the danger was likely minimal went some way toward calming his racing heart but he couldn't quite banish the sense of menace that came with whatever had brought a spider to her front door. Texas was known for its wild creatures, and his cowboy boots were way more practical than they were for show, but it was the mysterious doorbell that kept gnawing at him.

Did someone deliberately do this to scare Reese?

And why?

* * *

**We hope you enjoy the Midnight Pass,
Texas miniseries**

* * *

**If you're on Twitter, tell us what you
think of Harlequin Romantic Suspense!
#harlequinromsuspense**

Dear Reader,

Welcome back to Midnight Pass, Texas. For those of you who visited this past August, you know that this small town, nestled along the banks of the Rio Grande, is home to one of the biggest cattle ranches in Texas—Reynolds Station.

Youngest brother and former special ops soldier Hoyt Reynolds is known for his stoic (read: grumpy) attitude. That doesn't stop the whole town from swooning when he swaggers down Main Street in his jeans and boots. Nor has it stopped Reese Grantham from noticing Hoyt, well, pretty much her entire life.

She's still struggling to get past her father's suicide the prior spring, after his murderous ways were discovered, and Reese finds herself alone one night at the Border Line bar. That's where Hoyt finds her, and he's determined to take care of her and cheer her up if at all possible. Their evening turns into something more and, much to their mutual surprise, goes from a delicious memory to something even bigger—a baby.

When nameless, faceless threats endanger Reese, Hoyt knows he must protect the mother of his child at all costs. But will protecting her put him in the line of fire, as well?

I hope you enjoy *Special Ops Cowboy* and I look forward to sharing the stories of Hoyt's other two siblings, Ace and Arden, in future books. In the meantime, if you want to begin with the first in the series, *The Cowboy's Deadly Mission* is available now.

Best,

Addison Fox

SPECIAL OPS COWBOY

—

Addison Fox

HARLEQUIN®ROMANTIC SUSPENSE

Recycling programs
for this product may
not exist in your area.

ISBN-13: 978-1-335-66191-3

Special Ops Cowboy

Printed in U.S.A.

Addison Fox is a lifelong romance reader, addicted to happy-ever-afters. After discovering she found as much joy writing about romance as she did reading it, she's never looked back. Addison lives in New York with an apartment full of books, a laptop that's rarely out of sight and a wily beagle who keeps her running. You can find her at her home on the web at www.addisonfox.com or on Facebook (Facebook.com/addisonfoxauthor) and Twitter (@addisonfox).

Books by Addison Fox

Harlequin Romantic Suspense

Midnight Pass, Texas

The Cowboy's Deadly Mission
Special Ops Cowboy

The Coltons of Red Ridge

Colton's Deadly Engagement

The Coltons of Shadow Creek

Cold Case Colton

The Coltons of Texas

Colton's Surprise Heir

Dangerous in Dallas

Silken Threats
Tempting Target
The Professional
The Royal Spy's Redemption

Visit the Author Profile page at Harlequin.com.

In loving memory of Annette Deoria

1921–2018

I believe angels walk among us because of you.

Author's Note

For those of you familiar with cattle ranching, you will note I've played with the time of year cattle are branded. As calves are typically branded around two to three months of age, branding season is normally wrapped up by May, not early August. I hope you'll forgive the license I took in shifting the timeline to suit the story.

Chapter 1

Her mother had always said gossip was the devil's work. That the idle prattle of small towns had no place in their lives. Of course, Reese Grantham thought reflectively, her mother had offered up those pearls of wisdom before her father had turned into the devil incarnate, doing far worse than some dismissive chatter over produce bins at the market.

Whatever disaster Serena Grantham had hoped to avert by diligently avoiding discussion of the misfortunes of others throughout her life had all been for naught.

That fact became abundantly clear to Reese two months earlier, when Russ Grantham was transported to the morgue due to a self-inflicted gunshot to the head. Officers from the precinct he'd served for thirty years had solemnly carried out the transfer. And it was only that self-inflicted gunshot that had kept those same officers from hauling him into the police station on murder charges stemming from Russ's serial rampage killing drug dealers.

Some said Russ had snapped over the loss of his own son to drugs years before. Others whispered that it was bad blood, finally letting loose, hidden away all these years behind the noble facade of police captain. Still others—the ones who whispered in solemn tones—said it was a public service. Their small Texas border town, Midnight Pass, had been overrun by the drug trade and it was high time someone did something about it. So really, Reese acknowledged to herself as Tabasco Burns set down a beer and a whiskey chaser in front of her, what was a little gossip compared to all that?

"You sure you want this? I can still fix you a white wine spritzer like you usually order. Won't charge you for this." Tabasco waved a hand over the beer and whiskey, like a magician who could make it all go away.

Reese thought longingly of chardonnay but shook her head. She needed to forget and a watered-down glass of wine wasn't going to get her where she needed to go. It was the very reason she'd come to The Border Line for the evening. "I'm good, but thanks."

Tabasco looked about to argue but only nodded instead, his grizzled features going soft as he stared at her across the scarred bar. "I am glad to see you. It's been too long."

She nodded and reached for the beer, unable to acknowledge him with anything more for fear the lump in her throat would turn too swiftly to tears.

Tabasco took a few more beats to look at her before he moved on. He knew his customers well and had a keen sense for when they needed an open ear or a blind eye.

With the same determination that had her calling a car and heading to The Border Line bar on a hot summer Tuesday, Reese took a sip of her beer. No time like the present. She'd numb the pain while facing the gossip and maybe give half the damn town something to talk about other than her father's crimes and subsequent suicide.

She was done with being the perfect daughter in a family that seemed functionally unable to be halfway normal. Or what she had left of one.

Even if that meant she now had a life she'd worked hard for, a job that she loved teaching high school English and a small house on the opposite end of town from her parents, decorated to her exact specifications and bearing the stamps of her own self-sufficiency. A lawn mown each week by her own hand. Address stamps that had no one's name on them but hers. And a Christmas tree in her garage she'd put up the past two seasons all on her own.

Who knew it could feel so damn good to pay a mortgage each month?

And it did feel good. She wasn't a woman who drowned her sorrows—she'd always found the mental fortitude to deal with what life tossed her way, reading, thinking of her students and their future, or finding new interests to explore—but for some reason the little whisper that tantalized her earlier that day, suggesting a night away from her cares was in order, had taken root.

With that thought in mind, she reached for her drinks. Although she preferred wine, the beer went down smooth enough, a cool respite from the heat outside and the perpetually ashy, bitter taste that had coated her tongue for the better part of two months. She'd nearly convinced herself the whiskey would be as good, only to shoot the glass and nearly fall off her barstool in a choking fit.

"Hey there." A large hand covered her back while another steadied her arm. She jumped at the contact, even as a line of fire coated her throat, burning away anything that had been there.

Wide warm circles smoothed over her back and Reese accepted the gentle touch as one last racking cough shook her shoulders. The worst behind her, she lifted her gaze off the scarred wood and straight into the deep green eyes of Hoyt Reynolds.

Compelling, mysterious eyes, she thought, as their edges crinkled with a gentle smile. "You okay?"

"Sure." Her voice was still strained from the coughing. "Wrong pipe."

Hoyt's gaze shifted to the empty shot glass. "Wrong drink, I'd say."

Right drink, wrong drinker, her conscious taunted, but she kept it to herself, pushing bravado into her tone as her voice grew stronger. "It's what I wanted. And I think I'll have another."

The smile faded, replaced with something she didn't want to think about.

Pity.

She'd seen the same expression on the town's faces more than once in her life and she refused to get comfortable with it. This was her battle to fight and her long walk to take. She would get through this.

And still, something inside of her persisted. If she could only understand the reasons for her father's choices maybe she could push aside the awful well of sadness and anger and fury that came from the fact that Russ Grantham had thought it was acceptable to torture and kill others. Maybe she could push past the frustration that once again, her life had been thrown into chaos by the choices of her family and somehow, see her way past the wreckage.

Only she hadn't seen past anything. Not for one single minute in all the minutes that had come since the day her father kidnapped Annabelle Granger, a fellow police officer, for getting too close to the truth. The fact that he'd ultimately done the right thing and let Belle go hadn't mattered.

Nor had the gun he'd placed to his head.

In the blink of an eye, Reese was right back to those days in high school when all the effort in the world to do the right thing and get good grades and act perfect still couldn't make up for her older brother's drug addiction. When the sound of her mother's crying could be heard late at night, muffled softly from the living room in their small ranch house at the edge of town. When her father's stiff back and broad shoulders set beneath a uniform that bore captain's bars still couldn't keep Jamie Grantham out of trouble.

"You sure about that?" Hoyt asked, effectively cutting into her memories far better than her first shot.

"I am."

Hoyt let out a long sigh before taking the empty seat next to her. "Then I can't let you do it alone."

"I don't—" She broke off as Hoyt waved down Tabasco, circling his fingers in the signal for another round.

Undeterred by her protest and big enough that she

knew he'd be immovable once he sat down, Reese took the opportunity to look at him instead. She knew Hoyt Reynolds—they'd grown up in the same town—but she'd never spent much time with him beyond an occasional night out with mutual friends or enough to say hi at town functions. He was a loner by nature and had a grumpy, affectionately surly personality that had become somewhat legendary in the Pass.

Even without her personal connection—her father's last potential victim, Belle Granger, was engaged to Hoyt's brother, Tate—she'd have known Hoyt anywhere.

Everyone knew the Reynolds boys. The trio—along with their sister, Arden—ran Reynolds Station, one of the largest working beef ranches in the state. They'd run free as young men, but all had quickly settled down after their father's poor business practices had come to light about a decade before. Hoyt had been away in the service—marines, she thought—but had eventually come back, joining his family in the work of restoring the Reynolds name.

In the time since, the four of them had worked diligently to reclaim their role in the beef industry, all while carving a new path into the twenty-first century. They used sustainable practices, methods that were as humane as possible and focused on quality over quantity. She'd even taken a few of her high school classes to the ranch on field trips, pleased with the opportunity to both show off hardworking members of their town and help her students understand there were many paths available to them for their life's work.

She'd heard more than one teenage girl sigh on those tours over the cowboys who worked the land, but few had garnered as many sighs as the stoic, grim-faced man who blended the best of bad boy with cowboy.

Which made the gentle eyes and insistence on keeping her company that much more surprising.

Hoyt didn't do gentle. Or kind. Or congenial. He wasn't nasty, per se. He was just aloof. Separate.

Alone.

Hoyt Reynolds kept to himself. He wasn't a gossip and he wasn't prone to nosing into anyone's business.

Which, Reese figured, probably made him the perfect companion for her evening's adventure.

Hoyt Reynolds ignored the small licks of attraction that sizzled through his nerve endings, willing himself to focus on the bigger picture. Reese Grantham might be a gorgeous companion over a few drinks, but she was clearly in pain and it didn't take a genius to figure out that the way she was managing it wasn't the brightest idea.

Russ Grantham had surprised them all when his sins came to light this past spring. Hoyt's future sister-in-law had almost paid the biggest price, but something of the good man they'd all believed Russ to be must have finally shown through. Russ had let Belle go, taking his own life, and the secrets he'd buried deep along with him.

Hoyt didn't spent much time in town, but he'd seen Reese a few times, once at the gas station filling up her car and another over produce at the market. She'd been too many bays over at the gas station for him to say anything, but he hadn't missed the vacant look in her eyes or the emptiness that seemed to hover around her. A fact that was reinforced when he'd attempted conversation over the oranges.

She'd been polite and pleasant, but the wariness in her eyes was hard to miss. Whether it was from personal grief or their connection over Belle, he wasn't sure, but she'd hightailed it out of there with her cart as soon as she could politely flee.

Which brought them here. The drink she'd already had seemed to suppress the flight instinct, but there was a determination in her hazel gaze that was unmistakable.

Which meant he'd keep an eye on her, prevent her from drinking too much and see that she got home safe and sound.

Tabasco caught his eye as he set down two more beers along with two more whiskey chasers. Hoyt didn't miss the clear warning in the man's gaze, or the equally clear directive to watch out for her, and he simply nodded as Tabasco cleared Reese's empties.

He wasn't a hound dog. He might find her attractive but he hadn't done anything about it up to now; he sure as hell wasn't going to take advantage of her at a weak moment. He wasn't particularly successful at relationships—he preferred his own company and no one prying into his most personal thoughts—so he kept his dating out of the Pass and far away from local acquaintances.

But damn, she looked good.

Her hair fell in long dark waves down her back, the color a rich sable. She'd lost weight and was edging toward too skinny, but it didn't diminish the round swells of her breasts beneath a sleeveless tank or the lush curve of her hips beneath her jeans. Although she was seated, he knew the long, long legs that currently ended in sexy flip-flops that bared purple-painted toenails were a spectacular sight, whether she wore one of her conservative dresses for teaching or a pair of shorts for a town picnic.

Purple polish?

He had no idea why he found that cute since he could care less about nail polish or the varied colors it came in. Yet, on Reese Grantham it looked good. Everything looked good on her, from the outfit tonight to the more severe choices she wore while teaching. She was pretty and sexy, in a way that wasn't garish or overdone and...

And he'd do well to cut off that train before it got a head of steam.

No matter how good she looked, it couldn't erase the sadness that lingered in her eyes or the light smudges that filled in the hollows below them.

Nor could it erase the fact that one of her father's crimes had been committed on Reynolds land the prior spring. In the crime that had begun his descent into capture, Russ Grantham had killed his quarry at the edge of Reynolds property, seeking to make it look like a drug deal gone bad.

"What are you doing out on a Tuesday night?" Reese asked, reaching for her beer. The question was enough to jar him from the bleak direction of his thoughts and he reached out and hung on to it with both hands.

"I could ask you the same."

"I asked first."

She had a spine, something that had always intrigued him, and with a small nod, he answered her. "Figured I'd get a beer or two. Snag a few games of pool off anyone who was interested."

"Please don't let me stop you."

Although he heard no hint of the bum's rush, he couldn't resist teasing her a bit. "You trying to get rid of me?"

"No!" Those pretty hazel eyes widened as if she realized what she'd said. "I didn't mean you had to go away. I just meant you don't have to babysit me."

"Why's it babysitting?"

"Because I can already see the good cowboy routine. The nod to Tabasco that you'll take care of me. The whole you-can't-drink-alone stance. You feel sorry for me."

Although he knew she didn't have kids, it struck him in that moment that she spent her professional life around children and had clearly developed that legendary second set of eyes in the back of her head.

"You saw that?"

"What?" She inclined her head toward the opposite end of the bar. "The manly eye contact with Tabasco, ensuring you'd get me home?"

"Yeah. That one."

"Yes, I saw it."

He nearly laughed at the prim tone and the way her hands folded on the bar in front of her second round of beer and whiskey chasers, but held back. She was amusing, but he wasn't trying to make fun of her and for reasons he couldn't quite define, he wasn't sure she would understand the difference tonight.

Hell, he didn't even understand it. He'd headed in because he was restless and tired of his own company. A state that had become increasingly consistent over the past year. He hadn't felt this way in a while. The last time he could remember was his final year in special ops, when even three major wins, removing several terrorists in power hadn't settled his thoughts of home and the help he knew his family needed on the ranch. Before that, it had been the decision to enlist, escaping the confines of that same family and the sense that the world was bigger—and needed more of him—than simply raising cattle.

Oh, how things had changed.

Which had all brought him here.

A mindless night out had seemed like a good idea. He wasn't big on having his business spread around Midnight Pass like manure, so he hadn't put seducing a woman on the list of activities for the evening, but he'd be lying if he didn't acknowledge—only to himself— that he was enjoying her company.

He'd be lying even harder if that thread of sadness he saw in her eyes didn't pull him in.

"Well, I might be looking out for you but I'm not sitting here feeling sorry for you."

Her head tilted slightly, just enough to send her hair falling over her shoulder in a just-so motion that made him want to reach out and run the tips of his fingers through the strands. "Well, that's a surprise."

"Why?"

"Because that's exactly what I'm doing sitting here. Feeling sorry for myself."

"Whiskey's not the answer."

"You mean there's an answer?" Those pretty hazel eyes widened, her voice deadpan. "One that doesn't begin with 'you just have to take it day by day' or 'God has His plans, even if we can't understand them'?"

Hoyt knew those answers. Had lived them himself and dealt with the endless comments designed to be helpful and supportive. First when his mother had died of cancer, and later, when his father's bad business practices had come to light.

Instead of offering comfort, they'd been intrusive and taxing and designed to make the person saying them feel better, not the recipient.

He knew he had a reputation for being a cold, sullen jerk and he could hardly lay all that at his old man's feet. But he had definitely honed those personality traits after his father's actions had come to light.

Why talk to people when they really didn't want the truth? Each person's own version of events was far more interesting. And why make any effort to quell the gossip when the ones engaging in it were perfectly happy to keep whispering behind your back?

"No, I don't think there is an answer," he said. "And I know for a fact God's plans and how you take your days are not answers to that question."

"On that we are agreed." She lifted her whiskey shot and clinked it against his glass where it sat waiting on the bar. Liquid sloshed to the edges but she was obviously still steady enough not to spill. "Let's toast on it."

He lifted his shot glass, tapping it gently to hers. "To a lack of answers."

"Cheers."

Hoyt took his shot and braced himself for a second round of coughing—and the opportunity to settle his hands once more on the slender arch of her shoulders— but she held her whiskey. Her eyes did narrow into a determined squint, but she held on.

And why did he think that was sexy as hell?

She was a mystery to him. A woman who he'd known most of his life, had always found pretty enough and interesting enough, yet he'd never ventured even one single step in the direction of those waters. He wasn't the serious type in his relationships and he sure as hell didn't want forever.

Hoyt's own father had done a piss-poor job of convincing everyone he wanted forever and instead had done his level best to ruin whatever legacy his time on earth might have produced. Hoyt and his brothers and sister had lived with that truth, each learning to deal with it in their own way.

For Tate it was laughter. For Ace it was taking ownership of everything and everyone. And for Arden it was playing little mother and earth mother, all in one fell swoop.

He was the one who ran away. First with his emotions and later to his time in the service. When he'd come back, he'd settled on a single truth that had served him well: as a denizen of one of the smallest towns in the entire state of Texas, he knew better than to go peeing in the good, upstanding citizen pool of available women in Midnight Pass.

Reese Grantham was a high school teacher. She was the daughter of—up until recently—a well-respected, career police officer in Midnight Pass. And she was the surviving sibling of a drug addict gone very, very bad. She was a good girl and you simply didn't mess with women in that category. Especially if you weren't willing to see it all the way through with a ring, a promise and a lifelong commitment.

So why were those warm, wide-set eyes so compelling? And why did that restlessness that had dogged him all day—hell, all year—seem to have suddenly vanished in her presence?

"One more?" Her lips quirked into a smile as she tapped the bar.

"Not sure that's a good idea. And I know it won't be a good idea in the morning."

"Spoilsport." She stuck her tongue out but it was through smiling lips, a sure sign she wasn't as annoyed as her comment suggested.

"You are one ahead of me."

"Then maybe you need to catch up." She leaned forward and pointed a finger into his chest. The move should have been invasive—would have been on anyone else and if he'd been in his right mind—but his right mind had gone missing the moment he'd walked into The Border Line and seen Reese Grantham sitting at the bar.

Hoyt closed a hand over her finger, gently closing it so he could press her hand against his heart. "Or what?"

Heat lit up his chest where her hand lay pressed against his T-shirt and he could have sworn sparks were shooting off the place where their hands joined. "That's a very good question."

Reese looked over and tried to avoid goggling at the strong profile and flexed biceps of Hoyt Reynolds. She'd realized pretty quickly that she had a prime view from the passenger seat of his truck and had been shooting him furtive glances on the ride back to her house ever since they'd left The Border Line.

She had no idea how she'd ended up here, but one minute they were sitting in the bar shooting the breeze—and whiskey—and the next he was bundling her up to take her home.

She wasn't even very buzzed, although she could

have sworn she'd seen a sort of glow around Hoyt as he ushered her out of The Border Line. Had her vision gone funny? Or was she simply trying to figure out how a man she'd known her whole life could suddenly look different?

Better, somehow.

And if she were honest, he'd always looked pretty damn fine before.

"Are you sure you can drive?" The words popped out, a nervous filler to the silence that had taken over the truck.

If he'd noticed her watching him, he hadn't said anything, but did use the question to turn and look at her as they bumped over the two-lane road out of town toward her place. "I had one beer and one shot of whiskey. I'm good."

"People who drive drunk say that."

"Yes, they do. But there's one big difference. I'm not drunk."

"Oh."

"You're drunk."

"I am not! I only had a beer and a half and two whiskey shots."

"Which is why you're going home."

"Grumpy much?"

She had no idea why she was baiting him. He'd done her a favor—one she'd be fully prepared to acknowledge in the bright light of morning—but right now, all she wanted was…

To rile him up.

Which was ridiculous and childish and not at all like her. Yet, there you had it. There was just something about the way he'd swooped in and taken care of her that chafed. She was a grown woman, and she had a right to a night out to do whatever she wanted. She didn't need permission. And she didn't need anyone watching out for her. She was sick and tired of sitting in the home she loved day in and day out, feeling like a prisoner in the one place she'd created to be a haven. So she'd gone out, looking for a nice time and a fun evening and a few hours to forget about her life.

"I'm not grumpy. I'm just not interested in seeing Midnight Pass High School's favorite English teacher end up in trouble for puking her guts out in the Border Line parking lot. Or worse."

"My father's already done worse. So has my brother. It's a rather high bar."

Those attractive lips of his—thick and lush—had tightened back to a straight line. "I'm sorry about that. About your father."

"Why?"

"Some decisions—" Hoyt stopped and, after braking at a stop sign, turned toward her. "Some decisions can't be changed or reconsidered or amended. But he was once a good man. I know that."

"He killed someone on your property."

"So?" He phrased that single syllable more as a question than anything else and Reese momentarily found herself at a loss for words.

Didn't that bother him? Because it sure as hell bothered her.

Only she didn't say that. Instead, she focused on his bigger point. The one she'd struggled with for the past two months since her father's sins had come to light. "Well—"

From her vantage point, she watched as one lone

eyebrow lifted as he eyed her from the driver's seat. "Well what?"

"How can you say that about him? He broke, Hoyt. Broke in two and became a monster. That's not my definition of a good man. It's not my mother's. It's not even the expectations my father set for my brother and me from the time we were young."

The anger spilled out, again a product of all those years of trying to be perfect. She'd done as she was told. Had worked hard to be a model daughter. And yet, where had it gotten her?

The object of ridicule and gossip, and, if the quiet suggestion earlier that day while she selected a cantaloupe at the market was any indication, questions from the PTA asking if she was fit to keep her teaching job.

When Hoyt said nothing in response, just accelerated through the intersection, Reese realized she'd overstepped. And goodness, why had she gone there? Here he was being nothing but nice and she'd tossed out those little bons mots like they were candy. Worse, they were the creeping, dissatisfying secrets of her life.

"This your street?" he asked.

At her acknowledgment, he turned down her road and followed her directions to the driveway. In moments, he was parked and was already around the car, opening her door for her like a gentleman.

"You didn't need to do that," she said, in a lame attempt to defuse this damned awareness of him.

"According to you, I don't need to do a lot of things. Sit with you at The Border Line. Drive you home. Give a hand to someone who really needs one." As if to prove his point, he took her hand and helped her out of the high seat.

It hadn't seemed quite that high getting in, but the drop down to the ground was farther than she thought and she hit the driveway harder than expected, the backs of her heels thudding on concrete.

"Easy," Hoyt said, shifting his grip to steady her with his large hands.

Working man hands.

Capable hands.

She settled her palms where each of his hands rested on her hips, the moment changing with all the finesse of a spring storm.

The attraction that had simmered all night, kept at bay with her frustrations and embarrassment over the public nature of her family's downfall, suddenly had no place to go. Instead, all the pain and anger she'd bottled up for two long months—hell, for nearly a decade— needed a place to bubble up and land.

With his hands still cradling her hips and hers still pressed against the ridges of his knuckles, she ignored the little voice that always urged her to be careful and cautious and lifted her head toward his. It was a matter of inches that separated them and a quick reach on her tiptoes had their mouths meeting in the moonlight.

She expected resistance. Sexual tension had simmered between them all evening—she wasn't imagining that—but he'd also maintained a gentlemanly distance. A maddening distance, if she were honest.

Which meant the quick brush of lips that exploded into an inferno of hot carnal passion caught her just enough off guard that she barely had time to catch her breath. Even less time when she realized that she was being consumed, body and soul, by the delectable form of Hoyt Reynolds.

His mouth was hot on hers, his tongue filling the small *O* of surprise between her lips with smooth, effortless grace. His tongue was strong and persuasive and *welcome*, she admitted to herself. What should have felt like an intrusion was the exact opposite and as heat flared through her nerve endings like lightning, it filled every last inch of her body with the most delicious electricity.

Was this what it felt like to be kissed? Really and truly kissed?

She'd been kissed before, obviously. She'd had sex, too. If she'd considered it even an hour before, she'd have said those experiences were good ones. On a grading curve, satisfactory moving on toward excellent.

Oh, how little she'd understood.

Especially as every one of those experiences seemed to wash away in a sea of dull memory as Hoyt filled in its place. Nothing had ever felt like this. It was as if a sensual live wire lit her up, sparking from the inside out.

It was glorious.

It was heavenly.

And in that moment, she'd have gladly given up all she possessed to keep on kissing him.

Suddenly realizing she was doing way more analyzing than enjoying, Reese quickly fixed that, giving into the impulse that had her kissing him in the first place.

The strong shoulders beneath her palms flexed as he shifted his position, deepening the kiss and taking them another level. She took what he gave, all the while using her fingertips to explore the thick muscle and rounded curves of his shoulders. This was a man in his prime, of that there was no doubt. He was a product of hard, daily physical labor and she could hardly argue with the results.

Nor was she quite ready to let go yet.

Which made the lift of his head and the grim line of his mouth, more than evident in the glow of her front door light, that much harder to accept.

"I should get you to your door."

"Why?" That same tartness that had accompanied her comments on the ride home rose up to the fore. Which wasn't like her, yet seemed right for the moment.

"For all the reasons we talked about at Border Line."

"I thought we talked about answers."

That grim line of his mouth quirked up into a wry smile. "I thought we said there were no answers."

Reese wasn't sure if it was the smile or the heady feeling that still rode her bloodstream from his excellent kisses or something else she couldn't define or resist. The only thing she understood as the words tumbled past her lips, one after the other, was an overwhelming sense of rightness.

"Then why don't you stay?"

Chapter 2

*S*tay.

That lone word still shimmered between them, taking shape and form in the late night heat, as he walked her to her front porch. June in south Texas was always hot and this year had been no exception, with a few days already posting one hundred degrees plus. But tonight it felt different, somehow.

Hotter. More breathless. Anticipatory.

Reese Grantham tantalized and tempted, tugging at Hoyt in ways he'd never expected. And had certainly never predicted for the evening.

When had things changed?

They knew each other, sure. And he'd be a total liar if he didn't admit to himself that he'd always found her attractive. But what was it about this night?

This time?

What was it about *her*?

She was different from what Hoyt remembered and it wasn't simply because of what had happened a few months ago. She still had that beautiful face, the elegant cheekbones set off against smooth olive skin that already showed the evidence of a summer tan. She still had the long legs and mouthwatering curves that even right now tempted him and had his fingers itching to settle on her hips once again.

Maybe it was just right place at the right time.

But even that felt like an excuse as he turned the idea over in his mind.

She wasn't easy and he wasn't going to justify away this sudden shot of desire by trying to make himself feel better. There was something different about her but maybe there was also something different about him. Because after months of restless, aimless feelings, everything had suddenly settled in the past few hours in her company.

That strange dissatisfaction that had ridden him— one that wouldn't be assuaged by working the land or riding his horse or mending fences or any number of things he'd found to occupy his time—had vanished in the pretty face of Reese Grantham. It was like he'd had a perpetual buzzing in his ears for a year and now all he had was blessed silence.

"Hoyt." She whispered his name, pulling him from the aimless wandering of his mind.

"Yeah?"

Her lips feathered over his collarbone, drifting up his neck and on toward his ear. "I know this isn't the answer, either."

He hung on to his control by a shockingly thin

thread, but was willing to do it anyway to get out and leave her well enough alone. "No, it's not."

"Then we're agreed?"

He shifted back, pulling his skin away from the tantalizing strokes of her tongue so he could look down at her. "Agreed on what?"

"This might not be the answer to anything, but please don't leave."

"I need to go."

"Do you?" Something sharp and deliberate stuck beneath her words, part dare and all temptation. He saw it clearly in the flash of heat in her gaze and the sultry pout of her lips. Moonlight filled the sky and, combined with her front porch lights, made it easy to read every emotion on her face.

"You think I don't?" he asked, well aware he'd like nothing else than to follow her up those steps and on through the front door.

"All I know is we had a nice evening. We're two grown adults and we're both well able to determine how we want to spend the rest of it." She held up a hand. "And before you blame it on two whiskey chasers, I can assure you I'm making this decision, not a few shots of liquor."

"You seem sure about that."

"I'm beyond sure." She stepped back, removing her hands from his body, leaving a strange emptiness when she pulled away. "Aren't you?"

That dare grew stronger and Hoyt knew he wasn't immune to her words. Nor was he immune to the increasing heat that had nothing to do with the weather and everything to do with the woman who stood before him.

"Being sure about tonight isn't the problem."

"Then what is?"

"Tomorrow."

As excuses went, it was a cop out and Hoyt was gripping it with both hands. Hell, he'd claw at it with the tips of his fingernails if it would give him the ammunition he needed to hang on, get Reese Grantham through her front door and him back into his truck.

"I've spent far too many days of my life worried about tomorrow. It hasn't gotten me anywhere close to where I want. That's why I've decided to focus on a new strategy. It's called today."

"Why now?"

"I can't think of a better time to start."

Hoyt couldn't, either. Against his better judgment—and in support of his most fervent desires—he pulled her into his arms.

The bright moonlight that had revealed every emotion on Hoyt Reynolds's face was still in evidence when she walked with him into her room a short while later. Reese still wasn't sure how it had all happened—she certainly hadn't gone out looking for this tonight—but there was no way she was stopping.

Especially when it all felt so right.

It was why she'd pushed and poked at him with surprising persistence, even though she'd normally be unwilling to ask for what she wanted or be so brazen as to put voice to those thoughts.

How long had it been since she was attracted to a man? Not the cursory allure that came with light flirting or the occasional date that turned into a second, but real, bone-deep attraction and awareness.

And need.

It was the need that had tripped her up and had her pressing him to stay while they were out on her front porch. In all reality, his resistance was not only gentlemanly, but had far more foresight than she was feeling at the moment. There was nothing between them and one night of sex wasn't going to change that. Yet, for reasons that seemed a perfect fit with the evening, nothing about that bothered her.

Instead, it was freeing.

All her life, she'd been Reese Grantham, good girl. She'd done what was expected of her and, if she were honest, she was okay with that. She was also okay with a night of mindless sex with Hoyt Reynolds.

And wasn't that an amazing thought.

All that had come before—all the decisions she'd made because they were right for her—extended here as well. This was right. And since she had a hot, virile male standing before her, it was high time she enjoyed it.

With sure fingers, she reached for him, her hands playing along the hem of his untucked T-shirt. The cotton was soft and well-worn, heated from his skin, and she fisted her fingers in the material before dragging it over his head. Whatever she'd expected to see beneath, the hard abs, firm chest and impressively rounded shoulders were beyond her wildest imagination.

"Wow." The word was out on a hard exhale and Reese couldn't have stopped it if she'd tried. "Those are some impressive muscles."

A small smile tilted up the corner of one side of his mouth. "Not sure I've ever gotten a *wow* before."

"Oh, you've gotten plenty, of that I have no doubt."

She gave in to temptation and ran her hands over all that glorious muscle. "It likely just happened out of earshot."

"I'm not sure—" His words ended abruptly as her explorations had her hands dipping decidedly close to the waistband of his jeans, the pads of her fingers trailing along the line of his belt.

Pleased with the way his abs contracted beneath her touch, she lifted her head and pressed her lips against his, whispering as she did, "I'm quite sure."

Her initiative that had gotten them this far seemed to change in an instant. His willingness to stand still and take what she offered vanished as his arms wrapped around her, drawing her close. "You talk too much."

"I'm a teacher. It comes with the job description."

"Then let me teach you a new lesson."

Hoyt's words were full of delicious promise and Reese quieted as he made good on his instructions. The hands that had remained at his sides went into action, drawing her blouse up and over her head before working some fast, clever magic at the close of her bra. In a flash, her bra slipped to the floor and his fingers had replaced the cool air-conditioning, covering her breasts even as his thumbs found her nipples.

Heat arced through her, racing over her skin before settling low in her belly, pooling there. The sensation was so strong—so deep—she gasped at the need that sparked under her skin. With unspoken understanding, Hoyt pressed his lips to hers, his tongue filling her mouth in long, tantalizing strokes that matched the work of his hands.

Pleasure exploded beneath and around and over the heat, drawing a light moan from deep in her chest. The thoughts that had been crystal clear when she'd walked in had fragmented, floating in abstract images of warm skin and vivid green eyes that remained steady on her and a hard, firm body that pulled the darkest, most wicked sensations from her. But one thought did gain purchase, rooting deep.

This was right.

Real.

And there was nowhere else she wanted to be.

Reese kissed him back, willing all that *rightness* into the moment, determined to enjoy every single second of their time together.

Resuming her explorations, she reached for the button of his jeans, flipping open the closure and slipping beneath the waistband of both jeans and underwear. The solid strength of his erection met her hand, filling her palm as she gripped him more firmly. The stomach muscle contractions that had captured her attention flexed even harder in response to her touch, visible proof of what she already felt in her hands.

"Reese." He gripped her arm, firm yet easy in his hold, disengaging her from his body. "I'm not sure either of us are ready to end this too soon."

"I know I'm not."

"Then maybe you should let me set the pace."

Reese missed the feel of that warm flesh as he pulled her hand free and was nearly embarrassed for her eagerness until she caught sight of his cocky grin. "Are you laughing at me?"

"No, ma'am."

"Ma'am?" The sultry cocoon that had woven around them vanished like disintegrating cotton candy and Reese took several steps back. "Did you just *ma'am* me?"

"I did." Hoyt coughed. "Ma'am."

"That's the biggest insult I've ever—"

Before she could get the rest of it out, all those large muscles she'd so admired went into motion, wrapping her up and pulling her close. His lips hit hers with the same momentum as his hold, and heat and need and a delicious sort of lightness filled her before she realized she was floating in his arms, heading for the bed.

The momentum of his body carried them to the mattress with a heavy thud, his large form taking the brunt of her weight as she fell on top of him in a tangle of limbs.

It was awkward and silly and laughter rumbled in her chest. "Smooth, Reynolds."

He answered her with a smile of his own, one that lit up his features like the sun clearing the clouds. "I guess I'm just going to have to try harder. Smooth," he said as if to himself, before eyeing her with a wink. "I need to work on that."

And, oh, how he worked at it. He lifted his hands to thread through her hair, pulling her close for another kiss. The heat of his body pressed along hers, the delicious warmth of his chest against her breasts sensual and sexy and…right.

So very right.

And as far as smooth went… Hoyt certainly didn't have to try very hard. Everything about him was smooth. And perfect. And beyond her wildest imaginings.

Yes, she'd found him attractive. She'd be hard pressed to find a woman in the Pass or five surrounding counties who didn't think any of the Reynolds boys were attractive. It was sort of a rite of passage to get a head nod or hat tip from one of them in town or leaving church or attending the annual summer festivals in the town center.

But to be the recipient of all that sexiness up close? *Wow* was the understatement of the century.

No matter how successful he and his siblings became in business, that success was steeped in the fact that they worked their ranch. His body was prime evidence of that fact, the thick ropes of muscles and work-worn hands the proof. Even as she enjoyed the results, Reese knew it was more than just the physical.

He was a quiet man and while he was known for his surliness, she'd seen another side this evening. One that both warmed her and made her feel special. As if he'd pulled out that gentler side of his nature just for her.

Aware her thoughts were veering into sentimental territory, she pushed them all away. Tonight wasn't about analyzing the softer nature of hardworking cowboys or why said cowboy had decided to favor her with his time. It was about sex and a wonderful, mindless joining with another. She'd do well to remember that.

He momentarily shifted from the bed, reaching for his jeans and a condom stowed in his wallet. That quick slip from the bed went a long way toward reminding her even further of what this was.

Sex.

Clearly, he'd ensured he was prepared should the opportunity come his way and she wasn't going to get upset about it. Or think too hard about what it meant that she'd not considered protection at all.

For all her internal admonishments to not be affected, something must have shown on her face. His gaze met hers in the dimmed light of her room, a distinct blush creeping up his neck. "I. Um. That's been in there for a while."

She offered up a small smile before extending her

arms, welcoming him back to bed. "I'm glad, since I hadn't given protection much thought."

"You don't keep anything? In your house?"

"I think I may have something colored and vaguely dirty from a bachelorette party last year buried in the back of the medicine cabinet."

Hoyt resettled himself over her, holding his weight up on his forearms. "Dirty, you say?"

"Very."

"Since my wallet stash extends to one, perhaps we can go hunting in the back of your medicine cabinet later."

The indication he didn't have a stack of condoms waiting to be used on his person went the rest of the way toward defusing the situation and Reese deftly ignored the subtle sense of relief. Maybe he didn't do this every week. Or maybe even every month. And maybe she wasn't just a notch on his belt.

And maybe you need to stop thinking, Grantham, and get back to feeling.

Desperate for those gloriously mindless moments in his arms, Reese reached for the condom in Hoyt's hand and did the work of sheathing him herself. In moments, he was repositioned above her, fitted intimately inside of her.

It had been a while since she'd felt that delicious stretch of warm welcome, and she took him in, the thoughts that had dogged her fading as he began to move. And as pleasure once again took the place of thoughts or words, Reese gave herself up to the moment.

And the mindless oblivion of making love with Hoyt Reynolds.

* * *

The small, quiet neighborhood had settled down for the evening, the good citizens of Midnight Pass nestled snug in their beds. Normally, the small split-level with the neatly mowed lawn that sat toward the end of the lane housed the same. Front room lights that went on precisely each evening at eight o'clock and then snapped off promptly at eleven o'clock. A porch light that burned most evenings, whether the owner was home or not. And a driveway that remained persistently empty of guests.

Only not tonight.

The woman sat in her car, taking in the altered landscape and wondering what had finally made Reese Grantham snap out of that Prissy-Missy attitude and drag herself home a hot cowboy. If she didn't hate Reese so badly—or bear such a deep-seated grudge and anger—she might have actually cheered for the woman.

About damn time Prissy Missy got some.

The stick that sat perpetually lodged in her ass must get awfully uncomfortable.

But that large truck tucked up in the small driveway proved everyone had urges and needed to let 'em out for a walk every now and again.

The real question, the woman thought, was how she could use this to her advantage. It would be easy to whisper a few words in some well-placed PTA members' ears. Or drop a few hints down at the general store about what she'd seen.

But that would be easy. Crass, really. Besides, this game had gone on far too long to fold with such an easy hand.

Gossips got discovered. And someone always remembered where they heard something first.

As she pulled away from the curb and took one last pass in front of the house, that porch light still flaring bright this late at night, the woman knew what she needed to do.

Bide her time.

She'd waited this long, what was a bit more? The right moment would show itself. And when it did, she'd strike.

Swift. Immediate. And utterly remorseless.

Reese talked too much.

That was the first thought that drifted through his mind as Hoyt lay there, early morning summer sun beating over his eyelids. The second thought was that he couldn't seem to find the energy to mind. In fact, he thought, with no small shot of surprise, he sort of liked it.

Her voice was slightly husky—like just after she'd done that shot of whiskey—and drifted over him with a light, sultry drawl.

"Just in case you're concerned I have a big mouth, I won't say anything to anyone."

"I didn't think that."

"Good, because I'm not like that."

Hoyt often considered himself more perceptive than he usually let on—subtext wasn't nearly as hard to read as others often made it out to be—but he'd have had to have been deaf to miss what lay beneath Reese's words. Rolling to his side, he took in the flushed face and still-sleepy eyes. "I'm not worried about anyone finding out anything."

"But people saw us leave The Border Line."

"So?"

"And your truck's been in the driveway all night and now it's morning."

"And?"

He wasn't quite sure why he was enjoying this so much—gossip had a way of causing problems, no matter how deftly you ignored it—but something about the little furrow that creased the space between her eyes and the small frown that marred those incredibly kissable lips had him smiling.

"Hoyt Reynolds, tell me you're not that dense."

"I'm not dense at all. I'm just trying to figure out what happened between that convincing speech you gave me on the front porch last night and right now."

"What speech?"

"The *we're adults* speech. And it was rather convincing." Unable to help himself, he reached out and ran the tip of his index finger over her shoulder. Her skin was still warm from sleep and as soft as he remembered from throughout the night.

Something flickered in her gaze, erasing any lingering vestiges of sleep, but that small divide remained between her eyes. "It wasn't a speech."

"Monologue, then."

"I was hardly the host of a late-night comedy show."

"Soliloquy?"

"You're being—"

Hoyt struck quick, the move at odds with the contented, lazy feeling that still suffused his limbs. But damn it all, she was cute, with the confuzzled look and the worry about something they could neither change nor take back.

Something he had no interest in taking back.

That thought gripped him as he rolled her onto her back and covered her with his body. His lips found hers—ready, waiting and willing—and everything else seemed to vanish except for the two of them. Hoyt refused to think about the implications of that.

Or why those implications didn't bother him nearly as much as they should have.

It was a long while later that he lifted his head. They'd eventually hunted up the stash of party condoms in her bathroom and, even now, he couldn't help but smile to himself at the novelty of wearing neon green.

"That's a rather smug look?"

Since Reese wore one that matched his, he reached out and traced her full lower lip. "A look I think you're rather well acquainted with."

"I'm not smug."

"Smug and well loved. It's a good look on you." He leaned in and gave her one more kiss before she could protest, then pulled back. "My smile was for the vivid memory of a neon-green condom. I'm not sure I've ever seen one of those before."

"Clearly, you haven't spent much time around bachelorette parties."

"Maybe I need to start."

He got a light swat on his shoulder for the effort and leaned in, nuzzling her neck once more as his hands drifted over her shoulders and on down over her breasts. Damn, when was the last time he'd felt this good? He hadn't had sex in a while—he'd nearly tossed that condom in his wallet a few weeks ago—and had long stopped even considering a relationship or anything that smacked of permanence.

Or even semi-permanence.

But what had he given up because of it?

His evening with an interesting, engaging, pretty woman had been special. She had thoughts and ideas and hadn't been afraid to express them. They'd finally wandered into her kitchen around three o'clock, fixing sandwiches, and she'd shared her ideas on teaching and what she hoped for her students and chattered happily about one who'd recently written her after graduating from college.

He'd seen pride shining from her and a happiness for others that was rare. And beautiful. Reese had captivated him, that excitement and enthusiasm still shiny and bright, undimmed by the events with her father a few months back. It was awesome to behold, especially as someone who'd allowed his own parent's poor behavior to keep a firm grip on his emotions.

Maybe that had been the root of his displeasure of late. Reynolds Station was doing well—beyond his, Ace's, Tate's and Arden's wildest imaginings—yet, he hadn't found a way to enjoy any of it. He'd hit that very same point in the marines and then, later, in special ops. Years of working toward promotions and the respect that came with growing leadership had fulfilled him, and then one day it simply hadn't satisfied any longer. The orders and the structure and the reality that he was a chess piece on someone else's board had finally gotten to him.

In both cases, he'd lost the ability to take those precious moments of joy and pleasure and happiness at what his own hard work had produced.

It was a strange place to be, when all the hard work—work that was supposed to save you and occupy you and lift you up—simply didn't. Each accomplishment felt hollow, like it should mean more.

So why did he still feel empty?

"Hoyt?"

His name was a soft whisper in the room, but it was enough to pull him from his musings. "Yes?"

"I'm glad you stayed."

"No regrets?" The question was out before he could stop it and he was surprised to realize just how much he hoped the answer was no. Never.

"Not at all."

"Me, either."

"Thank you for being there. I'm glad you pulled the responsible cowboy routine on Tabasco."

"I'm glad I did, too."

"Then why don't you prove it to me before you have to head out for work."

He hadn't mentioned leaving or work or a timed departure, so it was with no small measure of surprise that Hoyt realized Reese had been thinking it.

As he lowered his lips to hers, once again wrapping himself up in her body, he knew it was stupid to feel even a shot of sadness. What man didn't want an easy exit after a night of unexpected sex? But as Reese shifted beneath him, drawing him close and setting the rhythm that had become intimately familiar overnight, Hoyt couldn't quite shake his disappointment.

She'd been unexpected, yes. But more welcome than he ever could have imagined.

Chapter 3

Two months later

"I'm sorry, Jake. Run that by me again?" She set the stapler down on her desk for fear the heavy object might become a weapon if her vision hazed any redder. Reese had learned a long time ago to never tell herself things couldn't get worse. It was one of the harshest lessons an addict had taught their family, and she'd had a crash course by the time she was a freshman at Midnight Pass High School.

Jamie had been the best of big brothers, but by the time she'd turned fourteen, their three-year age gap had made all the difference. What had been a bit of bad behavior—smoking marijuana at the end of the day or drinking too much out at the edge of town—had quickly become an addiction when his urges took a hard turn. Cocaine was plentiful in the Pass, brought up from South America by the drug runners who controlled the border, and her brother had been an easy mark.

But it was the heroin a year later that had sealed his fate.

By the time she'd started freshman year, her parents had already placed Jamie into two addiction programs and a solid amount of familial house arrest. Reese hadn't fully understood it at the time, but she'd done the only thing she had understood: acting the exact opposite of her brother.

Straight A's. A steady diet of after-school activities. And her role as the good girl of Midnight Pass. She never smoked, drank and hadn't even kissed a boy. They were traits that formed her and built the foundation of her life, and up until her late night foray with Hoyt Reynolds back in June, she hadn't deviated from that plan.

Oh, she'd been kissed since high school. And she certainly enjoyed liquor from time to time. Four years at the University of Texas had helped see her through both rites of passage. But the core of who she was—the good daughter of Serena and Russ Grantham—had stuck.

Which made the warning shots fired across her classroom that much harder to accept.

"Aww, come on, Reese. Don't make me say it again."

"No." She shook her head, even as her fingers itched to pick up the stapler once more. "I need to hear you say it. I want to make sure I got it right the first time."

Jacob Walters was a friend. He was about five years older than her, but they'd both taught in the English department until he was promoted to assistant principal two years before. It was that steady core of friendship—and the knowledge that Jake was an unfailingly kind human—that kept her in check.

And her hand off the stapler.

"The PTA is concerned," Jake said.

"Define *concerned*."

Jake sighed but kept his gaze level, his words simple and straightforward. "They're concerned your father's passing a few months back was too big a trauma not to take some time off."

"I took time when it happened. Mourned the passing of a parent good and proper, just as dictated in the union bylaws. Two whole weeks," Reese added for good measure, as if Jake had forgotten.

"They think you may need more."

"More what? Time to think about something I can't control or change?" She broke off on a hard exhale when a new thought filled her. "Has someone said something? Is my teaching lacking somehow?"

Reese fought the roiling of her stomach, refusing to let that steady layer of sickness that had accompanied her for six weeks have its way. "And why have they suddenly decided to bring it up now? After I've bought supplies for my classroom and set up for the new school year? Why is that, Jake?"

"Come on, Reese. Your father killed himself. After—" Jake hesitated. "Just after."

"After he killed four people, you mean. Tortured them, too."

"It's not a secret."

"No, it's not. Nor is the fact that I was teacher of the year two years ago. Or has that conveniently slipped everyone's mind?"

"No, it hasn't. Nor have I stopped reminding them every chance I get."

It was the stalwart support—which she *knew* she had from Jake—that finally had her standing down. Enough so that she physically sat down, dropping into the rolling chair behind her desk. "You really think they're going to fire me?"

"Leave of absence. That's all. They want the fuss to die down a bit more."

"That's a load of hogwash and you know it. The fuss has died down."

"It had until they found that other body."

The urge to shift her gaze was strong, but Reese kept her focus level with Jake's. She would not cower. Nor would she slink away in embarrassment. Her father's crimes were extensive enough—and repetitive enough—to be considered serial in nature. What she hadn't expected was that his choices in life would leave him a perpetual suspect each and every time a body bearing even the slightest resemblance to his victims was found.

Despite his death the prior spring, Russ Grantham had been considered for murders in El Paso, Houston and as far north as Waco. All crimes in which he was exonerated, but all of which had claimed front-page headlines and the lead focus on the nightly news.

"That wasn't him."

"But it made his crimes front and center once more. That scares people. Makes 'em skittish."

"Their small mindedness means I'm somehow at fault?"

"No, Reese. Not at all."

Well aware Jake was only doing his job, she opted

to play on his softer side. The PTA members had a voice, but they couldn't simply oust her from her role. Not without garnering a lot more support from a lot more people.

With that in mind, she pressed on.

"I need my job, Jake. My benefits. My salary. What else am I going to do? I have a contract."

"Which the district knows. You're locked in for the year. All I'm saying is take some bereavement leave and let this die down. By the time you come back, you'll have plenty of time to work your magic the next time contracts are being signed."

The urge to rant and rail at the unfairness of it all was strong, but Reese avoided saying anything further. Jake *was* just the messenger and he clearly hadn't taken any joy in delivering his missive. More, he was her friend and he was in her corner, two facts she refused to lose sight of. "Please tell me I don't need to make a decision today."

"Of course not. School doesn't start for nearly a month and the PTA doesn't have nearly the power it thinks it does. I wouldn't have taken this job if it did."

"Alright then." She nodded at Jake, surprised when he crossed around her desk and pulled her into a close hug.

"Take care of you, okay. As long as I'm here, there will be a job for you."

"Okay." She hugged her friend and knew his words for truth. It was only after he'd left her still-unfinished classroom that Reese let her gaze drift to the walls. She'd already begun decorating, her back bulletin board full of pictures of authors who were a mix of the classics, as well as the modern writers her students were reading in droves. She'd worked them all into her curriculum, too, ensuring her students would get as strong a dose of Jane Austen as Suzanne Collins.

Story was story and words were words, no matter where they got their enjoyment. Some of her best students had become that way because she'd encouraged them to read the things they enjoyed—pop fiction, sports almanacs and fashion magazines—well before they dived into the authors who'd been long dead.

That mattered, damn it. It mattered a lot. She was a good teacher. Even if...

Reese tamped down on the direction of her thoughts, resolutely refusing to go there. She was a good teacher—a hardworking, caring teacher—and she'd be damned if she was going to conflate that with her personal life. She wasn't responsible for her father's actions. And while she was responsible for her lone night of abandon with Hoyt Reynolds, that wasn't the town's business, either.

Even if she had heard the occasional whisper or two.

Jake had been too kind to say it, but she wasn't stupid. The PTA's inputs had begun in earnest after word had spread around town that she'd spent an interesting evening at The Border Line with Hoyt Reynolds. She'd ignored the implications—and, best she could tell, he'd done nothing to fuel the flames of innuendo and gossip—but it was out there all the same. She could only thank her lucky stars she lived on a quiet street and Hoyt had left early enough that no one had seemed to notice the large work truck that had taken up space in her driveway one summer evening.

A lone evening that had changed her life.

Reese stood and crossed to the bulletin board, remembering her excitement as she'd tacked up information about the various authors, their bios and covers of some of their most well-known stories. It was only as she reached Nathaniel Hawthorne that she stopped. She'd used the cover of his most renowned novel, *The Scarlet Letter*, for her board and Hester Prynne stood there in the illustration, back straight, face somber, staring right through Reese in all her puritanical glory.

Reese had never particularly enjoyed the original classic on slut shaming and repressed emotion, but had taught it along with the rest of the American canon of literature through the years. Of late, she'd paired it with *Pretty Little Liars* to identify the differences in cultural approach and storytelling and found her students to be both receptive and engaged in the discussions that came of both. Their ability to connect the injustice of the time with collective attitudes, regardless of the period, always made for lively discussion and Reese loved seeing their young faces light up when they made a connection or looked at the world in a new way. It was her greatest joy as a teacher.

Only now, someone was trying to take it away. While her choices were neither as dire nor as alienating as Hester's, Reese couldn't help it as her gaze flicked back once more to settle on that cover. For the first time in nearly a decade of teaching that book to her students, she'd gained a fresh connection of her own.

Only unlike Hester Prynne's literary child—a figment of Nathaniel Hawthorne's imagination and talent—Reese Grantham's was 100 percent real.

Hoyt dragged off his heavy work gloves and reached for the towel he'd stuffed in his back pocket earlier, running the thick terry cloth over his face and neck.

He hated branding day—knew there was nothing to be done about that, though—and considered what was still left to do.

They'd branded about half the new calves and would need at least another hour to work through the rest. The work was strenuous and tiring and made for a general sense of unease on the ranch the day they did it. The new calves hated it—and who could blame them?— and their protective mothers fussed over their young's distress.

"Earning our keep today." Tate's voice was husky from shouting orders over the loud sounds from anxious calves, and Hoyt didn't miss his brother's stiff shoulders and general unease as he took his place beside him at the corral fence.

"That we are," Hoyt agreed.

He, Tate, their brother Ace and their sister, Arden, were the fourth generation of ranchers and the current owners of Reynolds Station, a large and once-again prosperous Texas cattle ranch. Mismanagement and poor acts by their father had seen to the sell-off of some property and a decade-long process toward getting back on their feet.

And back they were.

Hoyt knew he should take pride in branding day and all it stood for—his father sure as hell had—but he could never muster up the stomach for it.

"Everything okay?" Tate's question was casual and his brother was wise enough to ask the question with no one in earshot, but Hoyt bristled all the same.

"I'm fine."

"You sure about that?"

Hoyt shoved the towel back into his pocket, pushing himself off the thick steel bars of the corral fence. "Why wouldn't I be?"

"I don't know." Tate shrugged, his casual motions at odds with the sharp focus that filled his green eyes. "Seems like you've been as skittish as those calves and as upset as their mamas for the past few months now."

Tate had never been the sibling to poke an emotional hornet's nest—Arden and Ace were far more adept at the chore—which made the fact his brother was standing there attempting to make inroads that much more of a surprise. "You're seriously comparing me to a cow?"

"Consider it illustrative."

"Or annoying."

"The fact you're evading the question only adds to my curiosity."

Hoyt ignored the unsettled feeling that scored his skin like barbed wire. His family usually gave him a wide berth emotionally and accepted his surly personality at face value, but even he knew he'd been worse than usual lately. Not that he was even remotely interested in mentioning that. Or the pretty, sweet woman who'd put him in that unbearably surly mood, with lingering memories of the softest skin and the sexiest kisses that refused to leave his thoughts for more than thirty seconds at a stretch.

He'd wanted to call her, and nearly had numerous times. But then he'd consider it and all he could conclude was that things would eventually grow messy. Something about Reese Grantham made him think about a commitment and a future and that scared the hell out of him.

So what else was a man supposed to do when his brother dug into choppy emotional waters?

Fight back for all he was worth.

"I know Belle Granger and I find it hard to believe she's down with all these feelings. What happened? She get sick of you so you're trying them out on me?" Hoyt said.

Tate's voice stayed level but the easy-going smile he'd worn faded. "Belle's got nothing to do with this."

"You sure? Because four months dating the woman and you're so wrapped around her little finger I'm surprised she even lets you out of the house. What's the matter? Leash getting tight?"

The remark was nasty—even for him—but Hoyt saw it the moment he met his mark. Tate was a big man, his large frame made even larger by ranch work, and all that muscle bunched up as he stepped back from the fence. Hoyt and his brothers had stopped pummeling each other into oblivion around the age of fourteen, but he had the immediate thought that perhaps old habits died hard.

"Belle has nothing to do with this. But I'm not sure you can say the same."

"Oh?" Hoyt asked, deliberate and slow. "Why's that?"

"I think you're the one walking a short leash. One held firmly in hand by Reese Grantham."

Whatever casual calm Hoyt had attempted as he stepped back from the fence faded as Tate's words hit a mark of their own.

Reese had imagined quite a lot as she drove over to Reynolds Station after leaving the high school. The secret that had gnawed steadily at her for over a month— the one that grew harder and harder to ignore as she spent a solid hour each morning desperately trying to keep down her bland breakfasts—needed air. It needed room to breathe.

And it needed its father to know of its existence.

After the initial shock had worn off, she'd been unable to suppress the sheer joy and happiness that filled her. She was pregnant.

Oh, the timing was off and the situation was far from ideal. The grief over her father was still fresh and the unsettling nature of his crimes had given her a few sleepless nights about what might be lurking in the DNA she was passing on to her child. She'd given the thoughts room to breathe, aware that addressing them was better than burying them, but in the end recognized the gift of life was just that. A gift. She'd be doing herself and her child a disservice if she let fear choke away her happiness.

Add on that she had no relationship to speak of with her child's father and the Midnight Pass PTA would go ballistic at the news, and she really shouldn't be this happy. Yet, even with that steady reality, she couldn't hide her contentment or the overwhelming sense of gratitude that had filled her the moment her gynecologist had confirmed the news. She hadn't once wavered since.

It was that surety—that absolute rightness—that had kept her focus steady and sure on the fact that she needed to tell Hoyt. She wouldn't hide this from him or try to keep him from knowing his child. If he chose not to embrace fatherhood that would be his call, but it wouldn't be from her lack of honesty.

She knew this. Felt it to her very core.

Yet, for the past month, the reality of getting in her

car and driving to Reynolds Station had seemed like a chore she could put off another day. Oh, she'd plotted and planned what she'd say, worked through the words and how she was going to say them. But she hadn't done it.

Jake's news about the PTA had only solidified the fact that she couldn't wait any longer.

Nor would the thickening of her stomach that was going to spill her secret unless she did the job first.

Truth and conviction pushed her on, through the large gates and enormous wrought-iron arch that announced the entrance to Reynolds Station. She drove down the immaculate concrete drive that seemed to stretch on for a mile, the ranch house rising up in the distance. That conviction never even wavered as she got out of the car and marched toward the side door that was the entrance to the kitchen and, as Arden had invited her in before, she knew was the preferred spot for family and friends to enter.

Ignoring the steady flutter in her stomach that was entirely different from morning sickness, yet nearly as harsh on the few contents still in there, she knocked on the door. A loud, masculine "Come in!" greeted her and she laid a hand on her stomach, willing what little was left to stay put.

And walked straight into chaos.

Ace Reynolds, the oldest brother and resident patriarch, stood in the middle of the kitchen like a football referee. Only instead of his arms extended in demonstrating football plays, each of his large hands was firmly planted on a shoulder. One belonging to Tate and the other to Hoyt.

Both men were filthy, layers of dust covering their

shirts and faces, blood dripping from various cuts.
Arden flitted around Hoyt with a first aid kit in hand
and Belle Granger, Tate's fiancée, hovered around his
head with an ice pack she kept trying to press to his
eye. A mix of low growls and muttered curses continued between the two patients which, best she could
tell, seemed to be the cause of Ace's firm and unwavering hold.

"Reese!" Arden's voice broke through the noise and
the greeting was enough to have Hoyt glancing sideways at her from beneath the steady pressure of a blood-
ied bandage. "Welcome to the O.K. Corral."

"There wasn't a gunfight," Hoyt muttered.

"And thank God for that," Arden said before lightly
smacking him on the back of the head.

Although it had been a long time since she'd swat-
ted at a man, Reese remembered the urge and couldn't
smother the smile. "It looks like I picked a bad time to
visit. I can come back later."

"Stay."

That lone word—firm and unyielding and without
even the hint of a grunt—left Hoyt's lips. The order
seemed to have an effect on everyone in the kitchen,
with puzzled looks coming from everyone except Tate.

Instead of uncertainty, a bright wide, *triumphant*
smile spread across Tate's face. That same sense of
triumph filled his words when he spoke. "Why don't
we give them a few minutes."

"But you're still—"

Tate cut off Belle with a squeeze of her hand over
the ice pack. "I'm fine. Or I will be, once Ace gets his
damn hands off me."

Reese knew it wasn't polite to laugh, but the harried exit of four adults, all of whom looked as if they'd rather stay and watch, fell firmly into sitcom territory. She wouldn't be half surprised if the four of them had considered taking up posts on the other side of the kitchen door to listen with empty glasses through the walls. In the end, though, it was Belle's firmly worded instructions to head outside that had everyone moving, the kitchen door slamming in their wake.

And then she was alone with Hoyt.

He had tossed the bandage Arden had held against his head, his wound obviously tender but no longer bleeding, in a garbage can by the edge of the counter before turning to look at her. "Sorry about that."

"About what?"

"The middle of our kitchen doesn't usually look like a MASH unit."

"Really?" Reese fought the butterflies that had suddenly taken flight in her stomach by picking up a box of bandages on the table and refitting them in the first aid kit. "With a working ranch full of cowboys, I figured this was par for the course."

"Maybe." He shrugged before a small grimace marred his firm, full lips. "But usually that's due to an accident and not a fight between brothers."

Although the tableau she'd walked in on—complete with Ace holding each man at bay—had suggested as much, it was curious that Hoyt would readily admit it. "What happened?"

"Nothing."

"That was some heavy duty first aid for nothing."

His grimace grew wider and for a moment, Reese was half convinced Hoyt wasn't going to say anything. "He suggested I've been in a mood," Hoyt said.

"At the risk of sounding indelicate, aren't you always in a mood?"

The surly look on his face broke wide open with a smile so dazzling Reese had to take a moment and simply stare. Good Lord, why hadn't she remembered just how attractive he was? Her fevered dreams each night had convinced her of just how handsome and good-looking he was, but nothing in those heated imaginings came close to the real thing. She'd thought more than once about calling him, but each time chalked it up to the whole one-night thing and left the situation alone. But now? With that broad smile? Oh, the man was lethal.

And she couldn't help wondering why she'd stayed away so long.

When he finally stopped laughing, his face settled into easier lines than when she'd first walked in. "Right you are. A point my brother was attempting to point out. I think."

"Why the fight?"

"Because he brought you up."

"Me? What's that supposed to mean? And why is it worthy of a brawl?"

"He had the nerve to suggest I've been a raging bastard for the past few months over you."

"Oh." She hesitated before pressing on. "Was he right?"

Hoyt seemed to consider the question before that gorgeous green gaze settled directly on hers. "Yeah. I think he is."

"What would I have to do with anything?"

"Reese." His voice stopped her, any hints of teasing gone. "You know what happened between us."

Knew?

Goodness, she'd lived with that knowledge each and every day since. She knew the moments they'd spent together—had watched them on the backs of her eyelids like a vivid film—and hadn't spent a single day since not thinking about him. While it hadn't been the only cause of her delayed visit, those vivid reimaginings were one of the reasons she'd stayed away. What had been intended as a casual evening, assuaging an adult need in a very adult fashion, had grown out of proportion in her mind.

Hoyt Reynolds wasn't her knight-errant come to save her from all the problems in her life. In fact, truth be told, he'd added a complication to her life that—while welcome—was absolutely an obstacle to getting her world back to normal.

Normal had vanished. It had begun back in the spring with her father's deeds and had only gotten more and more pronounced with her own choices. She was pregnant. And this time next year she'd have a small child utterly dependent on her. Life had changed and it wasn't ever going to return to where it had been.

"While I'm sorry you're injured and that I might have had any cause in that, I do need to talk to you."

"Sure." Hoyt nodded, pulling out a chair. "Sit down. What is it? Something with your father?"

His concern touched her, as did his immediate willingness to speak to the elephant in the room that most everyone else went out of their way to ignore.

"No, not my father. Although the PTA isn't crazy that the child of a killer is teaching their children."

The words popped out before she could stop them,

her discussion with Jake still bearing more residual anger than she'd realized.

Hoyt laid a hand over hers, folded on top of the kitchen table. "Reese. They don't matter. You can't believe they do. You're a great teacher. Surely they understand that."

That overwhelming support struck her hard and deep, like a punch to the chest. Only instead of pain, there was a strange warmth, filling her up even as she struggled to catch her breath at the kindness and ready support. "You going to go over and swing at them, too?"

"Will it work?"

"I doubt it. Although I'd pay big money to see Amanda Carneros take a punch to the nose."

"She still kicking around?"

"She's a fixture on the PTA. Eight kids have a way of doing that to a person."

Hoyt gave a mock shudder. "My condolences."

"Much as I appreciate the support and the diverting imagery, there's actually another reason I'm here."

"Sure." A soft smile had settled over his features, which nothing—even a split lower lip—could mar. "What is it?"

The stomach jitters ramped up as she accepted the fact that she bore life-altering news. News, she knew, that wouldn't change or grow any easier to hear by waiting another moment longer.

"I'm pregnant."

Chapter 4

He was going to be a father. That lone thought ran over and over in his mind, the impact like a sucker punch to the gut. Only unlike Tate's ham-handed fists, this one landed with far more power and a shocking degree of permanence.

It was the small tickle, though, that caught Hoyt up short. That light brush of something beneath his breastbone that was—shockingly—like joy.

Reese hadn't stopped talking since she dropped her bombshell ten minutes ago and Hoyt finally reached for her hand to quiet her. In that moment, the images that had haunted him for two months faded, replaced with the reality of her. She was beautiful. The dark hair that he'd imagined touching for these long weeks was once again in reach. And the soft arch of her cheekbones beckoned for his fingertips.

Hoyt touched neither, but he did give himself a moment to look his fill.

Although his lack of contact since would put their evening firmly in the realm of one-night stand territory, Hoyt had thought of their time together as anything but casual. In fact, it had scared him how many times he'd thought of getting in his truck and driving over to that small house on the other side of town, just to see if she was home or if she'd like to go grab dinner or spend some time together.

But he hadn't.

And now it had been up to her to make that same drive to share her news.

"How did this happen?" He kept his tone gentle. "We were careful."

"I suspect we should have paid closer attention to the word *novelty* on those neon-green condoms."

Hoyt had been lucky to even notice they were green—although that *was* hard to miss—let alone read the fine print on the side of the package. "Novelty?"

"Stupid," she muttered. "I know."

"I wouldn't quite go that far and if there's responsibility here, it's a shared one." He thought of the urgency and need that had gripped him and knew they equally shared the bad decision to attempt active birth control with something that looked like it was stamped out of a machine that made balloons.

"So what do we do?"

"I'm having the baby." Her chin shot up so fast—so defiant—that Hoyt had a moment of shock. A fierce possessiveness settled over her features, changing a gentle woman into a warrior.

"Of course you are. We are," he added for good measure. She might have had more time to get used to the idea, but he was warming up fast and he was going to be a father. While he'd actively looked to prevent it, now that the situation *existed*, it took no amount of time to decide he was all in.

"We?"

"Yes, we."

"When did we become a *we*?"

"I guess we just did," Hoyt said, suddenly realizing how true it was. Whatever had led them to those crazy moments together had created a life.

A child.

Their child.

And he was damned determined to be a hell of a lot better at raising said child than his father.

"I didn't come here expecting anything from you." Reese rubbed at a small spot on her cheek. "You deserve to know, and I want you to know—" She broke off and sighed. "All I'm trying to say is that I understand this is a bombshell and I know you weren't expecting it and I don't expect anything from you and, well, I just know it's a bomb. A big, crazy explosive one that's now detonated in your kitchen."

He knew bombs. And gunfire. And warfare. He'd seen his fair share in the military and knew what it was to lay waste to an area and destroy it all. Only nothing about this moment felt like destruction.

Change, yes. But destruction? Not even the slightest bit.

When she seemed poised to continue on her rant, he laid a hand on her arm to stop her. If he had to bet on it, Hoyt was quite sure the verbal rush wasn't anything she'd planned but recognized it as vintage Reese.

They might not know each other well—even if they had made a child—but one thing he knew with certainty about its mother was that words were her way of making sense of the world.

"I'd say this has been a rather sizable bombshell for both of us." He hesitated, only briefly, before pressing on. "A bombshell in a year of many for you."

"You mean my father?"

"Yeah. Of course. He changed your life, Reese. Changed it in ways you can never go back to. I realize a child is a joyous thing and his acts weren't, but it doesn't change the fact that your life is in upheaval once again. I'm sorry to be the cause of that."

"You're sorry we spent the night together?"

"No."

"But you're sorry we made a baby?"

"That's not what I'm saying."

The color of the small spot she'd rubbed on her cheek, already pink from her touch, deepened, as a spot on the other cheek heated rapidly. "I think that's exactly what you're saying. You came into that bar, you saw me and you felt sorry for me. Then we had a fun night. You were no more expecting to become a father than I was a mother. Let's not sugarcoat it or act like we're celebrating this joyous event."

Although Hoyt was known for his surly attitude, his temper rarely rumbled above a low simmer. He knew how to keep his irritation on a firm leash. So what was it about this one woman and these unfair, ping-ponging questions that had his ire up in a flash?

"Can we just calm down here a minute? Like you said, this is a big bombshell. Just because it's a surprise doesn't mean I don't want the child, nor does it mean

I can't pivot and accept the changes in my life. But to your point, let's not sugarcoat it."

"What are you trying to say?"

Hoyt took a deep breath. What was he aiming for? Love? Devotion? Or maybe just a moment to rewind and take in all she'd just shared.

"What I'm trying to say is hold on a damn minute. You've had a bit longer to get used to this than I have. Rash statements don't do either of us any good."

He knew rash. Had lived it himself over a decade ago when he and his family got stuck dealing with the after-effects of his father's poor business choices. While he might have moved on from those times and the anger that had fueled him to rebuild Reynolds Station, they weren't forgotten memories.

"Let me get us both a few waters and we can talk this through." Hoyt stood and crossed to the fridge, rubbing his midsection. Although he was well able to take a punch, Tate had landed a few good ones and his stomach was bruised from his brother's assertive fists.

"You okay?"

"I'd be a bit better if Tate hadn't decided to go all Terminator out in the paddock." Hoyt grabbed two bottles of water. "I'd feel even better about it if I hadn't been the one to punch first."

"Men worry about that?"

At the genuine innocence in her question, Hoyt couldn't hold back the smile that had continued to force its way into their conversation. Reese was having a baby.

His baby.

And for reasons he couldn't name or understand, everything in his upside-down world had just turned right-side up.

* * *

Reese knew men handled matters with their fists. She'd seen it enough growing up and had witnessed several school-yard fights since becoming a teacher. It wasn't an aspect of human behavior she liked, but she understood it.

It was an entirely different matter to know she'd been the root cause of a brawl. How was that even possible?

While she hadn't gone looking for a follow up evening despite wanting one, Hoyt had made no attempt to contact her over the past few months. If a small piece of her heart had been left bare and exposed at that, it served her right. She knew what she'd asked for that crazy Tuesday night in June.

Sex without strings.

It had felt important at the time. Grown-up. Mature. How humbling to realize after he'd left that she wasn't really designed for the whole one-night stand thing. But she could hardly change her mind after assuring him—repeatedly—that all she wanted was an evening of mutual fun between two consenting adults.

It had been the truth when the evening began. Even as she'd said the words, she'd believed each and every syllable herself. It had only been later—after—when she'd thought about all that she and Hoyt had shared that night. The sex had been amazing, but it had been so much more.

Camaraderie.

Kindness.

And a tender sweetness she'd never expected.

Was that the reason she'd found such joy in the discovery she was pregnant?

Even as she couldn't deny the lingering feelings for

her child's father, she knew that the joy of discovering she was pregnant was steeped in so much more. Based on her due date, in seven and a half more months she was going to be a mother. There was power there, and a most humbling realization that there would be an infant totally and completely dependent on her.

Her child.

With a glance toward Hoyt she amended that. *Their* child. A small ribbon of joy unfurled beneath her breastbone at that.

And his insistence on claiming his child.

"How long have you known?"

Hoyt's question put an end to her musing, meandering thoughts. "A little over a month."

If he thought that was too long to wait to tell him, he didn't show it. Instead, his direct gaze never wavered and his mouth remained set in a firm line. "How are you feeling?"

"Good days and bad. Mornings are tough," she admitted, happy to have someone to tell, especially since she hadn't dared mention it to her mother. "Some afternoons, I feel great and eat whatever I can get my hands on. Others, the thought of food has me running for the bathroom."

"I'm sorry you've carried this alone. Sorry that—"

Something silly and misguided leaped in her chest when he broke off.

Sorry that he what?

Hadn't called? Come around? Asked after her?

Or sorry about the baby?

Before she could ask, he finished his thought. "Sorry that you've had to face this by yourself."

"Yes, well. I wanted you to know." She stood, the

weight of the responsibility that lay between them heavier than it had been since the day she'd read that little plastic stick. "I'll get going now."

"You don't have to leave."

"Actually, I do. This changes a lot, but it doesn't change what's between us."

"And what's that?"

"We're not in a relationship," she said. The joy at his acceptance of her pregnancy faded in that stark reality. She'd reminded herself of it often enough. They had a child linking them together but they weren't in a relationship.

If she hadn't gotten pregnant using neon-green condoms, the two of them would still be going about their lives. Him on the ranch and her preparing for a new school year.

And they'd be apart.

It hurt, but the pain didn't make it any less true.

Although he was a man of economic motions, not prone to the exaggerated or expansive, Reese was surprised to see Hoyt go so still. As someone who had little ability to sit still, anyone who exhibited the behavior was impressive in her eyes.

But Hoyt's stillness was something else entirely.

"Hoyt?" When he said nothing, she pressed a bit harder. "What's the matter?"

"I'm trying to understand something."

"Of course."

"How is it that you could hold on to this secret for a month, not tell me and then when you finally decide to do so, race off like the hounds of hell are at your feet?"

"I'd hardly—"

"I'm not done." He held up a hand, the motion as

effective—maybe more so—as a gunshot. "You come over here, tell me the massive news that I'm going to be a father and think you're going to waltz out again."

"I'm not waltzing anywhere."

"Oh, no? Because if you're planning on walking away from me, you've got another think coming."

Whatever satisfaction he'd taken from pummeling on his brother had vanished, his skin as tight and his pulse as hard and thready as earlier. Hoyt wasn't sure how it had happened but this one woman had managed to turn his entire world on its ear.

Again.

He'd believed he'd get past their time together back in June. A crazy night of passion, not to be repeated or given a chance to sprout into anything serious. His aversion to commitment had been the only thing—the very thin tether—that had kept him from going back to her. The night after they were together and every night since.

It was out of character and more than that, it wasn't something he was looking for. He wasn't cut out for the whole lifetime with someone and a march toward forever after. He was a difficult person and whether it had become a personal shield—as Ace had hinted at often enough—or was just the reality of who he was, Hoyt knew he wasn't relationship material.

So why did this one woman have the odd ability to make him think otherwise?

Worse, to *want* otherwise.

"Walk away from you? I've never even walked toward you, Hoyt."

"The night we spent together suggests otherwise."

"Does it?"

Her question hovered between them, a living, breathing ball of fire that burned bright. "You don't think it does?"

"I think we were two adults who found something mutual in each other that night. Comfort. Release. The things grown-ups do in the dark. That's all."

Although it stung to have their night together painted in such raw terms, he was hardly about to share the confusion that had continued to haunt his dreams every time he thought about his night with Reese. Instead he nodded, keeping his gaze solemn. "Have you told anyone else?"

"No."

"Not even your mother?"

"She's—" Reese stopped. Sighed. "She's fragile right now. I've swung back and forth between the idea that a baby will give her something happy to focus on and the idea that she's going to go over the edge that her single daughter is having a baby out of wedlock."

"Any chance you're underestimating her?"

"Probably."

The discovery of Russ Grantham's crimes had shaken the very foundation of Midnight Pass. He could hardly expect the man's wife wasn't still reeling from living at the very epicenter of the situation. Even so, he found it hard to believe the prospect of a grandchild and a new generation would be met with anything but joy.

An image of Serena Grantham snuggling with her grandchild filled his mind's eye, at odds with the reality that his own mother would never see his child.

"You should tell her."

"I will. I'm running out of time to keep it a secret, anyway." Reese sighed. "Same goes for work."

"You're not expecting a positive reception there?"

"Hardly. A single, pregnant teacher? That's the stuff of nightmares for the PTA."

"It's no one's concern. Nor does your personal business have anything to do with your ability to teach."

"That won't keep tongues from wagging."

"Little does."

Little did stop the gossips but telling Reese to *screw 'em* was hardly the answer, either. Whether it made sense to him or not, Reese's reality wasn't his own and public scrutiny was a part of her job. Although he might be ignorant of her day-to-day challenges, it wasn't a stretch to realize a teacher of teenagers would receive a rather cold eye on any behavior that might—inadvertently or otherwise—influence those in her care.

And while she was right—they had acted as single adults—he couldn't help but feel she now bore a far bigger set of consequences.

"We could address it head on."

Reese let out a small bark of laughter. "Clearly, you've never met a determined Parent–Teacher Association and the fierce dragons who choose to run for the board."

"Focused parents?"

"Focused and often of the helicopter sort."

"Helicopter?"

"Sorry." She shook her head. "I suspect your exposure to rabid parents is minimal in the middle of a cattle ranch."

"'Fraid so."

"A helicopter parent is one who hovers and makes a considerable amount of noise while doing so."

The image connected and he nodded. "Got it. And you've got a few of those."

"A whole board full of them."

"Ouch."

He had no interest in parading his personal life around Midnight Pass, but he was hardly going to toss Reese to the wolves. If she needed help, he'd give it to her and he'd support her completely. "There has to be a way to make them see reason. You're a good teacher."

"Thank you. That's sweet of you." She stilled mid-tear of the label on her water bottle. "But how would you even know that?"

"That time you brought the kids here for a tour. I watched you. You're good with them. You didn't talk down to them and you treated them with respect."

"Thank you."

"Plus, you seem to really like what you do. You got into the discussion of careers and asked the ranch hands some really good questions."

"Thanks."

"You don't believe me?"

She shrugged. "It's not about belief, Hoyt. It's about the reality of standing up in front of a room full of teenagers, week after week, my stomach growing rounder and rounder. I'm supposed to set an example."

"And being a grown-up who's about to welcome a child into the world isn't a good example?"

"Not to the PTA and certainly not to my school board." She stood again. "Look. I don't expect you to understand the pressure or the magnitude of what I've created with this situation."

Her bleak expression tugged at something deep inside of him, even as a small flame of an idea flickered and flared to life. "Then explain it to me."

"I thought I just did. Parents of teenagers full of raging hormones are more than ready to take a pro-verbial pitchfork to anyone in a position to negatively influence their children."

"And having a baby is a negative influence?"

"It is when you're unmarried. When you add on the scandal of a serial killing father, the entire situation smacks of poor decisions and a pathway to losing my job."

"Let's kill the gossip then."

Her gaze flicked down to her still-flat stomach be-fore snapping back to his. "I'm keeping the baby."

His patience at an end, Hoyt's retort was sharper than he'd planned. "Yes. *We* are."

"We?"

"We. You might as well start getting used to it."

"Okay." She nodded, the fierce defense fading slightly. "We. That still doesn't change the situation."

"Let's change it then. Let's get married."

Chapter 5

Explain it to me.

We.

Let's get married.

Hoyt's demands hovered in the air playing over and over in her mind. But it was his final suggestion—the marriage one—that had her words sticking in her throat.

Married?

Why did that thought tantalize so much, like a dancing light playing just out of her reach? Something she wanted to touch—wanted to reach for with both hands—yet still couldn't quite grasp. So Reese did what she always did. What she'd done since she was a teenager with a family unit falling further and further apart day by day.

She fell back on practicality and reason.

"I can't marry you. I don't even know you."

"We're having a baby. Maybe it's time we started to know each other."

Hoyt's words tempted as they sunk in, that light dancing in the distance. Marriage? Getting to know each other? Having a baby together?

Did he have any idea what it meant to hear that? From the moment she'd discovered she was pregnant, there had been something other than that sticky coating of fear lining her throat. Yes, she was excited about the baby. Had been from the start.

But it was a joy that came with a shockingly deep price.

If she could keep the proverbial lions at bay—and she'd been a teacher long enough to know the PTA had very sharp teeth—she could adjust to her new reality. She could bring her child into the world and do it with the knowledge she wasn't destitute or risking unemployment once her annual contract ended.

It was a solution to her problems and it gave her time to plan her life.

But what would that mean for her heart?

Was she truly the type of person who could enter into a loveless marriage? A sham? It was that reality she couldn't reconcile, no matter how tempting his words.

"I agree, we need to know each other better. That doesn't mean we should get married."

"Why not? It will fix your problems at work."

"But we don't know each other," Reese tried again. "How do two people who don't know each other get married?"

"How did two people who don't know each other have sex and make a baby? We'll figure it out." Hoyt was so matter-of-fact. So sure of himself.

Reese fought not to get caught up in the moment, remembering exactly how well they'd figured it out. More, she tried desperately not to get caught up in that oh-so-wonderful vision of letting him take her away from the problem at hand.

And with that, came a new fear. And a new sadness.

She was a single mother, or would be one. She was prepared to face that alone. Marrying the father of her child—a man she didn't know—wasn't necessarily going to fix anything more than her optics problem with work, but she would still know the truth. She and Hoyt were strangers. Yes, they were two people who had found comfort in each other in the most intimate of ways, but it didn't change the facts.

As if reading her thoughts, Hoyt pressed on. "And it's not like we don't know each other. I've known you practically my whole life."

"As acquaintances in town or people who say hello at the grocery store. That's hardly marriage material."

He shrugged. "So we get married for a while. Get past the gossips and the innuendo and put on a show for everyone in town. They'll move on to a new subject soon enough."

"And then what?"

"We have to figure out how we're going to share our child. This will give us time to do that, too."

The warm, comforting visions that had begun to roost in her mind of their own accord vanished in the space of a heartbeat. "How to share our child? What's that supposed to mean? This is *my* baby."

"And mine. I'm going to have a role in my child's life. I'm not looking for visiting rights once a week, Reese. We will share custody."

Whether once a week or once a year, the thought of parting with her baby for even a moment filled her with dread.

"I can't believe I came here."

A small line furrowed Hoyt's brow as his eyebrows made tight slashes across his forehead. "What is that supposed to mean?"

"This is my baby. I'm not giving him or her up."

"I'm not suggesting anything about giving anyone up. The baby is mine, too. Would you keep me from him or her?"

"No." When he said it that way, Reese felt small. This was his child, too.

That reality was one they were both going to have to come to terms with, and quickly. They were having a child. And that life belonged to both of them.

Impetuous and brusque. Careless. Hard.

He'd been all those things and more.

Hoyt replayed his kitchen conversation with Reese over and over in his mind as he covered ground in the north pasture on his mustang, Stinkbug. The horse had long outgrown his name—one granted to him by the odd fondness he'd initially had for the small bugs littered around the corral his first summer at Reynolds Station—but the moniker had stuck.

Sort of like Hoyt's attitude.

What should he have said to Reese? Because clearly a desire to share parenting duties and an offer of marriage weren't it.

Their conversation at an impasse, the woman had made her excuses and ducked out as fast as she'd come in. He'd thought to follow her—he likely should have—

but damn it, he needed some time, too. The baby bomb was a large one, but oddly he'd found himself warming to it almost immediately. It was the other component that had settled more restlessly on his shoulders.

The reality of his child's mother.

He was having a baby with Reese Grantham.

Hoyt had only ever felt this unsure of himself one other time in his life. The day he had discovered his father's sins, via a phone call from his brother Ace. That day of discovery—and the sinking reality of what was to come—had been crystal clear. It had upended his life and that of his siblings, and it had forged the man he'd become.

He'd believed the marines, and later special ops, had played that role. Determined to enlist after high school, he'd proudly worn a uniform and happily gone off to basic training. His time on the ranch, both the physical strength it brought and the willingness to follow the routine of tending and caring for animals on a daily basis, had set him up well. His military service and his ultimate selection of something more dangerous yet even more rewarding had honed who and what he already was—a competent, effective leader.

His father's betrayal had taken all that and turned it on its ear.

It didn't matter how competent you were; when you stared down the barrel of bad business practices, cheated partners and overall distrust in your product, the world took notice. And they weren't interested in how many skirmishes you managed or how devoted you were to your fellow soldiers if they had been swindled by a bad deal.

On that day of Ace's call, Hoyt had understood the

gravity of it all, even if he hadn't been able to put words to it. The ground that he stood on and the life he'd believed he had were gone. And something new had been about to take its place.

Where that time had been fraught with confusion and anger and a lingering shock at his father's deceit, today was different. Today there was excitement, anticipation and, admittedly, a raw sense of fear that wouldn't unclench his gut.

A baby.

Someone small and helpless and utterly dependent on him. For shelter and for sustenance and, as he or she grew, for learning all there was to life. An awesome responsibility that, while scary, was far more exciting than he'd ever considered. What he hadn't considered was what had come next.

A marriage proposal. Scratch that, he amended as he turned Stink toward a small grazing area he knew the horse liked. He'd offered up a ham-handed and clumsy marriage proposal. No wonder the woman had rejected him outright.

What had he been thinking? Unconventional relationship with Reese Grantham or not, people had babies every day. Sometimes that child came into the world with married parents, and sometimes it didn't. What may have carried a stigma in years past wasn't nearly the same any longer. Yet the first place his mind had gone was to give his child his name.

Arden would call him a Neanderthal. Was she wrong? Or was something else at play? Questions without answers. Or maybe, he reflected, questions *with* answers.

Maybe he was a Neanderthal, but he wanted his

child. And he wanted that child to have his name. The name Reynolds stood for something. He, Ace, Tate and Arden had seen to that. This land, the ranch and all he was paid tribute to that name.

And he wanted his child to carry it on.

"There you are."

Tate's loud greeting floated toward him as Hoyt turned to see his brother silhouetted in the sun. The second of the three Reynolds sons, Tate had always worn life the easiest on his shoulders. As the eldest, Ace carried the responsibility and Hoyt—despite being the youngest son—had never been easygoing or light-hearted. Tate made up for all of it.

The fact that they'd been tussling on the ground a few hours before and now his brother sat easy in his saddle, a broad grin splitting his face, only reinforced that simple fact.

As Tate rode closer, Hoyt gave himself a moment to look. There was a red bruise over Tate's left eye, heading on toward purple, and even with the easy ride in the saddle, it was obvious his brother favored his right-side ribs. The side, Hoyt remembered, where he'd gotten in a solid punch.

"You look awful damn cheery."

"I am," Tate affirmed as he patted his own mount's neck. "Tot and I felt like a ride and it's a pretty day for one."

"It's beastly hot and if we don't get back to it, we'll only have half the herd branded."

"Ever the cheerful one, little brother. I'd have thought beating on me would have gotten rid of that stick up your ass but clearly I was mistaken." Tate rode closer. "And I already told everyone to take an extra hour and then we'd get back to it. Everyone seems grateful for the rest. That was until Arden began racing around with full canisters of bug spray and sunscreen."

Hoyt smiled in spite of himself. "They're going to be running back toward the cows."

"Which, I suspect, is all part of Arden's devious plan," Tate said with a smile. "Protection from the elements and a team of men anxious to get back to unpleasant work. She's also promised apple pie for dinner."

"She did?"

"Yep. She had about a bushel of apples on the kitchen table, which I was more than happy to leave her to."

Jokes about their family and apple pie. Just like that, Tate had made all that had come earlier vanish. It was easy. Simple.

Forgiven.

It had always been like that with his brother. And without thinking, the words he usually had so much trouble conjuring up spilled from his lips in a rush.

"I'm sorry. About before. You didn't deserve any of it."

Tate shrugged. "It's forgotten."

"Maybe for you, but not for me. You deserve better."

"Why don't you talk to me instead?"

"I'm going to be a father."

Hoyt's rarely riled brother went stock-still in the saddle before letting out a huge whoop. "Hot damn! How'd you swing that one?"

"The usual way."

"With Reese Grantham, I suppose."

"How'd you guess?"

"Tabasco mentioned it by mistake a few weeks ago."

"Tabasco?" The news was a surprise, as Tabasco Burns was known for his vault-like confidence.

"He was embarrassed about it, too, after he realized Belle and I didn't know what he was talking about. Mentioned he hadn't seen you for a while and hoped that it meant you two had hit it off after meeting up at his place a month before that."

Although he had no interest in being part of the gossip grapevine Reese had mentioned that first night at The Border Line, Hoyt had to admit he was relieved by the source. If Tabasco had said something to Tate, then it wasn't designed to be malicious. He had to admit equal surprise that Belle and Tate had both hung on to the information for as long as they had.

Tate shot him a side eye before pressing on. "What, exactly, do you have going on with Reese? Besides a child."

And just like that, his brother had struck at the very heart of the matter.

"Hell if I know."

"What do you *want* to have going on with Reese?"

The questions were fair. Even with his decided lack of verbal communication, he'd have asked the same if the positions had been reversed. And yet...

"What are you? Oprah?"

Tate only grinned harder before slapping one of his riding gloves against his leg. "You'd better practice on me, little brother. Because once Arden and Belle get a load of this news, the questions are going to fly fast and furious."

"It's none of their business."

The easy, jovial manner vanished as Tate's dark

green eyes, so like Hoyt's own, filled with something unmistakable.

Something fierce.

The Reynolds family protected their own and nothing would ever change that.

"This child is their family. Of course it's their business."

Once again, with little effort, his brother put him right back in his place. "Okay. I get it."

"We're behind you. And we're here for you."

"I know that."

"Do you?" Any trace of humor had vanished as Tate stared at him, long and hard. "Because you seem determined to fight every single battle all by yourself."

"They're mine to fight."

Tate shook his head. "That's where you're wrong. By the time a man goes to battle, he needs an army marching right along with him. You have that. Don't forget it."

He'd do anything for his family and quickly fell into line as a foot soldier in that Reynolds army Tate spoke of. So why did he find it so hard to accept the support in return?

They sat their horses for several long moments, the animals seeming content to stand in the sunlight, soaking up the day. Both Tate's mount, Tot, and Hoyt's own Stink were trained workhorses in addition to being pampered and well-loved pets. Their ability to blend into the family dynamic—and remain unfazed by the tension that refused to lift from Hoyt's shoulders—was a testament to their training.

But it was Stink's soft whinny when Hoyt laid a hand on his neck that reinforced the family Tate spoke of.

The child he and Reese Grantham were bringing

into the world had a family and a support system just waiting for him or her.

Now it was a matter of convincing Reese of that fact.

Marriage?

The idea still lingered in her thoughts hours later as Reese scrubbed her kitchen sink to a high polish. She'd read a few pregnancy websites and each had mentioned the nesting phase. But as she attacked the stainless steel with another round of cleaning liquid she admitted this went *way* beyond nesting.

This was anger, pure and simple.

How had she gotten herself into this situation?

And why, no matter how many different ways she spun it, couldn't she whip up any sense of remorse or desire to go back and do things differently?

Go back.

How enticing that thought had been, one that had lived with her for the past several months, since her father's awful crimes had been discovered. What if they could go back and change her brother, Jamie? What if they could go back and be a different family? What if she could have had a different childhood?

Reese had learned a long time ago that what-ifs did little good but, oh, how tempting they were to imagine. Especially in those dark hours between midnight and dawn when questions seemed to be the only thing she had.

She loved her family. Despite all that had happened—every horrifying bit of it—she loved them. But she was also honest enough to admit that she'd change them if she could. Her brother's illness, one that grew worse and worse as addiction racked his body and his actions. Her father and his twisted inability to deal with the reality of his child's life.

And her mother.

Had she known? Sensed it somewhere? Abstractly, Reese laid a hand on her stomach. Wouldn't a mother know every aspect of her child?

Reese flipped on the water, washing the cleaner down the drain. In the end, none of it mattered. Not the questions. Not the memories that lingered and haunted. Not the graves that now sat in the Midnight Pass cemetery, proclaiming the lives of Jamie and Russ Grantham.

If only they could have been different.

If her brother's decisions had been different.

And if only her father had found justice through the channels he'd been trained to use.

Oh, she understood remorse, and the desire for things to change. Or for things to never have happened. But she didn't feel the same way about the baby. Nor did she feel that way about its father.

That lone night with Hoyt had played over and over in her mind in those same restless hours before dawn. The simplicity of it all, and the ease with which the two of them had come together. Although not a stranger to sex, she didn't have a huge repertoire of partners. She considered herself proficient, she thought with a smile, but had never seen herself as a wild woman in bed. Her actions with Hoyt that night suggested otherwise.

Yet even for the casual nature of their coupling, there was a connection. Something deeper. She thought it was just herself, or her memories of their night together, but seeing him again today made her question that. Was there something between them?

And why had he been fighting with his brother over her?

The initial news had surprised her and by the time they got into the discussion over the baby, she'd forgotten to ask. Now it was all she could think about.

The scrubbing at an end, she poured herself a fresh glass of water, adding a few lemon slices she kept in the fridge. It was beastly hot outside but she was sick of her own company and wanted a bit of fresh air. Heading out back, she settled into her favorite lounger on her small screened-in porch. The space welcomed, full of the happy things she liked to surround herself with. Several plants bloomed along the section of the porch that gathered the most morning sun and she flipped on the large paddle fan that kept the air moving even on a day as hot as this one.

The water was cool on her throat as she sipped and took her seat, curling her legs up beneath her. The scent of hot grass wafted through the screens, a reminder she needed to get out and mow this weekend. She was grateful that, other than the bouts of morning sickness, her checkups to date had been excellent. Her pregnancy hadn't slowed down other aspects of her life and she could easily run the mower around her small patch of land. An hour and she'd be done.

Alone.

Accomplished, but alone all the same.

The thought hit with a thud, reminding her she was no further along in fixing the problems of her life than she had been that morning. Yes, Hoyt knew and that was a start. But there was still the conversation with her mother to be had, then one more with the school. Not to mention all the well-meaning townsfolk who would notice and comment on her growing baby bump.

Let's change it then. Let's get married.

Hoyt's words had raced through her mind, over and over. They comforted and infuriated in equal measure, but at that moment, the lazy turn of the fan smoothing the air above her, she had to admit they did something else.

They offered a way out.

Was it a path she could take?

Despite her maudlin moments, she was perfectly capable and absolutely prepared to care for her child on her own. She was strong and determined. She had a job and she had her savings if something went sideways.

She could—and would—find her way forward. For both of them.

Reese laid a hand on her stomach. Although she didn't have a bump yet, she had noticed a thickening in her waistline. She might make it through the first few weeks of school, hiding the evidence with large shirts or flowy dresses, but by homecoming, everyone would know she was pregnant.

The air changed. It was the last thing Reese thought before a deep resonant voice floated toward her through the screen.

"It's pretty out here. Care for some company?"

Chapter 6

Early evening sunlight filtered through the screens, highlighting Reese in a golden glow. It was still hot— August in Texas was never anything else—but even the heat haze only added to the sense of stillness and contemplation.

That's how Hoyt found her, her eyes distant and dreamy and her hand pressed protectively over her midsection.

Had he ever seen anything more beautiful?

The spell broken with his greeting, her arm fell to her side as she stood and she gestured him toward the door. "Come on in."

The afternoon had been as tiring as he expected, so it had been a surprise when he heard himself rejecting the large barbecue dinner their bunkhouse cook had ordered up along with Arden's apple pie, and headed instead for his room to clean up. Branding cattle was hard work, and it worked up an appetite, yet he found he had none.

Now that he saw Reese, highlighted in that beautiful evening sunlight, Hoyt realized just how wrong he'd been. He did have a hunger—for *her.*

"Can I get you anything?" she asked.

"No, thank you."

"You sure? I have some beer in the fridge," she smiled. "It's been sitting there and hasn't had much use."

"That'd be nice."

Reese ducked back into the house, the door closing gently behind her. It gave him a moment to look around, her small backyard spreading out before him through the expansive screens. It was a nice house, he thought. Welcoming. He'd thought so back in June when she brought him here, even though he hadn't spent much time looking around.

But now that he had the chance, he looked his fill. The house was small but well appointed, as he remembered, with pretty furnishings and brightly colored rooms. She'd obviously taken great pride in crafting the place just to her own specifications. He turned to watch her through the window that overlooked the porch. She moved easily around the kitchen and he saw once again the updated granite counters and deeply polished cherrywood cabinets he'd observed briefly in June.

"You have a great house," he said as she walked back through the door, a beer in hand.

"Thank you. It's home."

"This used to be the Baxter place, wasn't it?"

"This was where Old Mrs. Baxter lived the last ten years of her life."

"How did you find out about it?"

She smiled. "My dad and Bruce Baxter were good friends and hunting buddies. After Bruce's mom passed away, he told my dad first that they were putting the house on the market. They sold it to me without even listing it."

"It's got great bones, and it's obvious that you put in the work to update it." Hoyt took a long swallow of his beer as he looked around the porch. "This screened-in porch space is great."

"My dad helped me with it. We renovated it the first spring I was here. Before—" Her voice faded off. "Just before."

Before the murders.

The reminder of Russ Grantham's crimes seemed to hang there, in the thick air between them, stiff and unmoving despite the overhead fan.

"It's okay to talk about him, you know."

"Is it?"

"Of course it is. He's your father."

She laughed, the sound anything but gentle. "Then you are the rare individual in this town. Any mention of Russ Grantham, no matter the reason, is met with frowns and hissed responses."

"It hardly seems fair."

"Fairness flies out the window when we're talking about murder. It makes people decidedly uneasy."

Even as he wondered at her words, Hoyt knew what she spoke of. While Russ's crimes were far worse than Hoyt's own father's, both men had still committed crimes, made choices that had hurt others and betrayed trust and confidence. He would never suggest to Reese that the situations were identical—not only would it be insensitive, but he would also never compare bad criminal business practices with killing others—but he did understand the disgrace.

The whispered comments.

And the shame.

It was the shame, Hoyt admitted to himself, that was the hardest to explain or get over. Behavior that wasn't your own yet reflected on you with a bright shiny light.

How many times had he questioned it? The overwhelming guilt and embarrassment for something he hadn't done. Shouldn't he have known, somehow? Shouldn't he have sensed it?

Surely that's what others asked. How could the son, a member of the same family and same family business, not be complicit?

"Hoyt?"

Reese's question pulled him from his thoughts and he lifted his beer, tipping it toward her. "Well, you don't have to keep quiet around me."

"Thanks." She took a sip of her water, her eyes focused on him. "I'm glad you're here. I don't like the way we left things. Before."

"Neither do I."

She seemed to hesitate before pressing on. Open. Honest. And seeming more than willing to stand her ground. "I know what I had to tell you was a surprise. Maybe with a bit of time, we can talk about it with cooler heads."

"That's why I'm here."

The afternoon, both the talk with Tate and the work with the cattle, had given him some time to process things. His mind had worked as hard as his body, but rather than being mentally exhausted, he found he was almost too keyed up to sit still.

"Before we get into it, are you hungry?" he asked.

"You want to go to dinner?"

He did want to go to dinner. Wanted to spend time with her. That strange craving that had hit him at odd moments over the past two months—the one that made him want to drive over to her place—had finally been given free rein.

"Yes, I do."

"Oh, okay. Yes, I'd like that."

"You up for Mexican food? Tate and Belle keep raving about this place a few towns away."

"I live in Texas." She smiled broadly. "I'm always up for Mexican food."

"Then let's go."

Reese buckled herself up in Hoyt's truck and ignored the images that assailed her of the last time she'd done the same. The heated looks that had passed between them. The increasing awareness of the strong, stoic cowboy with the compelling green eyes. And the increasing reality filling her mind's eye of exactly what she wanted to have happen between them.

She'd gotten her wish and then some.

And now here they were again.

They made small talk on the drive, focused on any number of topics. All of it was light and easy, none of it fraught with the sexual tension and underlying need that had underpinned their last drive together.

Reese kept her thoughts to herself, but she had seen the change in him. It was strange, she realized, because discussion of Russ Grantham always made people uncomfortable. Yet with Hoyt, it was different.

He understood her father's crimes, probably better than most others, since one of them had been committed on his property. But he didn't seem to judge her. Nor did she see that cold, fear-based censure deep in his eyes. Instead, he seemed to want her to find the good.

It was unexpected and, if she was honest with herself, encouraging. Even her mother had tried to avoid any and all talk of her father. It was lonely and alienating and gave all the power to the last year of Russ Grantham's life instead of the sixty or so that had come before.

"You're quiet," Hoyt said.

"I was thinking about before."

"And?"

"And it's nice when I talk to you about my father. That you don't, in your mind, seem to be jumping to the fact that he was a murderer."

"Maybe because I'm not."

"It's rare."

He kept his focus on the road but she felt his unyielding attention as keenly as if he were staring right at her. "I suppose it is. I don't think people do it to be unkind or to make you uncomfortable. I think it's their discomfort and their lack of knowledge of what to say."

"You mean you don't think it's because he tortured and killed several people?"

"Reese—"

"No, wait." She held up a hand. "Please hear me out."

"Okay."

"I've had a lot of months to get used to this, and even though I know I should understand by now, I don't. I don't know how to reconcile the man that I knew with the man who committed those crimes."

"How could you? He was your father."

"He was a monster."

"I think—" He broke off, then started again. His voice was hesitant, before growing stronger. "I think that's too easy. As humans, we want to paint things in black-and-white and while decisive action can't be changed, what led to it is often a mystery."

"Murder is a rather decisive action."

He turned toward her, that gaze that she had imagined staring right through her. "You keep going back to that same place. Part defense, part sharp taunt. It's like you feel you must keep reminding me that he killed people."

"Because he did."

"He was also a father. A lawman. He supported his community. He wasn't all bad, Reese."

"But he became bad. What if that lives inside of me? Inside of my child?"

The words were out before she could stop them. A great gushing well of sadness that haunted her in the moments that she allowed it to claw and dig too deeply into her mind. A fear so big—so giant—that she feared to even put it into words.

Only now she had.

The sign for Manuel's Kitchen came up on the right-hand side of the road, a beacon beckoning them in, and Hoyt kept his silence until he turned into the parking lot and found a spot. Once he did, he cut the ignition and turned in his seat, reaching for her hand.

"Listen to me. I can't change how you feel, nor can I ever fully understand it. But something I know. I *know* it, Reese. You aren't your father. Our child isn't your father. What he did, what he felt compelled to do, isn't genetic and it isn't living in your DNA, waiting to come out. It was a terrible product of living with grief."

"How do you know?"

"Because I know it the same way I understand a Texas sky at dusk, the way it gets all purpley and gold. The same way I know when one of my cattle is going to calve. The same way I know how badly I want to be a father. Russ's crimes don't live in you and they don't live in our child."

She wanted to believe him. As she listened to him, she did believe him. She saw her future and she knew, to the depths of her soul, that her child was good. That the baby she carried had a future and a still-to-be-fulfilled life ahead of him or her. That her father's sins didn't and couldn't taint that innocent life.

So why was she so afraid?

The position in the empty, sparsely wooded lot behind Reese Grantham's house didn't provide much cover, but it had been enough. Although she'd rushed back there to get out of sight, the field had ended up providing a perfect view to see the back of the house. And the surprising coming and going that had included Hoyt Reynolds.

Interesting.

Where she had expected minimal chance of being caught, her ability to claim PTA business was a ready excuse if she had been found out and around the house.

Well, gee, I knocked on the door and no one answered, so I went around the back to that pretty screened-in porch to see if I could find Ms. Grantham.

If only Reynolds hadn't beat her to it.

What was he doing suddenly hanging around again? Since one of Russ Grantham's crimes had been committed on Reynolds land, it was hard to imagine the Reynolds family carried anything but a vendetta because of it. A murder on their property didn't make folks feel all that safe.

Yet, somehow the town had rallied, she mused. Likely it had something to do with one of the other Reynolds boys. Tate, she thought—but who could keep their attractive asses straight?—who'd taken up with the cop. Seeing as how that cop had been the one to catch Grantham and end his crime spree, folks had eased up a bit.

She still figured it didn't mean the Reynolds family was set to become buddy-buddy with what was left of the Grantham clan. Yet, there he was—another Reynolds brother—looking amazingly attentive as he escorted Reese back into the house from the porch. Whatever they'd been talking about, it had looked serious. More talk of murder?

Or had the two of them decided to scratch an itch again?

She made it her business to know what was going on in town and news of something romantic between those two hadn't reached her at all. And she'd been listening since seeing them back in June. But if there *was* something romantic, well…that changed things.

It changed a lot of things.

She'd finally decided to do something about Reese Grantham, the all-around goody-goody of Midnight Pass. The woman had been a thorn in her side for years, her lack of remorse for her brother's death like a wound that never healed. The whole damn town loved Reese Grantham, and she was the only one who knew the truth.

What had started out as a silver thread of anger had grown, expanded, and now colored the way she saw the world.

The buzz of her phone had her reaching for the front pocket of her shorts. A text from her ex, complaining that he needed to get the kids back early. It figured. Paul was about as reliable as Texas weather in spring, and that gave way too much credit to Mother Nature's unpredictability.

On a small sigh, she texted back that she'd meet him at the house in fifteen minutes.

And she set off to greet her kids.

Reese took one whiff of the beef-and-cheese enchiladas that her waitress sat down in front of her and offered up a silent prayer of thanks that the only thing her stomach did was growl.

Loudly.

"You okay?" Hoyt glanced up from his burrito smothered in cheese.

"I am. Sorry," she said on a small smile. "Lately, I'm just never quite sure with food."

"Was this a bad idea?"

"No, not at all. It seems to be a game-time decision if the baby is going to welcome dinner or reject it out of hand. I'm hungry, so that seems to help."

He smiled in return, the motion lighting up his face. It was funny, Reese realized, but he wasn't a man who smiled very often. On some level, she knew that. It wasn't exactly a secret that Hoyt Reynolds had a quiet

and stoic demeanor. Even with that knowledge, she realized that she'd never quite associated his personality
with smiling.

But to suddenly be the object of that broad, bold
grin…

It was heady.

And it shot a load of butterflies to her stomach that
had nothing to do with morning sickness and everything to do with attraction.

Attraction, she quickly reminded herself, that had
no place to land.

"I thought they call that morning sickness because
it only happens in the morning?"

"I think that's the biggest old wives' tale of them all."
She took a small bite of her enchilada, savoring the rich
flavors. "I've been sick at all different times, with no
rhyme or reason when it strikes."

"Is there anything that particularly bothers you?"

"Chicken," she quickly said and barely avoided the
shiver that skated down her spine.

"Really?"

"Oh, yeah. I didn't even look at that section of the
menu."

"But beef's okay?"

"I crave it, actually."

Something lit deep in his green eyes. Although
they'd been placed in a quiet corner of the restaurant,
it was hard to miss the sudden spark. "You do realize
that's the highest compliment to a beef producer."

"I guess it would be. It's been particularly strange
for me, since I'm actually not a big beef eater normally.
I like a burger occasionally, but I usually lean toward
the salad or fish options on a menu."

"Hmm," he said. "Reynolds Station might have its new advertising campaign."

She did laugh at that. "The number one beef for pregnant women?"

"Hey," Hoyt said. "If it's good enough for my baby, it's good enough for anybody else's baby."

His baby.

She knew that. Obviously, she knew the father of her child. But hearing the words come out of his mouth— *his baby*—made her go completely still.

"You don't like my ad campaign?"

"No. No, I like it just fine. It's just—"

What could she say? Things hadn't changed from the words they'd exchanged earlier in his kitchen. They didn't have a relationship. They could barely even call themselves lovers, other than that one special night together. Yet, she was having his child.

His baby.

"It's just what?"

"For the past several weeks I've been thinking about it as my baby. It's just different to hear you say it as well."

"Because this is my baby. I know I came off heavy-handed before, at my house. I didn't say it to upset you or to suggest I would do anything against your wishes. But this is my child, too."

He was right. She might be carrying this child, and she might've had the benefit of a few extra weeks of knowledge, but that didn't mean she could ignore that he was also going to be a parent. Nor did it deny the fact that he had a right to see his child and be a part of raising the baby.

"I know that and, to be honest, I'm grateful that you

feel that way. Not every woman in my situation is quite that lucky."

Her honest assessment seemed to hover over them for a few moments and Hoyt looked about to say something before he closed his mouth.

"What?" she asked. "You can tell me how you feel."

"What do you mean, other women?"

"Not every couple is happy to have a child. It's a burden or it's unexpected or it doesn't fit into their life plan. Plenty of men have walked away from a child they've created." She stopped, recognizing the reality wasn't simply from a male point of view. "Plenty of women have done the same."

"I realize that we're not in a relationship." He said the words slowly, as if he were trying to find the right ones, syllable by syllable. "But that doesn't change how I feel, or my responsibility to this child."

"I know."

"More than that, it's not even about responsibility. I hadn't planned on becoming a father at this point in my life, but now that it's a reality, I want it more than I can say."

"I do know what you mean." And she did. After those few preliminary moments of shock when she had stared down at the positive pregnancy test, the reality of becoming a mother had begun to sink in. And in those moments between surprise and reality—when the ground seemed to shift beneath her—Reese had known the exact feeling he spoke of.

Happiness. Joy. And a sudden realization that regardless of what life *had* been like, the new direction was tremendously welcome.

"If you feel that way, then why were you so quick to reject my marriage proposal?"

Marriage? They were back to that. "Hoyt—"

"Wait." He held up a hand. "Hear me out."

Hear him out? Give him the chance to convince her? Because between the raging hormones and that sly, subtle attraction that refused to let go of her, the thought of a marriage proposal kept getting more and more enticing.

"Okay."

"I know marriage isn't ideal between two people who really don't know each other. But we do have a bond and you do have a place in this community as a teacher. There's a connection between us. One that's big enough to get us through the hurdle of not knowing each other that well. I don't need you to make a decision today, but tell me you'll think about it."

Think about it? All she had done was think about it. From the drive back from Reynolds Station, to the cleaning frenzy once she'd arrived home, to those lazy minutes on the porch.

Oh, how she had thought about it.

He'd avoided saying they weren't in love and that stung, but the rest of it swirled around her like a whirlpool, pulling her down into the spinning vortex.

"Please?" he asked.

"Please what?"

"Please tell me you'll consider becoming my wife."

Chapter 7

The summer nights were growing shorter, day by day, but streaks of red and gold still filled the edge of the sky as Hoyt pulled back into Reese's driveway. Dinner had been a revelation. For the past few months, his memories of her had veered more toward the outcome of their evening rather than the start. Admittedly, he'd forgotten how much he'd enjoyed her company in those initial hours at The Border Line.

She was smart and funny, with a sharp sense of the world around her. She had a kind heart but she wasn't syrupy with it. Instead, she seemed to have a keen sense of human nature, yet genuinely liked other people despite their flaws.

Or maybe in spite of them.

In fact, he had to admit to himself, the only quiet moments at dinner had come when he'd pressed his marriage proposal. She'd seemed to close up then, and while he wasn't ready to drop the subject, he did back off. And had continued to back off ever since, keeping their conversation light.

"You really passed the kid?" He'd come around to her door and held it open, taking her hand to help her down from his truck. The feel of her fingers closing around his momentarily had him forgetting his question or the young football player whose grades had allowed him to pass with flying colors.

"He earned it. And not because the coach came by my office almost daily, begging me to give the kid a good grade."

"Football in Texas is sacrosanct."

She shot him a sharp eye as she stood beside him, her hand still wrapped in his. "Funny, but so is learning."

"Spoken like a true teacher."

"I'd like to think the coach and I both won, but in the end it wasn't about either of us."

"Oh, no?" Hoyt thought about the bright lights that filled the Midnight Pass High School football stadium so many Friday nights during the fall, and questioned how passing the kid wasn't clearly a win.

"Not at all. It was Spence Long who really won. The boy wrote a damn fine paper, ended up with a B and a shot at a scholarship to college. And with the extra tutoring hours we put in together he's got more confidence in his schoolwork, which will ensure that college tuition isn't wasted by only putting him on a football field. That's the definition of a win-win in my book."

"Let me amend that. Spoken like a true educator. You gave him the gift of knowledge and that's something he won't age out of or risk with an injury."

The smile that lit her face in a warm glow was the best reply he could have received. "That's exactly how I feel."

He wanted to kiss her. The hand still wrapped in his was warm and soft. The smile that beamed in his direction was welcoming and oh-so-enticing.

But it was the look deep in her eyes—the one that turned those hazel eyes a deep, soft gold—that pushed him over.

Before he could check the impulse, he bent his head, his lips grazing hers with a light touch. She responded, her fingers tightening around his as she opened that lush mouth pressed against him. Hoyt deepened the kiss, taking them from a sort of gentle persuasion to heated exploration in a matter of heartbeats.

The evening heat was thick and still, but instead of being cloying, it enfolded them in a cocoon. All he felt was Reese and, as the kiss deepened, he wrapped his other arm around her, pulling her close. With her free hand, she settled her fingers over his nape, holding him to her for their kiss.

She was as warm and welcoming as he remembered, even as he sensed something different than the last time they were together. There was knowledge here that went beyond the carnal. They'd created a life, and the intimacy that came with that—and the understanding that they shared a bond that would never be broken—had changed the dynamic.

His body responded in kind, the slow pull of desire mixing with a deep protectiveness he'd never felt before in his life.

How was it possible to want a woman like this?

Sexual need, he understood. But that pull between a

man and a woman, which was as natural as breathing, had suddenly become something more.

More intense. More powerful. And more deeply felt than he could ever have imagined.

This was the mother of his child.

But even more than that, this was the woman he needed.

The streets were familiar, hot and dusty to match the air that swirled around him. Innately, Hoyt knew the moment wasn't real. That it was a figment of his imagination, conjured back to the forefront of his thoughts from some of the hardest days of his life.

He'd been good at special ops. His innate athleticism and understanding of nature—how it sounded, how it settled at night and how it felt when something disturbed it—had added to his almost preternatural sense of his surroundings and had served him well on past ops.

This one, however, was different.

He'd walked this street up and down, dressed in his fatigues with a gun on his hip, to send a message. That the town was being watched. Scrutinized. Studied.

He and his fellow soldiers had been instructed to show themselves and make their presence known by day for one simple reason. The real prize was just outside of town and it was his leaders' most fervent hope that a visual presence during the day would keep civilians in their homes at night.

Away from the action and the danger.

Away from the mission.

Hoyt did it willingly. And while he didn't care for

the heat, especially clad in another fifty pounds of gear, he was from Texas and knew what August weather felt like. He'd survive.

In the way of dreams, day faded into night. While the air wasn't any fresher, the relenting sun had gone down, providing a modicum of relief. Hoyt followed the backs of his fellow soldiers, their forms hazy before him as dream blended with memory. At times, he followed. At others, he led. But each step took him closer and closer to the inevitable end.

To the goal of their mission.

Crouched low, he spied the small, squat dwelling. Dim light showed from the windows before being doused, as if the occupants knew they were being watched. Not that it mattered. The equipment in his hands lit up with the reality of body heat inside the dwelling and Hoyt knew he'd found his quarry.

Holding still, he waited. Wasn't that the part no one ever told you? How much waiting you'd do in the military. Waiting for orders. Waiting for something to happen. Waiting for something not to happen.

Until it did. In wild, often explosive bursts of activity.

Just like home.

He'd waited his whole life to take over the ranch, only to find out from Ace's call that there was precious little to wait for. Their father had ruined everything and had nearly run them into ground in the process.

Would this be his last mission because of it? Was he ready to give it up? And could he really see his way to staying when his brothers needed him?

Before he could dwell on the seemingly endless questions, everything shifted into motion. Shouts and screams, live fire and the scent of smoke from a well-

placed grenade. Hoyt forgot about his questions and focused on the moment. He'd trained for this and now it
was the time to depend on that training for his life and
the lives of his fellow soldiers.

One moment he was under cover of night and the
next he was at the edge of the dwelling, visible through
his night goggles. Shouts sounded from inside and he
listened, absorbing them as he staked the perimeter.
With careful movements, always watching for any hint
of the enemy, he sidestepped his way along the building
until he was at the door, slipping inside.

The air was still fetid with smoke but all shouts had
vanished. He was alone.

He dragged off his goggles and turned on his heel,
assessing every part of the room and shocked to find
it all empty.

Where was everyone? Why had the fighting stopped?
And if the gunfire had ended, where were the bodies?

More questions, their possible answers as confus-
ing as the ones he'd asked himself outside in the bush.

Only then did he see another light, tugging at him as
if it'd show him answers. As if the light would show the
way. Hoyt walked down a small hall that looked surprisingly like the one at home. From the kitchen to the
living room, he followed it, the light growing brighter
and brighter before he found himself in another kitchen.

His kitchen. He could still see his mother in it if he
squinted hard enough. Could still picture his father,
seated at the head of the table as they all ate dinner.

The bright overhead light gave way to the softer light
of late afternoon, flooding the room with a golden glow.
It was only in that softening that he saw the figures he

was meant to see, strapped to chairs in the middle of the room, with twin gunshots between the eyes.

His father and Russ Grantham.

Hoyt woke on a harsh scream, tangled in the sheets.

The familiar sight of his bedroom came back to him quickly, moonlight streaming through the outline of his windows. He fought to even his breathing, the scent of war and the stark image of his father tied to a chair fading with each inhale and exhale.

It didn't take a genius to figure out the direction of his thoughts or the momentous reason for them. But damn, he hadn't had a dream quite that vivid since his first year out of special ops.

Settling back onto his pillow, Hoyt replayed the evening in his mind. He thought he'd made several good arguments for marriage and had been encouraged by the heated kiss he and Reese had shared when he dropped her off, but had also figured it paid to make a hasty retreat. He'd seen her to her door and after pressing one last kiss to her forehead, left for the evening.

He'd driven around for a while, restless with his thoughts and the overwhelming shift in his reality. He had a future. One that was clear and defined.

A child.

The image of that new life filled him with joy in the deepest of ways.

It also scared the hell out of him.

He was responsible for a child. Or would be in a matter of months. Did he have what it took to be a father? He had a miserable example for one, but that didn't mean he couldn't do it. Couldn't be a good one. Right?

He lay there for a long time, staring toward the window, as that question played over and over in his mind.

* * *

Reese stared at her computer, her eyes reading and rereading the words she'd typed in earlier for her first week of lesson plans, but seeing nothing.

It had been a week.

A week since she'd driven over to Hoyt's and told him about the baby. A week since they'd gone to dinner and talked. And seven very long days since she'd kissed him in her driveway.

They'd talked every day and the past weekend he'd come over to mow her lawn, but there hadn't been any more kissing. Nor had there even been any suggestion of it. He'd kept his physical distance and hadn't shown the slightest sign of coming in close for one.

Which was fine with her. She didn't need the heartache or confusion kissing the damn man seemed to gin up.

Like now.

She had lesson plans to write and another dive back into the first book she was teaching this year, *The Scarlet Letter*. The irony wasn't lost on her, and as much as she might want to avoid teaching that classic this year, Nathaniel Hawthorne was a requirement for high school English. Add on that she knew that the scarlet *A* inevitably made it into state testing exams and she didn't dare skip the book.

As she did each year, she reread every book on her syllabus, seeking new ways to teach the information or new tactics she could draw on to make her lessons fresh. Funny how her own personal understanding of Arthur Dimmesdale and Hester Prynne had changed so radically this year. Where she'd always seen both characters as tragic figures, in this latest review of the work she saw something else.

Courage.

It was an odd thought and one that she hadn't expected. Nor was it quite the tone she wanted to strike with impressionable teenagers who inevitably found forbidden love dangerous and exciting, yet she wanted to find a way to bring her new understanding to her lessons.

With a renewed focus on her computer, she read through her lesson plans. She expected the normal moaning and groaning when she announced the fact they'd read seven books this year, but had made an effort to mix the historic with the present. *The Scarlet Letter* might be on her lesson plan, but so were *The Hunger Games* and *The Maze Runner*. Books she anticipated would make up for puritanical Massachusetts.

The doorbell pulled her from thoughts of a dystopian future and she headed for the front door. Had Hoyt come over unexpectedly?

While she didn't expect him in the middle of the day—he'd talked enough about his work on the ranch to give her a sense that there was very little downtime during the day—hope sprang in her breast all the same.

She enjoyed seeing him and no amount of trying to temper those thoughts seemed to be working.

A glance through the small peephole on her front door didn't show anyone there. She wasn't waiting on the delivery of any online packages and the mailman didn't usually arrive this early anyway, but who had rung the door?

Even more curious, she tugged open the door and

scanned her front lawn, continuing on across the street. Reese saw nothing, not even a light breeze to mar the stillness in the air. Which made the light brush along her toes that much sharper.

When she glanced down, she saw the large spider that even now moved another inch farther up her foot.

Reese struggled to catch her breath as she fumbled for her keys. Her throat was still raw from the screams that had filled her at the sight of the spider and she couldn't get rid of that creepy-crawly feeling that still covered her bare flip-flopped foot.

Despite the unpleasant feeling, she couldn't fault the eight years of soccer that had carried her from elementary school clear through to her own senior year at Midnight Pass High School. Her still-powerful kick had dislodged the unwelcome visitor and landed it somewhere near the center of her lawn.

And now she had to figure out what to do.

Her first instinct was to drive over to Reynolds Station and share the trauma with Hoyt, but that initial need was beginning to fade. What would she say? A big bug (and she knew an arachnid was technically not a bug) had paid her a call on her front porch. The damn thing was big enough that it might have rung the bell all on its own.

Which only made her feel more stupid.

And vulnerable.

Who *had* rung the bell? It could hardly be coincidence the front door had buzzed and a spider was there waiting for her. Which meant someone had put it there. Deliberately.

Reese was almost tempted to brush it off until some

shred of common sense buzzed through: the need to protect her child. Someone had played a cruel and deliberate trick on her. No, on her and her baby. She deserved to go for help.

She toyed with looking up answers online but decided the front doorbell required a bit more urgency. Besides, who knew what horrific images would lodge in her mind once she went down the internet rabbit hole?

Hitting the button on her garage door opener, she pulled slowly away from the house and down her driveway, her attention focused on the center of her lawn where she'd drop-kicked the spider. It was large enough that she'd have expected to see the shape of its body over her freshly mowed lawn, but nothing stood out. She hit the door opener once more, her attention focused on the driveway to ensure her new "friend" didn't find its way back in. With the door down and satisfied the spider wouldn't be in her garage to greet her when she arrived home, Reese pulled out and headed for the familiar police station downtown.

How many times had she gone there to see her father, stopping in after a long day at school or running in a cup of coffee on the mornings she popped in to the town barista for a morning fix?

She hadn't been back since before his death. Since before the murders.

The thought of going back filled her with an unpleasant mix of dread and sadness that thickened in her midsection like cement. But she ignored it all as she headed toward town, determined to find help.

The lingering threat of death by arachnid began to

fade as she drove down the street, her thoughts roiling of who would have done such a thing.

It kept her from looking back to see the dark sedan parked at the bottom of the hill.

Hoyt brushed down Stinkbug, feeding him sugar cubes as he worked a currycomb over the horse's neck and shoulders. A wild-caught mustang, Stink hadn't spent much of his formative years being groomed or brushed, but had caught on quickly as Hoyt had worked to tame and temper the animal.

They'd met while Hoyt had been on a ranch exchange in Arizona, learning some new sustainability techniques by day and bored out of his mind after each session had ended. The ranch owner had taken in several mustangs from a rescue organization and Hoyt had bonded with Stink, the horse providing a ready distraction. When the owner had seen how well they fit, he'd given Hoyt the horse for the simple price of paying to transport Stink back to Texas.

The brushing and grooming had been one of the things that had connected them early, and Hoyt had always felt the time spent in making the animal feel comfort, attention and, ultimately, love had done more to bond them than any amount of training ever could.

An animal trainer would have dubbed it domestication, but Hoyt preferred to look at it as mutual affection and a desire to work together. Whatever you wanted to call it, the outcome had paid dividends in spades. He had a working partner on the ranch who understood him, what he needed to manage the land and was a ready listener on the rare days Hoyt chose to talk.

And had he spilled his guts this morning.

The same dream had visited him for several nights in a row, each as vivid as the last. First he'd be on active duty, that time morphing into a special ops mission, then in his home, then he'd discover the bodies of his father and Reese's father. It never wavered, and even as he knew he ghost-walked through the nightmare, he couldn't seem to shake himself out of it.

Couldn't seem to forge his way to a new outcome.

Why now?

While he wouldn't say he was immune to what he'd dealt with in special ops, he'd done the work for his country and had believed in it. He dealt with the occasional memory from time to time and when they got too heavy to handle he had a doctor a few towns over he wasn't ashamed to go and talk to. Pride in his job didn't mean he'd refuse help.

But it did mean the dream had caught him off guard. Especially the addition of his father. He'd likely give Ted a call and see if he could fit him in this week because the dreams weren't getting better and the ball in the pit of his stomach was getting worse.

In the meantime, he had Stink. And the work.

The western pasture had been their destination, and a day spent inspecting fence line, as well as checking on several of the new calves they'd recently branded, had given Hoyt a lot of time with his thoughts. Though tedious work, inspecting fence line was hardly interesting or mentally taxing and it had given him more than ample time to think about Reese Grantham.

It had been a week since their dinner and the explosive kiss—or kisses—they'd shared on her front driveway. He'd wanted more—the thought of *more* was inevitable when he was around her—but he had pulled back, settling for a mini make-out session instead.

His body had cursed him for the choice and he'd stood under more than a few cold showers this past week, but he wasn't sorry for his decision. Moving forward into a physical relationship with Reese came with expectation. On his part and definitely on hers. He had to decide if he was all in and what exactly that would even mean.

And besides, she still hadn't given him an answer on his marriage proposal. She hadn't even brought the subject up, as a matter of fact.

A fact, he reflected as he offered up another sugar cube to Stink, that was beginning to stick in his craw.

It was a simple matter of giving him a yes or no. Ignoring the subject was akin to leaving an elephant standing in the middle of her living room. An elephant they'd both sidestepped when he went over on Sunday to mow her lawn.

The invisible pachyderm they both also sidestepped each evening when he called her to see how she was doing.

Stink's ears had perked as Hoyt had spilled all this earlier and he'd have sworn the horse even nodded his head a few times, so it made little sense to rehash it.

But damn it, why was the woman being so stubborn?

And why was that subtle itch beneath his skin—to be on a firm path toward their future—growing stronger and stronger each day?

They didn't know each other. Yet, every time he tried that rational argument on himself he got nowhere.

He'd nearly launched into another diatribe to Stink when the sound of female voices filled the barn. The last thing he needed was his sister or his soon-to-be sister-in-law, Belle, hearing him talking to himself. They'd both already been keeping a suspiciously close eye on him every time they were in each other's company and he didn't need any more of the new family pastime: "let's psychoanalyze Hoyt."

"I'm fine, Belle. Really, I am."

Was that Reese?

Hoyt stuck his head out of Stink's stall and dropped the currycomb, moving toward Belle and Reese at a run. Belle's arm was draped over Reese's shoulders in an unmistakable sign of support.

"What's wrong?" He already had his hands out and was pulling Reese into his arms. "What happened?"

"Just a scare." Belle's voice moved firmly into authority territory as she crossed over to close Stink's stall door. "But why don't you give Reese a chance to tell you?"

"Tell me what?"

Reese's cheekbones arched high over hollowed cheeks and her tan had visibly faded in the paling of her skin. "It's nothing."

"You don't look like it's nothing. Nor does walking in here with a member of the Midnight Pass PD set my mind at ease that whatever happened is nothing."

"Last time I checked, a spider isn't a criminal offense."

"What?"

"Reese," Belle said gently. "Why don't you start from the beginning?"

Hoyt moved them over toward a small bench at the end of a row of stalls and pulled Reese down onto the seat next to him. "What happened?"

It didn't take long to get a picture of her front porch visitor and the scare a large spider would give anyone. What troubled him was the idea of the doorbell ringing that had preceded the incident.

"And you didn't see anyone?"

"No." Reese shook her head. "Not through the peephole or across the street."

"What about when you left the house to go to the police?"

"I didn't—" She broke off and stared down at her hands, a light blush filling in those hollows. "I didn't even think to look."

He put his arm around her shoulders and pulled her close, catching sight of Belle over the top of Reese's head. Although Belle was kind and mothering when needed, she was also a hard-nosed cop, who had a keen eye and a strong sense of right and wrong.

"Do you think this is anything?" Hoyt asked.

"I think it's strange," Belle said. "That's for sure. I'm also suspicious on the timing."

Before she could say anything more, the phone at her belt began to ring and Belle excused herself to take the call.

"You sure you're okay?"

"Yes." Reese nodded, straightening up from where she'd taken comfort against his chest. "I'm perfectly fine and beginning to feel really stupid for overreacting."

"You were scared. And I'm still bothered by the doorbell."

"Probably a few kids being kids."

"Last time I checked, teenage troublemakers aren't

exactly quiet. And you said there wasn't even a hint of sound when you opened the door."

"No, there wasn't."

"Is the spider dangerous?"

"I know our biology teacher pretty well. Fred would know if the spider is dangerous or not, but I don't think that it is. I did some research and while horribly ugly, there's not much reason to think a tarantula is poisonous."

"That's what it was?"

"I think," she said, and Hoyt felt her shudder beneath his arm.

"I'm not sure waiting to be bitten is the way to find that out," Hoyt said, his imagination already racing toward harm to Reese and the baby.

"Well, I wasn't bitten. And we have a few at the high school. I'd hardly think the school board would appreciate having poisonous animals around the kids."

The thought that the danger was likely minimal went some way toward calming his racing heart but he couldn't quite calm away the sense of menace that had brought a spider to her front door. Texas was known for its wild creatures and his cowboy boots were way more practical than they were for show, but it was the mysterious doorbell ring that kept gnawing at him.

Did someone deliberately do this to scare Reese?

And why?

"Are you sure you're okay?"

Hoyt was still trying to catch his own breath, the mix of fear and concern still tripping his heartbeat every time he thought about what had awaited Reese on her front porch.

"I'm sure. It was gross, I'm not going to lie about

that," Reese said with a smile. "But I do teach teenagers for a living. I'm made of sterner stuff."

Wasn't that the heart of the matter?

The woman was made of stern stuff. She'd shown that, over and over again. Surviving and thriving during and after her brother's addiction and death. Surviving and thriving again after the news of her father. It would've been very easy for Reese to go into hiding, but she'd done the exact opposite.

She had pressed on and continued with her life, her head held high.

"You're pretty amazing, do you know that?" Unable to hold back, he reached out and ran his fingers over the edge of her hair, teasing one of the tendrils into a curl around his index finger.

"It was just a spider." Even as she said it, her voice softened and her gaze went a little hazy.

"No. I know what I know. You deal with spiders as easily as you've dealt with news that's changed your life. You *are* amazing."

"Aren't you sweet."

"I don't feel sweet." He leaned in, his lips hovering near the edge of her ear. "In fact, I don't feel sweet at all."

"How do you feel?" That softness in her voice had morphed, becoming breathy and shallow as his lips moved over the rim of her ear.

"Edgy."

"Maybe… Maybe there's something we can do about that."

"You think so?"

Reese was prevented from answering as Belle stomped back across the stable.

"What is it?" Hoyt was already on his feet, moving forward toward Belle. "What happened?"

"That was the biology teacher. Fred McNamara. I left him a message and he was kind enough to call me back."

"You called Fred?" Reese asked.

"I did," Belle said. "You mentioned him when we were talking in my office, so I gave him a quick call."

"What did you ask him?"

"I wanted to know if the two spiders he keeps in his classroom are still there."

Hoyt saw the ready set of Belle's face and knew the answer before she even spoke. "What did Fred say?"

"From the sounds of it, those spiders are his pride and joy. The man panicked when I suggested one or both of them might be missing, and drove straight over to the school to check."

"Fred left a spider at my door?" Reese shook her head. "That's not possible."

"No. Fred didn't leave anything at your door. But from the looks of it, someone did go into his classroom and take one of the two tarantulas."

"Well, then it has to be a kid," Reese said, her voice triumphant, as if the news clearly eased her mind on the subject. "This is the exact kind of thing a teenager would do. It's the end of summer and they've got too much time on their hands."

"What's a kid doing hanging around school a few weeks early?" Hoyt asked. "Aren't they trying to avoid it?"

"But what else could it be?" That eager readiness to put a solution on the problem visibly ebbed, a frown tipping the corners of Reese's mouth down.

"I'm going to look at some of the security footage from around the school, but I don't think it's a kid." Belle still held her phone, and slapped it against her thigh. "Fred doesn't think it is, either. He was at the school most of yesterday getting his classroom set up, and the spiders were there the whole time."

"So somebody broke into the school after hours just to steal a spider? It doesn't make sense."

Whether it was a matter of trying to mentally prepare herself for the news or the sheer inability to believe the safe haven she called the Midnight Pass High School had suddenly put her at risk, Hoyt didn't know why Reese was in denial.

But he kept his voice gentle when he pressed Reese further. "I think what Belle is trying to say is that someone broke into Fred's classroom with the intention to steal that spider and scare you or do you harm."

"The scaring, I understand. They're teenagers, Hoyt. They dare each other and engage in dumb rituals that make no sense to anyone over the age of twenty. I'm the English teacher and someone probably got wind of the fact I'm going to make them read seven books this year. No one meant me any harm."

Reese's expectant gaze shifted from him to Belle before landing back on him. "Come on. It's no big deal."

"Or it is a big deal, it's not a kid and it's someone who's trying to hurt you."

Chapter 8

Reese was still trying to digest the events of her day an hour later as she peeled carrots at the sink in the middle of Hoyt's kitchen. To be fair, it was Ace, Tate and Arden's kitchen, too, but after telling Hoyt he was going to be a father at that very table, she'd sort of equated the room with him.

And now she was taking part in a Reynolds family dinner.

Hoyt and Belle had both insisted she stay and Reese had figured out pretty quickly it was useless to argue. Hoyt had called his brothers and headed out after he was confident she was settled into the kitchen; Belle and Arden's arrival a few minutes later had sealed the deal.

"Are you okay?" Arden had drawn her into a tight hug before stepping back. "And the baby, too?"

That was all it had taken for the conversation to

turn personal, with a series of coos and squeals and feminine laughter that a new baby was coming into the family.

So here she was. Peeling carrots and struggling to keep the tears at bay because of how tight Belle and Arden had hung on.

Darn hormones.

She fought the lump in her throat and just peeled harder, attempting to ease her frustrations with an ever-growing pile of shaved carrots.

"Whoa, there. I think we have enough." Arden reached over and took the peeler from her hands. "But you're definitely our girl when we prep for next year's Fourth of July party."

Next year.

Arden's tone was so easy and matter-of-fact that Reese barely held back the tears she'd struggled with for the past half hour.

Arden spoke as if there would be a next year.

Well, there would be a next year and a year after that and millennia more, but that wasn't what had the tears thickening her throat and filling her eyes. It was the idea that there would be a scenario where she was a part of the lives of Hoyt Reynolds and his family.

"Come on, why don't you sit down with me?" Belle said, gesturing toward the empty seat next to her.

Reese took the offered seat, well aware sitting next to Belle Granger likely wasn't going to do a whole lot for her tears. Up until now, the baby had managed to stifle the elephant in the room, but it wasn't going to take that long for them to swing back around to it.

Her father had been Belle's boss at the police department.

Her father had also been the one to kidnap Belle, scaring everyone with the thought that he would hurt her or worse—kill her—as his hostage.

And then in an apparent change of heart, it was her father who'd killed himself within a few feet of Belle.

Yep, Reese thought to herself, that elephant was awfully large, its trunk up and damn near ready to trumpet.

"Tell us about the baby. How are you feeling? How long have you known?" Belle's voice interrupted the imagined sounds.

"A little over a month. I'd suspected, but…" Reese trailed off, memories of those days between wondering if she was pregnant and actually taking the test still fresh in her mind. "I've known a little over a month."

Arden turned from where she stood at the counter. "It's so wonderful. Babies are happy news."

"If I'm honest, that's not quite the reaction I was expecting." While Reese wasn't looking for trouble, she'd hardly expected coming into Hoyt's home as his unmarried non-girlfriend *and* the woman carrying his baby was going to be met with open arms.

Yet, here they were.

And Arden's arms seemed rather open.

"What were you expecting?" Belle's voice was gentle, her gaze equally so.

"I don't know. But I know my family isn't necessarily the town favorite. And since Hoyt and I don't have a relationship, news like this is, well…surprising."

"I'll give you that." Arden smiled, taking one of the empty seats at the large family table. "Not the town favorite part, but the non-relationship with Hoyt. But you must know that doesn't make the news any less welcome, Reese. I hope you can come to understand that."

"Does your mom know yet?" Belle asked.

"No, not yet. I want to tell her, but I felt Hoyt deserved to know first. Now that he does, she'll definitely be next."

"Oh, she's going to be so excited," Belle said. "I can see her already, with her warm smile, gazing down at the new baby."

Although Reese had seen similar images in her own mind, fervently hoping reality would come to match it, she'd also seen her mother in her more recent days. Sadness and emptiness, loss of hope and that terrible, seemingly bereft loss of spirit that seemed to surround her.

Maybe a baby would help those things. A new life that brought new hope and renewed feelings toward the future.

It was a lot to lay at a child's feet, but maybe it was what they all needed to begin to move on.

"So how did you and Hoyt get together?" A small smile danced around Arden's lips, sheer curiosity filling her vivid blue eyes. "I mean, I'm happy about it. I've always thought you two would make a great match."

"You have?" Reese couldn't have hidden her surprise if she tried. "Hoyt? And me?"

"Oh, yeah. There's something about the two of you that just seems to fit. And that time you came here with your class…" Arden's voice drifted off. "Yes, I've always thought you two would make a great match."

Arden's assessment was not only unexpected, but it was a funny thought to think someone had seen her connection with another and she hadn't. She and Hoyt lived in the same town and had both grown up there. But for someone—his sister, no less—to have seen something between?

"Well, I don't know," Reese said, hedging. "I'm not sure I'd go envisioning cupids just yet."

Arden looked about to argue before she stopped, a sharp look from Belle clearly adding to her decision.

"I think what Arden is really saying is that we all think this is a great idea." Belle pulled her close for a hug, the side-armed support going a long way toward assuaging the tension that continued to fill Reese.

But it was the rest of it, the sheer anxiety of it all, that spilled out next. "I promise I don't want anything from him. Well, I mean, I want Hoyt to be a part of his child's life. But this isn't about money or, well, trapping him."

"Of course it isn't."

"We don't think that." Arden was the first to respond but Belle's protest was quickly on her heels.

"We know you, Reese. Do you understand that?" Arden asked, her blue gaze bright and earnest. "We don't have any judgment about this. Or about you."

They were words she needed to hear, but in a small corner of her heart, Reese recognized she wasn't quite yet ready to believe them. So instead, she did what she'd been doing for months. She put on a small smile, nodded her head in affirmation and pretended like everything was okay.

"Thank you. That means more than you'll ever know."

"It'd better," Belle said with a smile. "Because I expect a lot of cuddles and snuggles with my new niece or nephew."

Hoyt spent the rest of the afternoon scouring every inch of Reese's house, inside and out, with Ace and

Tate. They'd been thorough and diligent, so it chafed two hours later when they'd found no evidence of anything. Nor had they found the large hairy spider that had been used to torment Reese from her front porch.

Not that he was surprised on the spider. Now free from its glass prison, the animal had likely hightailed it for wherever it could get. Although a part of him had still hoped the sun-warmed concrete that made up Reese's front porch might have lulled the animal for a time.

From the looks of it, the science teacher's pet had taken freedom over safety and a warm spot to perch.

While he'd have liked to have found the hairy intruder, he couldn't deny some relief that the threat had passed. What was harder to work through was the way he'd left things with Reese. She'd been so determined to believe the spider was the work of some kids horsing around that he hated to be the one to suggest something far more sinister was afoot.

Was he overreacting?

He'd turned the idea over and over in his mind, from gathering up his brothers to the drive to Reese's to the unlikely scavenger hunt he'd executed over the past few hours. While a small part of him kept thinking he'd overdramatized the whole situation, a much bigger part of him was worried. He had a pretty finely honed sense of intuition. It had served him well in special ops, where sometimes instinct was all you had to go on. He found the skill equally productive working with animals in the great wide open of Reynolds Station. Split seconds of intuition meant the difference between surviving and...not.

So the fact that he couldn't conjure up a casual, relaxed attitude to Reese's front porch visitor told him something.

Why would someone want to harm her?

Sure, kids could be the culprits. And it wasn't unheard of for a student to hold a grudge against a teacher. Yet, something kept veering him off that track.

Reese hadn't mentioned any problems with anyone at school besides her worry that the PTA would freak out. Add on that it was summer vacation. Were kids really likely to randomly go after a teacher during the months they were free and clear from the classroom? The fact that she was well liked made that seem like an even bigger stretch.

Which left her father.

Was someone trying to avenge Russ Grantham's crimes? Someone who believed he should have served time instead of ending things his own way? Someone who felt the child should pay for the sins of the father?

Hadn't Reese paid enough?

"You find anything?" Ace asked as he came around the corner of the house.

Hoyt shook his head, his dark thoughts scattering as he scanned the porch and surrounding bushes once more in hopes he'd overlooked something. "Nothing. You?"

"Other than the fact that the woman keeps a ruthlessly organized shed and the cleanest, most well-oiled lawn mower I've ever seen? Nope."

Hoyt had observed the same. But now that he was actually looking, moving through her things and peeking inside her cabinets, seeking a furry stowaway, it was even more evident how neat and organized she was. "The woman does have an orderly streak."

"Orderly?" Ace raised his eyebrows. "I'd say she's military-grade orderly and if I hadn't known her my whole life, would have assumed she'd spent time in army boot camp."

While it certainly might have been her personality, Hoyt couldn't help wondering if that rigorous, practically ruthless organization wasn't tied to something else. The woman hadn't exactly had a drama-free life. Her brother's addiction—especially coming on when Reese was still in school—would have forced one of two outcomes: a child equally matched with the same devil-may-care attitude as her brother or what seemingly came out instead.

Neatness. Order. Perfection.

If the rest of your life was out of control, the one place you *could* control was your personal space.

"You ready to get out of here?" Ace asked.

"Sure. We'll grab Tate and head out."

"I think he was checking the trees out at the back of her property." Ace hesitated for the briefest moment, lines settling in his forehead just over his eyebrows. Hoyt knew those lines. They were his eldest brother's tell and it meant he was both uncomfortable as hell and determined to pursue a line of questioning, anyway.

"I know what you're going to ask." Hoyt beat Ace to the punch.

"What's that?"

"You're going to ask why Reese Grantham. Why now. And why a baby."

Ace didn't quite smile, but the lines softened, smoothing out and reminding Hoyt his brother was still only a few months shy of thirty-five. "You pegged a few of my questions."

"What'd I miss?"

"I'm not questioning why Reese. That part's obvious."

Obvious? What could possibly be obvious about a woman he barely knew? "Obvious how?"

"You're crazy about each other. I'm not saying the news of a baby hasn't been a surprise, but you and Reese? That part's easy."

If Ace had whipped out a show tune and begun a soft shoe on Reese's front porch, Hoyt would have been less stunned. "Me and Reese are easy?"

"Sure are, little brother. You've always had a thing for her."

"How could I have a thing for a woman I've barely spoken a sum total of twenty sentences to before she and I hooked up a few months ago?"

"Ahh." Ace nodded his head knowingly. "So that explains it."

"Why I've been a raging ass?"

"Why you've been more of a raging ass than usual." Tate's voice boomed out from behind Hoyt as his other brother took the last few steps toward the front porch.

Although he'd opened the door, Hoyt couldn't quite give his brothers the room to keep poking at what had happened back in June. Or his behavior since. "I'm surly and grumpy. You all like me that way."

The twin snorts didn't require his response but Hoyt decided to press on anyway. "And for the record, I don't have a thing for Reese Grantham. She's a beautiful woman and things sort of progressed a few months back. We're two single, unattached people. Stuff happens between two single, unattached people."

"Like babies," Ace said.

"And house raids to trap the school pet," Tate added.

"And sex," his brothers said in unison.

"You're both high on ranch fertilizer if you think there's anything else there."

"You keep telling yourself that, little brother." Ace slapped him on the back. "And know we're here for you on that day you realize we're right."

Hoyt was still chewing over his time at Reese's house an hour later, after he'd washed up and was heading down to the kitchen for dinner. He might have cleaned away the day's grime, but his brothers' knowing smiles, glances and smug words hadn't rinsed away so easily.

In fact, if he were being honest, they'd stuck in his mind like glue and didn't seem to have any intention of budging.

Especially since Reese was waiting for him in the kitchen. He'd spoken to her briefly when they'd returned, reassuring her that her home was safe. They'd looked for the spider and while it might have found a soft place to land outside, it hadn't made its home inside hers. She'd seemed resigned to the lack of discovery and had promised to call her fellow teacher and break the bad news that his science classroom would be missing one of its pets for the start of the new school year.

So here he was, stalling in his bathroom, anticipating seeing her again and recognizing they'd be the object of his family's attention.

Did he blame them?

While he'd tried to play it cool and keep his nose out of it, he hadn't been immune to the recently burgeoning relationship between Tate and Belle. The entire ranch had recognized that spring was both in the air and working its magic on his brother's love life with his first—and only—love. He'd be a hypocrite if he didn't anticipate the same scrutiny on him and Reese.

The problem was, everyone wanted to see the same outcome.

Yes, they were having a baby. And while it seemed like a complication on the surface, he had every confidence they'd make raising a child together work. That didn't mean the two of them had some great love story just waiting to unfold.

"Hell. We don't have a love story at all," he muttered to himself before slamming his towel over the top of the shower and heading for the door to his room. He wasn't hiding up here and he'd be damned if he was going to let whatever was in his family's collective heads mess up his. He knew who he was. He also knew what he and Reese had, and it wasn't some grand romance.

His wing of the ranch house was one floor up and located at the opposite end of the house from the kitchen, so it wasn't until he was narrowing in on the front staircase that led down to the living areas that he heard voices.

Reese's voice, in particular.

"I'm feeling good. Mornings can be tough and several afternoons, too, but other than that it hasn't been too bad."

Arden offered up some teas that she knew to be good for anything upsetting digestive balance and Hoyt let that sink in. His baby sister was giving the mother of his child tips on helping morning sickness.

How had that happened?

And then he remembered how it all had happened, a flush of heat coursing through his body at the remembered hours with Reese Grantham in his arms. Whatever had come since, that lone night hadn't been far from his thoughts.

Or just how right it had felt to hold her close.

Reese settled her napkin onto her lap and took a moment to look around the table. Hoyt's siblings were a raucous bunch; everyone seemed to be talking at once. Belle Granger certainly had no problem inserting herself in the mix, her conversation easy as she teased Ace about an article he'd appeared in for a national ranching magazine before shifting gears to ask Arden when she was doing another vinyasa class down at the Midnight Pass Community Center.

"Sorry if they're a bit overwhelming." Hoyt leaned in from her left, handing her a basket brimming with warm yeast-scented rolls.

"They're not—" Reese turned to face him, their heads coming close, and plum forgot what she wanted to say. The stress of the day, coupled with the seesawing fears that his family would accept her or think her a money-grubbing schemer faded away in the depths of those vivid green eyes.

She could get lost there.

And, as she remembered the child they'd made, realized she *had* gotten lost there. One lonely night at the local bar and pool hall and in the glorious hours that had followed.

Shifting her focus to the basket of rolls, she selected one and used that time to collect her thoughts. "They're wonderful."

"I'm not quite sure I'd go that far." When she looked back up, prepared to argue, he stopped her with a broad smile. Laying a hand over hers where it rested on the table, he said, "They are pretty great, a fact I'm well aware of. And while being overbearing seems to be a gene that comes with the Reynolds name, they have my back. And now they have yours, too. I hope you know that."

"I do."

Funny enough, for all the swings of emotion, the one thing that had been more than evident in her conversation with Arden and Belle, and even later, once Ace and Tate had come back in with Hoyt, was that sense of belonging.

Of being one of them.

The Reynolds siblings had closed ranks over a decade ago when their father had been accused and found guilty of illegal ranching practices. The whole town had seen it and marveled on the fact that the children of Andrew Reynolds could still hold their heads high, while they all worked tirelessly to rebuild the ranch, its product and its reputation.

Maybe it had been her own personal hell with Jamie's addiction and how desperately she didn't want her family to be judged for her brother's illness. Perhaps it had been her friendship with Arden and how she understood the embarrassment her friend had suffered, struggling to find her place in Midnight Pass once the Reynolds name had a blight over it.

Or maybe it had even been more superficial, after all those years in school when she, along with the rest of the female student population, had found the Reynolds boys the object of more than a few appreciative sighs.

Like she'd done with the movie stars she loved to read about, she'd always placed the brothers in a special category of male beauty and charisma, their cowboy boots and tipped hats making them seem larger than life.

It was hard to say now, because it was likely all those things, as well as a lifetime of sharing this same small, square plot of Texas, that had influenced how she saw the Reynolds family. They'd all been raised under the same bright blue skies and on land that had stood under six flags. They'd all run wild as children like the mustangs that used to roam this land.

But like the mustangs that had long since vanished, so had their childhood. Youth had been lost to the harsh realities of life, whether it was addiction or crime or greed, and adulthood had come far too early.

Funny how it all faded in the camaraderie that filled the table and the support she felt from each and every one there.

Her child had a future. And while she and its father might not share anything more than a heated night and—perhaps—genuine affection, they also shared mutual respect and a willingness to raise their child with love.

It would be enough.

It would have to be.

Chapter 9

"You don't have to walk me inside." Reese heard her prim tone and tried not to wince. "I mean, it's nice if you do but you don't have to."

Hoyt laid a hand over hers, waiting quietly until she tore her gaze from her closed garage door, visible through the windshield of his truck. "Reese."

"Yes?"

"You don't need to do this alone."

Sure, I do. I always have.

The thought hit so hard it cratered through her, leaving a strange emptiness in its wake. She was alone and had been for far longer than she wanted to admit. Even now, when she and her mother should have found some measure of comfort in their shared experiences, they'd each gone their own direction, like two magnets repelling at the poles.

Since the darkness of Hoyt's truck, after an emotional day and evening, would have been the perfect place to settle in and say all she felt, she pushed herself in the opposite direction and reached for the door. No use trying to take comfort when it had a limited shelf life. A fact she understood to the depths of her toes.

They'd shared one amazing night, but they weren't married or even remotely attached to each other. Both their lives would go on and he'd find someone else, a woman who likely wouldn't appreciate Hoyt Reynolds's past indiscretion or the living evidence of it all nosing around the edges of their new life.

The door slammed harder than she intended and Reese made her way to the front door. In spite of her swinging moods, she was touched to see he'd left the porch lights on after his earlier visit with his brothers and reveled in that small measure of thoughtfulness.

"We didn't touch much. Just enough to search every area thoroughly." Hoyt spoke from behind her, his large form radiating heat at her back.

Damn the man, didn't he understand her need for space? How was it he kept pushing, even when she was at her very worst, pushing him away? Pasting on a smile she didn't feel, Reese fell back on her manners and the "good girl" that was ingrained in her personality. "I wasn't worried. Besides, there's not much to touch."

"Oh, I don't know. You might not have a lot, but what you have you take care of. There's something to be said for that."

She flipped on the hallway lights, continuing on toward her kitchen. Since he was clearly following her in, she kept up the inane conversation. "I'm a hopeless perfectionist. If I'm given something, I appreciate it. If

I buy something, I take care of it. A personal curse but I long stopped trying to explain it or fight it."

"Nothing wrong with taking care of what you have. It shows character."

She came to a stop at the counter and turned, amazed once again to see how his large form just seemed to fill up the space. He was a presence—a real, tangible presence—and it still stunned her to realize all that they'd shared. And would still share in the form of their child. Even with that knowledge, she couldn't help poking at his words. "Piling my perfectly folded dish towels in a drawer I vacuum out every month shows character?"

"Sure it does."

"Liar."

"There are worse things in the world to be than neat. And there's not a force on earth that will stop me from folding my corners with military precision, if it makes you feel any better."

Only it didn't make her feel any better.

While the conversation was light and innocuous, she couldn't shake the feeling that there was something else hovering beneath. Talking to a hot man in her kitchen about her neatly folded dish towels and his precisely folded bedsheets was hardly entertaining conversation. Yet, she sensed his interest and, beneath his limited words, something else.

"Like a serial killer?"

"Excuse me?" Hoyt's eyes grew wide, that vivid green going a hard, dark emerald.

"Oh, I think you heard me. My father was meticulous, too. He was careful and focused and paid attention to his tasks. For many years, it was keeping a neat shed and a sparkling garage and hunting lodge. Then he decided to expand and found he could still be neat and sparkling and freaking meticulous when he tortured and killed four people. That we know of," she added for good measure.

"What's this about?"

"Here you are praising me for my neat home, acting like we're comrades in arms, and somehow I can sense there's something hovering there that's not about a neat house or clean cabinets at all."

"I was thinking more along the lines of an orderly home gives you some sense of control and ownership in a world that provides little."

"Thanks for the psych profile, Dr. Reynolds."

"What's this about?"

She had no earthly idea what it was about. All she knew was that, after an evening where she'd felt welcome and included, it was suddenly, desperately important to make sure Hoyt Reynolds understood all the ways her life was a mess and that she did a damn fine job handling it all. Just like she'd handle having a baby and raising their child.

She was fine.

Capable.

And more than able to handle whatever life tossed at her all by herself.

"You tell me," she shot back.

"It sure as hell isn't about dish towels."

Before she could reply or argue or protest or continue on this ridiculous hill she'd decided to die on, he was there, in her space and pulling her close. One moment she was bound and determined to stand alone, battling whatever came her way, and the next she was in Hoyt's arms, being devoured by his mouth and his hands and...*him*.

He walked her back a few steps, so her back pressed against the counter, lifting her once they were close enough and seating her on the cool marble. She felt the cold through the light capris she wore and it did nothing to diminish the wall of heat that consumed her.

This was what she'd been missing. For two long months, she'd dreamt of their night together. But no matter how vivid or heated her traitorous memories, nothing compared to this. The broad shoulders she gripped tight beneath her fingers, an anchor she could hold as she rode the deep devouring kisses. The large, well-muscled form that pressed against hers, hard and solid to her curves and the increasing softness as her body made room for their child. And that firm, lush mouth, normally so stoic in life yet animated and determined as he kissed her.

He recognized her life was ordered and controlled, but he made her want to forget every bit of it. Because nothing about her feelings and reaction and *need* for Hoyt Reynolds made sense. In fact, these feelings were the perfect definition of out of control and she had no idea what to do about it.

Or him.

Or the fervent need to be with him again.

With sudden force, her hands that curled around his shoulders pressed, palm first, against the rounded curve of hard muscle to push him back. Away. And out of temptation's reach.

"What's wrong?"

"This. All of it." The words spilled from her lips in a torrent, misery quickly taking their place as she acknowledged to herself how she'd rather hang on tight and welcome him into her bed. But they'd already done that and it hadn't fixed anything. In fact, it had only added complicated layers they were only beginning to understand.

"We can't do this, Hoyt."

He opened his mouth as if to respond before closing it, his only answer a terse nod.

"Thank you for the lovely dinner and for bringing me home. I enjoyed spending time with your family."

The polite sentiments dripped from her lips, still swollen and stung from his kisses. Determined, she kept on, falling back on the polite platitudes and congenial air she'd perfected so many years ago. "Their ready acceptance and excitement over the baby, I appreciate it more than you can know. Especially to know my child will always have a safe place. It matters."

"You have one, too, Reese." He seemed to hesitate, warring with himself before he lifted a hand and ran the back of his index finger over her cheek. "You always have a safe place with us, too."

Now it was her turn to nod.

And wait for the tears to fall after the rumble of his truck had faded into the night.

Despite a nearly sleepless night, interspersed with limited stretches of sleep that were dominated by vivid carnal dreams of Hoyt that gave no sense of rest, Reese dragged herself out of bed the next morning. It had been far too long since she'd seen her mother and it was time to fix that.

And time to tell her about the baby.

It felt wrong, somehow, that Hoyt's family knew of her pregnancy and her own mother didn't.

Dressing carefully, she did her makeup—light enough to matter and not heavy enough to draw a mother's notice—and laughed to herself as she imagined the conversations she might have with her own daughter. Assuming, of course, the baby was a girl.

Would they argue over hair and makeup? Probably. Nail length and color? Likely.

Hopes and dreams and goals? Reese was determined the answer to that would be never, whether her child was a boy or a girl. She wanted those conversations to be full of nothing but love and support and respect for her child's decisions. Perhaps it was a dream—their relationship would have its ups and downs like any other—but it was one she wanted to hold on to.

The drive was familiar and quick, and as Reese got out of the car with the small bouquet she'd picked up in town, she fortified herself with the underlying reality that the news she shared was happy. Even if it would be hard as hell to look her mother in the eye and tell her she was having a baby with a man she barely knew.

Willing any hint of the negative away—even if it were only in her own mind—she gathered up the pink roses and headed for the door. Although she knew without a doubt that she was welcome, she gave a light knock before pushing open the door.

"Mom!" Silence greeted her, but Reese moved in closer and hollered again. "Mom!"

A thready response floated toward her from the back of the house. "In the family room."

Reese headed for the rec room that dominated the back of her parents' house, glancing at the layer of dust on the small curio cabinet that had stood in that hallway longer than she'd been alive. The carpet had needed replacing for at least five years. Now, it wasn't simply threadbare but layered with a fine film of dirt, the carpet fibers crushed and flat.

She took both in and resisted the shot of remorse at how long it had been since she'd been there. At least a month, or was it more like six weeks? Reese fought down the lingering sense of shame that she'd stayed away so long and closed the last few feet to the family room. "Hey, Mom."

"Reese."

Serena Grantham smiled from the rocking chair she sat in, the emotion not reaching her eyes. "What brings you over here today?"

"I wanted to talk to you, Mom." Reese thought about all the words she'd practiced on the way over, and mentally fortified herself with the thought that she could do this. "I have some things to tell you. Some news to share."

"You do? Something about work?"

Serena's gaze had brightened a bit at the announcement of some news, but other than that slight glimmer, her grief seemed so firmly etched in place that there was no room for any other emotion to break through. Lines carved her face, grooving her despair and sadness in clear unfettered marks.

While Reese didn't want to be discouraged by the question, she couldn't quite hold back the small shot of disappointment that the only news in her life her mother could possibly come up with had something to do with work. "No. Not exactly."

Her mother gestured her forward, pointing at the

empty couch. The TV droned in the background, a talk show in full swing. The set wasn't quite loud enough to hear, yet not quite low enough to be missed. "Well come on, then, sweetie. I want to hear all about it."

Reese took the offered seat, glancing around the room as she sat down. Her mother had often spoken of the years before she married and had children. She'd been a smoker in high school and college and even in the early days of her marriage. But once she'd had Jamie, she stopped cold turkey. She claimed that it'd been the hardest but easiest thing she'd ever done because she'd done it for her child and Reese had always believed her.

There'd been a time, shortly after Jamie's death, when Reese had seen a fresh pack of cigarettes buried in the kitchen drawer, unopened. It'd taken her several days, but she finally worked up the courage to ask her mother about them. Serena had looked at the pack, sadness in her eyes, and talked of how she longed for a hit. And how quickly the demon of addiction had come back when times were so utterly horrible.

Yet, she'd held out and that pack had stayed right where it was, unopened, in the drawer for years. But then one day, about three years ago, Reese hadn't seen them when she'd gone hunting for a stamp. She'd asked her mother and Serena had whispered that it was time to let go. That she had made a commitment to herself when she quit smoking before having children, and she wasn't going to give in to her addiction simply because Jamie had died. It would be a betrayal of him and of her vow to stay healthy for her children.

So it was less with surprise, and more with sadness, that Reese noticed the full ashtray that now sat next to her mother's chair, brimming with ash and filtered tips; it was clear that the loss of Russ Grantham had finally taken its toll. That whatever vow her mother had made to herself had long since vanished.

"What's your news?" her mother asked.

"I know this is going to be a bit of a surprise but, well—" Reese hesitated, taking a deep breath for a final shot of courage "—I'm having a baby."

"You're what?" The question hovered in the air between them, the tone not one of censure and certainly not excitement. "How? I mean, I know we haven't seen each other for a while, but I wasn't aware you were dating anyone."

"Well, I'm not exactly."

"It certainly sounds like you're seeing someone," her mother pointed out. "Who is the father?"

"Hoyt Reynolds. He and I had an evening together earlier in the summer. And well, things just sort of happened."

"Reynolds?"

Reese wasn't sure what stung more: her mother's seeming lack of excitement at the news of the baby, or the way she had zeroed in on Hoyt's last name. Reynolds. Owners of Reynolds Station, the site of one of her father's crimes.

Worse, the crime that had begun his downfall.

"We've known each other forever," Reese said carefully. "We grew up together."

"Sure. You and everyone else in town."

"He's an attractive man, Mom. I'm sure you can see that. We had a connection and as two single adults, we acted on that. He's a good man."

"Right. A good man. Such a good man he got you pregnant."

"It wasn't like I wasn't an active participant."

Her mother reached for the soft pack, crumpling it when she realized it was empty of cigarettes. Tossing the pack back on the end table, her mother's gaze swung back toward her, pinning her in place. "What is this, Reesie? You come in here telling me you're having a baby. With a Reynolds boy of all people."

The Reynolds boy? What were they—a couple of fifteen-year-olds who'd been caught necking in the park after curfew?

"I'm not exactly a child. I'll be thirty by the time it's born. I thought you'd be happy about a baby."

"What's there to be happy about? You're having a baby with a man who is at the root of our family's downfall."

"I thought that sat squarely on Dad's shoulders."

"Excuse me?"

Reese knew the moment she'd overstepped, yet she couldn't hold back. "Dad made his own situation. That has nothing to do with Hoyt Reynolds or anyone else."

"Your father broke, and the Reynolds family, along with that Annabelle Granger, are the reason he's gone. He bore up under the weight of Jamie's death, doing what was right, anyway, as a leader of the police department. All those years spent following the law and locking up criminals who always got out in the end, who always got a future when all his son got was a cold grave. And what did he get for it?"

"Caught, Mom. He got caught." *Which was right and just*, she added silently, not quite ready to poke what had obviously been a slumbering bear.

Was this what her mother had been harboring for the past four months? Sitting here, day in and day out, twisting the truth of her father's crimes into some sort of moral exercise over right and wrong? Or worse, painting Russ Grantham as some sort of avenging angel and excusing his decision to kill criminals?

Reese struggled to process it all and while some part of her knew she needed to stay and battle it out, forcing her mother to see reason, another part of her was far too hurt about Serena's reaction to the news of becoming a grandmother. In the end, it was the hurt that won out.

"I'd better be going."

"I don't think—" Her mother stopped, her gaze settling back onto the TV. "Maybe that's for the best."

"I guess it is."

Reese followed the well-worn tread of footprints in the threadbare carpet, refusing to look back as she left the room. Her mother might be harboring a lifetime of disappointment, but she'd finally given Serena Grantham something to be happy about and it had been tossed in her face like some dirty secret.

Her child wasn't shameful, nor was the decision to sleep with Hoyt Reynolds. And if the one person who was supposed to support her couldn't see that, there really wasn't anything else to say.

Hoyt walked in the front door of Midnight Pass High School and wondered how it was possible a place he'd barely thought of for more than ten years could feel so immediately familiar.

Why was he even here?

Yes, he'd spent a sleepless night, the feel of Reese

in his arms and on his lips haunting him like a physical presence. And yes, he understood pursuing that desire that always seemed to hover on a low throttle between them could come to nothing good. Even if they felt so damn right together.

And even if they'd made something very good in the form of a child.

That thought—and the image of holding his son or daughter in his arms by the time spring rolled around—stopped Hoyt short. A child. Fatherhood. An unbreakable bond for the rest of his life with Reese Grantham.

Moving on, determined to shake off the conflicting and somewhat overwhelming emotions, Hoyt dragged off his hat and headed down the hall. Unresolved yearning aside, he wanted to see that she was okay. And he also wanted to do a bit more digging on the science teacher's spider.

He'd spoken to Belle and gained her promise to come over and check things out, but knew it would have to be a lower priority in her long list of duties. She had mentioned that MPHS kept a regular rotation of security on staff and he'd decided to come talk to them about any possible video they might have captured over the past few days.

While an active security presence was new since he'd been in high school, Hoyt suspected there were reasons. The drug problem that refused to abate—any number of substances readily available on the path from South America, through Mexico and on into the US—needed tight controls and steady vigilance. Sadly, that extended to high school kids.

Jamie Grantham's hadn't been the first—or last—

death from drugs in the Pass and teenagers could be, unfortunately, easy marks.

He took a quick right into the school office, where he was greeted by the same dragon-faced Mrs. Larson who'd stood guard over the front desk during the years he attended MPHS. He had it on good authority she'd been there even longer, watching over Tate's class, Ace's class and, if rumor were correct, all the way back to the founding fathers of Midnight Pass.

Or something like that.

Holding his hat against his chest, he nodded and put on his most charming self. "Good afternoon, ma'am."

"How may I help you?" While she didn't fully smile, he was pleased to see a small twinkle in the deep brown eyes that looked out over her half-moon spectacles. "Mr. Reynolds."

"You remember me?"

"I remember every student who went to this school. You're no exception."

"Well then. Ma'am," he added for good measure. "I'd like to speak with someone who manages security."

"What's the problem?"

"I'd prefer not to say."

Humor fled that dark gaze, something steely and hard taking its place. If he'd been fifteen years younger, he'd have said she was trying to scare him. But with age had come wisdom and he saw what was really happening instead: she was taking his measure. "Very well. Retired Officer Zacks is in the office next door. I'll let him know he has a visitor."

Hoyt followed her directions and walked into the room he remembered as a computer lab. The room still had computers, but it had been converted into some sort of central security office, replete with computers, video feeds of various parts of the grounds highlighted on TV monitors and a large wall of maps and what looked like bus routes.

"Officer Zacks?" Hoyt called out from the door.

An older man looked up from one of the computers and waved him in. Years had etched themselves in a face that looked like it had seen more than a few dirty fights, but even around the crooked nose and scarred chin, Hoyt couldn't miss the sharp eyes and even sharper focus. "You found me. Though I think it'll be fine if you just call me Alan."

Hoyt shook the man's extended hand. "Hoyt Reynolds. It's good to meet you, Alan."

"What can I do for you? We don't get many cowboys wandering these hallowed halls."

Hoyt glanced down at his jeans and boots and realized what he must have looked like: someone heading in, just off the ranch. "I usually clean up a bit when I'm headed into town but I had an idea and I wanted to run it by you."

"Oh?"

It might have been many years since Alan Zacks wore a uniform, but Hoyt got the same sense with him as he got with Belle: unwavering attention and a determination to do what was right. With that in the forefront of his thoughts, he filled Alan in on the events of the past few days, including his concerns over a spider from the bio lab that magically found its way out of a secured school.

"Let's take a look then." Alan waved him over toward the wall of monitors and a rather sophisticated-looking desk console. "I have to tell you, I had my concerns when I was offered this job. Watching over kids with cameras and security guards and the like, it doesn't sit all that well with me. I have come to appreciate the necessity, though."

"Things sure have changed since my siblings and I went here."

"That they have. And they changed fast. All the good and bad that comes with technological advancement."

Hoyt knew there were limits—safe or not, kids were going to be kids and deserved to get away with a certain amount of hijinks—but he also couldn't deny how much better he felt knowing Reese was safe. That any possible threat made here could be managed and likely contained.

Alan busied himself with the monitors and Hoyt could see the date and time changing at the bottom of the screen. "When Belle spoke with the science teacher, he said both spiders were in his classroom as late as Monday afternoon."

Alan shook his head. "Let me see what we can find."

The retired officer might wish things were different with school security, but Hoyt couldn't fault him for his ability to quickly move through the tools at his disposal. In a matter of minutes, he had various feeds from around the campus lined up on monitors.

"I'm going to fast forward through the evening hours for now since we have different alarms set to capture motion around the school after dark."

It took another twenty minutes, but by the time he and Alan had reviewed various angles around the school, all they'd seen were adults coming and going from the building. No one looked suspicious or like they didn't belong. Alan even knew most of them by name.

"Other than that small group of students here yesterday morning for football practice, not a kid's been around," Alan said.

"And all of those students were confined to the practice field. Not a single one appeared suspicious or to be carrying something he ought not to be?"

"Not a one."

Alan paused the screen and turned to face Hoyt. "Any chance this is just a weird coincidence? Critters can be a problem in this part of Texas. Heck, my wife screamed so loud they heard her in El Paso last weekend when I ran over a snake mowing the lawn."

Hoyt knew it was true. It was the reason he wore boots that went up to his calf. Everyone in the Pass shared their home with some unsavory animals and it was useless to pretend otherwise. "I suppose you're right." Hoyt picked up his hat off a nearby desk. "I appreciate your time, Alan. I really do."

"You can be sure I'll keep an eye out, though. And an extra one on Miss Grantham."

Before Hoyt could add a final word of thanks, the object of his concern filled the doorway to the security office. "And just what has prompted this?"

Chapter 10

If there was one thing Reese hated the most about small-town life, it was the endless scrutiny. She'd always loathed being the object of that focused attention, but she did take some small solace when that scrutiny worked out in her favor.

Or when it at least gave her advance warning of impending doom.

It had taken Alma Larson all of eighty-seven seconds to alert Jake Walters to the fact that Hoyt Reynolds was nosing around the building, asking to speak to the security office. It had taken him even less time to figure out that the presence of a Reynolds at MPHS was likely associated with Reese and he'd hightailed it down to her classroom to tell her privately before Alma could make much more of the situation.

After her assistant principal left, Reese had sat quietly and fumed for a few minutes, determined to focus on what she'd come to school to do and finish setting up her classroom. But Hoyt's unexpected visit, coupled with her mother's disinterest and even distaste for the subject of becoming a grandmother, already had her raw. What was supposed to be a quiet afternoon for herself, designed to get some of her equilibrium back, had taken a sharp turn off My-Life's-A-Mess Lane straight into Life-Sucks Ville. And to think she had expected a quiet afternoon at the high school after that disastrous visit to her mother.

If Alma caught on that Hoyt was somehow involved with her, she might as well kiss her privacy goodbye and put a for-sale sign on her house now. That was still a likely possibility when the PTA ran her out of town with pitchforks once its members discovered they had a young, unwed, soon-to-be single mother on their teaching roster.

Which was the only reason she'd stayed in her classroom for twenty-seven additional minutes after Jake departed before rushing down to Officer Zacks's office. It still prickled her that they even had to have a security center, but she pushed that ongoing grumble aside as she marched into the small room where she'd learned to use a computer and which now served as Security Central at Midnight Pass High School.

The object of her ire was there, just as rumored, leaning over a computer monitor with sweet Officer Zacks. Although the older man had told her to call him Alan more times than she could count, she still remembered him as Officer Zacks, a man who her father had always respected and worked under during his early days on the force. She'd grown up seeing him around town, and calling him by his first name seemed weird and disrespectful. Yet another by-product of small-town life.

Everyone knew everyone and even becoming an adult didn't guarantee you felt like one on the inside.

"Hi, Reese." Alan waved her in, his expression serious. "Hoyt here was just telling me about that situation with a spider on your front porch."

She avoided shooting eye daggers at Hoyt—just barely—and kept her smile firmly in place for Officer Zacks. "I think Mr. Reynolds has made a bit too much of this."

"Maybe, maybe not." Alan pointed to the screen. "But I take seriously anyone who would steal while on school grounds and, creepy or not, that animal is Fred McNamara's property."

"Of course."

Reese wasn't quite ready to back down, but Alan did have a point. Moving farther into the room, she kept her gaze focused on the screens. "Did you find anything?"

"No." Hoyt spoke first, his frustration more than evident in that lone syllable. What really got her, though, was the sullen, oddly defeated set of his shoulders. He stood there, so stiff and straight she could practically see the tension quivering off him like heat waves.

"Well, I still say it's kids pulling a prank," she started in, convinced if she said it often enough she could make it true. "I know we have cameras and I'm grateful for you taking a look into this, but I think we're going to have to chalk this up to summer hijinks and leave it at that."

Alan Zacks nodded. "Don't think I won't still be keeping an eye out."

"I appreciate that," she assured him before nodding

to Hoyt. "If we're done here, I'd like to borrow Hoyt for a few minutes. I have a high spot on my bulletin board I can't reach and you've shown up just in time. Room one forty-two."

"Of course."

Reese waved and headed out, more than anxious to avoid any possible lurking from Alma. It was only when she cleared the left turn for her classroom's hallway that she let out her first easy breath.

Why was Hoyt making such a big deal out of this? And why did he refuse to accept her explanation that it was likely just a prank? It was almost like he was trying to make the scare on her front porch more than it was.

And why are you trying to make it less?

That light nudge from her conscience grew in intensity as she thought of her child. At the idea that she was downplaying a threat, she laid a protective hand over her still-flat midsection and gave Hoyt's concerns a moment to roost.

Could someone be trying to hurt her?

It seemed far-fetched, but it wasn't impossible. There were a lot of crazies out there and her father's actions had ensured the name Grantham was known across Texas and even the US. Had she taken things too lightly, believing the fuss would die down as the news cycle continued its relentless tide?

"I haven't been here in years. This is old Mrs. Sinestra's classroom, isn't it?"

Reese shifted from contemplating the parking lot through the window and thoughts of the mysterious threat that possibly lurked and turned to find six feet two inches of cowboy standing in her classroom doorway. Goodness, did he practice that pose? Casual, with a side of lazy grace to top it off?

Helpless to resist, her gaze traveled from the top of his wide-brimmed hat, over the firm lines of his jaw, down over the blue button-down shirt that had to add thirty degrees in the August heat. Her perusal continued, over the slim hips, the distressed denim that fit those hips like a glove and on down to the boots. Pointy-toed and well-worn, they were the boots of a man who knew what he was about. A man who worked hard and had a body to show for it.

And good Lord, when had she grown so fanciful that all she could imagine was grabbing handfuls of chambray, pulling him close against her and losing herself in all that strength?

This was a special brand of hormone-induced madness; one that heightened the senses, even as it dulled every bit of impulse restraint she possessed. And she well knew she couldn't even blame it on the baby. Oh, no. Hoyt Reynolds managed to rile up her hormones all by his lonesome, sexy self.

Once more imagining the wagging tongue of Alma Larson, Reese pulled herself out of the fantasy of losing herself in big strong arms and settled into the matter at hand.

"Thanks for coming to help me." Reese pointed to the back of her classroom. "I would appreciate an extra pair of hands on the very top of that bulletin board."

"I didn't realize you were here."

"Would it have stopped you from coming?" Reese knew damn well when she was putting her personal shields up and this conversation certainly warranted that. Add on the fact that her hormones were still rac-

ing around her bloodstream with all the finesse of a
cat in heat, and she needed all the help she could get.

"Hardly. But I'd have come in to say hi first and tell
you what I was about."

"My car's out in the driveway."

"I'm around the side in visitor parking. I didn't see
your car."

"Oh."

Hoyt stepped fully into the classroom, closing the
thick metal door behind him with a hard snick. "I'm
worried about you and, whether you get all prickly
about it or not, I'm not going to change my mind. I'm
going to see to it that you're safe."

"Even if I think you're making much too big a deal
about all this." She waved a hand to encompass the *all
this* and was surprised when Hoyt reached out, neatly
capturing that hand in his larger one.

"If all this is worrying about you and my child then
yes, all this." He leaned closer, his lips hovering near
to her forehead as his voice dropped to a softer, lower
register. "If that makes me overprotective and overbearing, I'm willing to accept it. I've certainly been called
overbearing before and I'm sure I will be again."

"And overprotective?"

His voice remained low and he stood in place, close
but not so close that his lips were against her skin. It
was only when he used his thumb to stroke against the
back of her hand that she let a distinct shiver roll down
her spine. "It's a new one for me."

"It's a waste of time."

"Oh, I don't know about that. I find I sort of like it."

"What if I don't?"

"Then I'd say you'd better find a way to get used to it."

Reese wanted to push back. She wanted to rant and rail and all-around piss and moan about his bossy ways and his sudden territorial takeover of her life.

She wanted to do all those things.

But she didn't. Instead, she stood there, their faces not quite touching, and reveled in the warm moment. And allowed herself the fantasy that maybe the father of her child cared about her just a little bit.

Belle Granger was used to taking charge. It was an expected part of her job as a member of the Midnight Pass Police Department, and it had been ingrained in her at an even younger age as she lived the life of a child of an addict. Her mother's alcoholism had ensured that Belle knew how to cook dinner, pay bills and basically act as the grown-up in their relationship by the time she was ten.

That same relationship had ensured she saw far more than she let on to others, and she wasn't afraid to confront someone to hash it out.

And right now, Reese Grantham was at the top of her list.

She'd given things time to settle, especially after Reese got the full-court press Tuesday night over dinner at the Reynolds ranch house. Dinner with the four Reynolds siblings could shake anyone, no matter how firm their foundation, but Belle knew Reese was on a bit of shaky ground. A surprise baby with a man she wasn't exactly in a relationship with could do that to a woman.

Which bugged Belle, too, and she'd already started working on Tate over that one. What was wrong with his brother? He might have the hardest head in south Texas, but couldn't Hoyt see how perfect Reese was for him?

Tate had done his level best to shut her up with steamy kisses and some distracting kitchen sex, but she'd won out in the end, pushing and poking at him until he finally gave in and agreed to talk to his little brother again.

Score one, Granger. Score zero, Reynolds.

Unless, she admitted to herself with a sly smile, you acknowledged just how well they both scored.

With memories of outstanding kitchen sex still humming in her veins, Belle rang Reese's doorbell. A little Friday afternoon visit was in order and she wasn't leaving until she said what she had to.

And saw to it that Reese fully understood she had a support system that wasn't going anywhere.

"Belle!" Reese gestured her into the house, her smile wide. "It's good to see you."

Belle didn't miss the momentary puzzlement that stamped itself on Reese's face, nor the quick efforts she made to hide her surprise. "I'm sorry to just drop in but I've been wanting to visit and when I hit the wall on paperwork, I figured it was the universe telling me it was time to go visit my friend."

"Does that mean you're off duty?"

"Technically, yes."

"Then can I offer you some wine? It's getting lonely on my shelf all by itself and it'll give me a chance to stare at you longingly as you drink it. Maybe a few of those tannins will even waft in my direction if I breathe deep enough."

Belle took the reference to Reese's pregnancy in

stride, secretly pleased the woman had given her such an easy entrée. "Sounds perfect."

She'd been to Reese's home several times and had always enjoyed the cozy feeling she got when she was there. Everything was neatly in its place, yet that sense of order couldn't detract from the pervasive sense of welcome.

As Belle meandered into the kitchen, Reese already had a bottle out of a small wine rack built into the lower side of her cabinets and was fitting a corkscrew into the top.

"It's been hard to give up alcohol?" Belle asked, warming to her subject.

"Not as hard as you might think. It's a heck of a lot easier when you have a good reason." Reese patted her stomach, still devoid of any visible bump. "But I do miss it from time to time."

"You really don't need to open that just for me."

"Nonsense. We'll cork it up, and I'm sending it home with you."

Belle took the offered glass and waited until Reese had poured a fresh club soda for herself before proposing a toast. "To my future niece or nephew."

"And to my child's future aunt," Reese added, a delighted twinkle filling her eyes.

"I'll toast to that." Belle lifted her wine.

"Cheers." The light clink of glasses filled the kitchen before Belle was gestured into a seat. "So paperwork, huh?"

"It's about as constant as death and taxes. And proof that whatever cop shows make people think police work is all about is a dirty, rotten lie."

"No stakeouts with sexy partners?"

"Not a one," Belle said, shaking off an unbidden image of her forty-four-year-old partner, Jared, in silky boxers and nothing else. With the ensuing shudder that rolled down her back, Belle reached for her drink and took a good long swallow. "Not ever."

"My dad was always pretty down on cop shows. Said they were about as true to life as superheroes and vigilante jus—"

Reese stumbled over the last word, clearly catching herself on the image of an unsupervised individual meting out justice as they saw fit. The happy, light conversation that had carried them to the kitchen and through their afternoon toast faded away.

"Justice," Belle said quietly, finishing Reese's sentence.

"A concept I stopped believing in quite a while ago."

"Are you sure about that?"

Reese looked up from her determined focus on wiping beads of condensation off her glass. "Positive."

Reese fought the urge to flee—highly unlikely in her own home *and* with a MPPD cop present—and tried desperately to get that lighthearted sense of friendship back. Only there wasn't any getting it back.

Just like she'd never get her father back. Would never get a chance to ask him herself what he could possibly have been thinking to go so out of bounds like he had. To turn so determinedly toward the darkest aspects of his nature.

And worst of all, to decide that it was not only permissible but that it was somehow his right to take the lives of others.

"I think justice still exists. It's not always easy to

find and it's often blind for a reason, but it's there all the same."

Reese shrugged. "If you say so."

They sat there for a few minutes, the silence filling up with all the things she wanted to say. Or ask, really. What had those last minutes been like, between Belle and her father? Had Russ told her why he'd made such horrible choices? Or had Belle been so focused on fighting for her life that she hadn't even asked?

Although the realities of that last day had been explained to her by the Feds, their descriptions had been almost clinical in nature. The family of a confessed serial killer, it seemed, were meant to get explanations but weren't given the room or the time to express their grief or ask their own questions about their loved one.

"Do you know what the worst part is?" The question came out in a whisper, almost as if she were afraid to voice the words. Yet, in that moment, Reese knew she had to push forward. Had to get some answers to the questions that refused to abate.

"What?"

"He seemed so normal. Through it all, he'd remained so calm. So *him*. Why didn't we know? Or maybe, more to the point, *how* didn't we know? Two weeks before it all happened we'd been at the cabin, cleaning it out for spring. That cabin—" She broke off, the reality of the place where Russ Grantham had kidnapped and taken Belle swallowing her up. The place where he'd then taken his own life.

"He was a good man," Belle said.

The tears Reese had been determined to hold in welled up, hot and fiery behind her eyes. Hoyt had said the same about Russ. And funny enough, her mother had used the same words as she sneered over Hoyt's role as father to Reese's child.

Good man.

What did that even mean anymore?

"No, Belle, he wasn't. Not in the end. Not when it mattered."

"I know what I know."

"And so do I. And what I can't seem to reconcile is why you all seem so bound and determined to excuse his behavior. Or worse, to attempt to exonerate him somehow."

"I'm not excusing anything."

"Oh, no?" Reese stood then, unable to sit still any longer. "You're not? Or more to the point, is that your way of excusing yourself? You were more than happy to go after him. Is this now your way of making yourself feel better about it?"

Unbidden, her mother's words from earlier that week came back to her.

He bore up under the weight of Jamie's death, doing what was right, anyway, as a leader of the police department. All those years spent following the law and locking up criminals who always got out in the end, who always got a future when all his son got was a cold grave. And what did he get for it?

What *did* he get for it?

What had any of them gotten for it?

Suddenly exhausted, she dropped back into her chair, laying her head on her crossed forearms. Had she, even for a moment, entertained the same train of thought her mother had jumped on? That somehow Russ had been driven to his behavior and everyone else was to blame?

Because whatever she thought—and she thought a

lot—she didn't believe his actions should be blamed on anyone else.

But, oh, how she missed him anyway.

She'd lost her father and everyone thought she should just move on, accept the bad and forget all about the good. To forget about all that had come before the good went away.

To accept that he was a soul who'd lived entirely in darkness.

"I don't have any excuses, Reese." A warm hand covered hers where it lay folded over her arm. "I don't need them. I stand by my decisions and that includes the very difficult decision to go after Russ once I believed he was at fault. I can't and won't apologize for that."

Although the words hurt, there was something soothing in their honesty. More, there was the acknowledgment that Belle had suffered, even if she'd still pushed forward to do what was right.

"But none of that means I can't see that you're hurting and that you have every right to the warm, loving memories of your father. No one has a right to take that away from you."

Reese lifted her head up, her gaze meeting soft, understanding blue. "That's been the worst part. It's like a switch flipped and all that came before doesn't exist. As hard as it was, it wasn't like that with Jamie. We were allowed to grieve. Allowed to remember him in the time before his addiction without that being tainted by what he'd become."

"You're still allowed to grieve. You can with me. And I know you can with Hoyt and his family."

Oh, how she wanted to believe Belle. That the events this past spring could somehow be overlooked if there were enough understanding and acceptance. That if she only wished hard enough, the very people who'd been confronted with her father's demons could make all the pain go away.

"How can you say that? From the accounts shared with my mother and me, he was going to take you down with him, only changing his mind there at the end."

"But he did change his mind. As hard as all this has been, that's what I can't let go of or forget. In the end, he did change, Reese."

Overwhelmed with the lack of artifice or any sense of lingering anger from a place where there should have been plenty, Reese struggled to put it all together. And once again found herself confiding in Belle instead.

"My mother's not very excited about the baby."

"When did you tell her?"

"Wednesday. After telling Hoyt and the rest of you all, it felt wrong that she didn't know."

"And she didn't handle it well?" Belle toyed with the stem of her wineglass, her voice never wavering from the same warm and gentle cadence she'd used since sitting down.

"Best I can tell, she's not handling anything these days."

"I tried to go see her. About a month ago. She wasn't having any of it."

"You tried to—" Of course Belle would have. She was one of the strongest people Reese had ever met and clearly was the type to go talk to Serena Grantham. "You tried?"

"I did. But she wasn't ready to talk to me or hear what I had to say. Maybe she never will be, but I don't think the same can be said for news of her grandchild."

"I don't know. She seemed pretty fixated on the un-married part. And if that weren't enough, the whole Hoyt-Reynolds-is-the-father part just about put her over the edge."

"She doesn't like Hoyt?"

"Which brings us back to where we started. Since the Reynolds family is now tainted with my father's crimes, I'm some sort of emotional traitor."

Belle's eyebrows winged up. "She said all that?"

"I inferred it." Reese played with the edge of her napkin where it sat below her sweating glass. "But I know I'm right."

"Well, I know I'm right, too. A baby's happy news, no matter the circumstances. You just need to give her a bit of time to work her way around to it."

"And if she doesn't?"

That warm, soothing hand came down over hers again. "Not gonna happen. Just like I knew your father, I know your mother. Give her some time to get used to the idea. Once she does, I know this baby's going to do a lot to help put the bad where it belongs."

"And where's that?" Reese asked, amazed at how easy it was to believe in Belle's certainty.

"In the past. Firmly and finally in the past."

Chapter 11

Heavy, thumping bass echoed from the front of Reese's house, nearly shaking the windows with the deep, steady rhythm. Whatever Hoyt had pictured in his mind, Reese Grantham as a heavy metal lover was not it.

Not it at all.

Yet, here he stood, the evidence obvious as he caught sight of her silhouette through the front curtain, her head bobbing up and down to the music.

"Reese!" He pounded on the door, trying to get her attention. When the head bouncing only continued, he pressed a finger to the doorbell and refused to let off the ringer.

"What the—" Reese's shout floated over his head as the door swung open, the music spilling out over him like a wave.

He pulled his finger off the small white button. "I tried the bell. And knocking. And yelling—"

She cut him off with a wave of her hand and ran down the hall toward what could only be called the hell-mouth. The music cut off abruptly, even as the air still seemed to shimmer around him. He stuck a finger in his ear and jiggled, not sure if he'd ever fully hear again. And briefly wondered how developed his child's hearing was at this stage.

He'd have to look it up. Just like he'd been looking up its size and shape and developmental goals each day, amazed at the idea that his baby was somewhere around the size of a grape at the moment.

Thoughts of babies and auditory development faded as images of that spider on her front porch filled his mind's eye. He'd been willing to give her some room to think it was a high school prank, but nothing about the incident sat well with him.

He glanced over his shoulder, but all he saw was the bucolic neighborhood in the throes of Texas summer. Grass browned by the sun. A light breeze drifting through trees. And sun so hot he could see shimmering waves emanating off the pavement.

Reese ran back down the hall, her bare legs and feet visible beneath a pair of old UT shorts. He pulled his gaze off her street as an unmitigated shot of lust curled in his belly.

"Don't run." He stepped into the house, escaping the early evening heat for the cooler air-conditioning.

"I can still do that, you know. It's good for me."

"Pregnant women are supposed to be running from one end of the house to the other?"

"Why not? If it was good for me before, it should still be good for me now."

Hoyt wasn't so sure about that—he'd have to check

the baby website—but he could hardly argue with the lithe form and strong sexy legs that he still hadn't managed to tear his gaze from.

"You're a heavy metal fan?"

"Guilty."

"Neighbors don't mind?"

"I think it scares them away." Reese smiled. "Plus, old Mrs. Campbell next door needs hearing aids and the family on the other side uses that house as their second home, so I'm sort of exempt from annoyed neighbors."

"Lucky for you." *Or them*, Hoyt added silently to himself.

"What's going on?"

Hoyt fought the shot of irritation that something had to be *going on* for him to show up, but buried it under the same steady annoyance that had accompanied him all day. Hell, half the week, if he were honest.

He'd gone to the high school to help her and the damn woman had shrugged him off like a nuisance. Like his concerns were extreme at best and paranoid at worse. He wasn't paranoid. And it galled him that she wasn't taking things seriously.

And hell, what really bothered him was that Belle had been out here all afternoon, talking to Reese about any number of things, and Reese hadn't bothered to call him or text him since Wednesday.

Not that he'd called or texted, either, but that was beside the damn point.

"I wanted to see you. Does something have to be going on?"

"No, not at—"

The rest of her sentence was effectively swallowed by his mouth as he pulled her close, anxious and needy to get his hands on her. And his mouth. And whatever else she was willing to let him put on her because damn, the woman was under his skin and nothing seemed to change that.

In fact, Hoyt admitted to himself as he settled his hands at her hips while her arms wrapped themselves around his neck, it kept getting worse.

Way worse.

Somehow, he couldn't find a way to complain about it when her lush lips opened, her tongue wrapping around his in long, lapping strokes. Hoyt gave himself a moment to simply drink her in. The taste of her. The feel of her. And the strange, calming effect she had on him, even as his body drew tauter and tauter under the sensual onslaught.

Long moments spun out between them, a balm after a long week spent working the ranch, riding Stink all over their property and worrying like an old grandma over Reese's safety.

He'd believed he could handle it. No, damn it, he *would* handle it. But it was nice to feel all of it recede as this thing between him and Reese tightened its hold even further.

She broke the kiss first, even as her arms stayed in place around his neck. "That's quite a hello. Maybe I'll ignore my doorbell more often."

"Hello to you, too."

"Why don't I start over? Instead of asking why you're here, I'll tell you what I really wanted to say."

The fact that she started again warmed something inside his chest. Something that only grew warmer when he realized that she'd understood how frustrated he'd been by her greeting. "What's that?"

"I'm glad you're here and would you like to join me for dinner? I was about to order a pizza, just as soon as I finished vacuuming."

"I'd like that."

"Then let's get to it. The vacuum isn't quite as much fun without a bit of Metallica in the background, but I'll make do."

She'd nearly turned back to the vacuum when his hand snaked out, pulling her close. "No way. I'll finish the floor. You go order the pizza."

"How will they hear my order over the racket?"

"That's your problem." Hoyt shrugged his shoulders, feeling lighter than he had in days. "I've got some cleaning to do."

The woman watched from the clearing in the field. She'd already sent the kids off with her ex, well aware that they'd be back later. Especially when Paul caught wind that she'd sent Ben over with an ear infection and a runny nose.

Paul didn't do runny noses. Or sick kids. Or kids, really, at all.

He'd been her big mistake and she now paid for it each and every day. That and the fact that Paul wasn't Jamie. He never had been, but she'd pretended to herself that he could be. That if she tried hard enough and took care of him well enough that she'd bring him around. All she'd done was give herself a miserable decade of marriage and two kids who had a father who wanted as little as possible to do with them.

The antithesis of Jamie Grantham.

Oh, if only Jamie had lived. If only things had been different and she'd found a way that last year in high school to help him. His family sure as hell hadn't, which only meant she should have tried harder.

He'd hidden the drugs from her at first. Or maybe not hidden, exactly, but he had concealed the depth of what he was doing. They'd smoke pot and it was only after he'd drop her off at home after their dates that he'd go find the harder stuff. Not that it would have made a difference, she knew. She was in love with him, and there was nothing he could have done that would have changed her mind.

Nothing at all.

And then he'd gone and died, taking too much too fast and wrapping his car around that tree. Her mother had cried for days, so grateful that her daughter had already been dropped off at home that night and wasn't anywhere near *that death trap of a car*. Her friends had told her over and over how lucky she was to have escaped Jamie's drug addiction. And poor Mrs. Grantham had cried on her shoulder and hugged her tight at the funeral, sick at the loss of her son. Even Jamie's father had hugged her and thanked her for being such a good influence on Jamie.

Only Reese had stood back, distant and cold.

High and mighty Reese Grantham, who thought she was above it all. She'd stood there quietly at the funeral, staring through everyone and never shedding a tear. In the months after Jamie died, they'd seen each other from time to time and Reese never even acknowledged the loss. She'd simply moved on, as if she'd never had a brother. As if nothing had happened and no one had died. Above it all like some regal queen.

And now she was doing it again.

While Jamie had raged on about his old man, complaining that his father was too uptight to ever understand him and what made him tick, she'd come to understand Russ Grantham differently. Officer Grantham had been an okay guy. He'd always been nice to her when he'd seen her around town and wished her well after she and Paul got married. He'd always ask her how she was doing and never assumed she had simply gotten over her high school boyfriend or the shock of how he died.

And then he'd figured out how to get back a piece of Jamie.

Oh, the town was all aflutter with how awful it was, but there was a piece of her—a surprisingly big piece—that understood. Even cheered him a bit. He had made a choice to act and take out some of the scum who infected this part of Texas with their drugs and their empty promises.

He was a *hero.*

It was one thing for no one in the Pass to understand that, but his own daughter? Her father had died and Reese had proven herself once again to have a heart of ice. She walked around all regal and proud, above the sympathy and the kind words and the grief.

This was the example they were setting for the students of Midnight Pass? No way.

She'd had enough.

It was high time Reese Grantham started paying a bit more attention. Time she stepped off that block of ice, slipped off the crown of indifference and understood what was expected of her.

She hadn't finalized her approach, but her access to the high school made it easy to walk the floor and time out how long it would take to carry out her plans.

Reese Grantham thought she could ignore her family and move on with her life.

So there was no better place to take her down than the places she believed she was safe.

A lesson she was going to start teaching tonight.

Reese set out the dishes, napkins and forks and knives, amused to still hear the vacuum running up and down her hallway. It shouldn't be funny—she hardly subscribed to gender roles and Hoyt was as capable of running her vacuum as she was—but there was something about that large powerful body, clad in jeans and a black T-shirt, that seemed incongruous with a Friday-night cleaning session.

Less amusing and far more serious was the kiss he'd laid on her shortly after arriving. She could still feel the imprint of his lips and the twin brands where his hands had settled at her hips.

Goodness, the man was lethal. Whether he was in full-on cowboy mode like the other day at school, or dressed in his military uniform on Memorial Day crossing through the town square, or here, dressed for a casual Friday night, it didn't seem to matter. Her mouth watered at all of it.

Even if it had begun to go way beyond attraction.

Like now, she admitted to herself. It would be so easy to make the evening all about how he looked: as American as apple pie and infinitely more scrumptious. Only he was so much more than that. While she did revel in teasing him, his concern for her health was touching. The fact that he paid attention and worried over her was endearing and sweet.

He'd been the same way after he'd stopped into her classroom. The quiet moments between them, so heavy with need and longing, had faded after she stepped away, putting those feelings firmly back into that small place in her heart where she kept them hidden. And then he'd gone and helped her, hanging pieces from the highest corners of her bulletin board and asking her questions about her lesson plans.

Questions he seemed genuinely interested in knowing the answers to.

Did the kids really enjoy reading *A Tale of Two Cities*? And if she honest-to-goodness liked *Pride and Prejudice* or if she taught it because she had to? And even more interesting, when she told him she taught the first Harry Potter book along with *A Separate Peace*, he'd launched into a soliloquy of how much he loved the entire Harry Potter series.

Yes, the man was a surprise. The more she learned about him, the more she wanted to know. He wasn't just a handsome cowboy in well-fitted jeans. Well, she amended, he was that, but he was so much more.

And wasn't that just the most amazing thing?

"Pizza's here," Hoyt hollered down the hall, the vacuum shutting off just before his heavy tread faded as he moved toward the door. She'd planned to buy dinner and had already laid out money on the hall table in her entryway, but he ignored the money, pulling out his wallet as he opened the door.

"Hoyt. Money for the pizza's on the hall table."

"I've got it." He waved her off and while she appreciated the gesture, something in it poked at her. She could pay for her own dinner and his, too. And damn it, why did he seem to feel he had to pay for everything?

They weren't dating.

And hell, even if they were, she wouldn't expect him to buy every meal then, either.

It's just a pizza, Reese. Find another sword to fall on.

She took a few deep breaths before following him into the kitchen. It *was* just a pizza, after all; they weren't sharing a gourmet meal. The rich scents of cheese and warm sauce wafted toward her, effectively pulling her those last few steps into the kitchen. "What do you want to drink?"

"A soda's fine."

She pulled out a cola for him and got herself some water and settled both on the table. The scene was oddly domestic, made only more so by their shared cleaning moments before.

"Living room's ready for inspection after dinner." It was hard to remain irritated in the face of that smile and the small puff of his chest. "I roll a mean vacuum."

"I'll hold you to that."

"See that you do." Hoyt took a big bite of his pizza and chewed, his expression thoughtful. "Belle said she'd visited earlier."

"She did." Reese took a bite of her own, wondering where he was going with his observation. If he wanted to know something, he could ask. Which was curious because underneath the casual comment she suspected that Belle's visit had bothered him.

Which made no sense at all.

Why would he care if his soon-to-be sister-in-law stopped over? Add on that she and Belle had been friends since they were kids and his curiosity seemed misplaced.

"I guess I didn't realize you two visited regularly."

"I haven't seen her as much over the past year, but we are friends." And if their conversation earlier was any indication, she and Belle were on a path to getting that friendship back in place. Reese had naturally backed away after the events of the spring and it was healing to know she didn't need to.

Especially after her mother's dismal reaction to the baby. Belle seemed sure that Serena would come around, but Reese wasn't so certain. And amidst that insecurity, it was wonderful to know she had a friend to lean on.

Which made Hoyt's seeming upset that much more difficult. Suddenly as prickly as she'd felt over the money for the pizza, Reese pressed a bit harder. "Does it upset you that Belle came over?"

"No." Hoyt quickly took another bite of pizza, stuffing his mouth and effectively stalling his side of the conversation.

"You sure about that?"

"Of course I'm sure." Hoyt got up and crossed to the counter for another slice. "Would you like any?"

Reese waved her pizza in the air, still only half eaten. "I'm good at the moment."

"Okay."

She nearly laughed at his sullen expression when he returned to his seat. Despite their absolutely riveting conversation, she sensed she was nearing a breakthrough and decided to push on. "I've got a question, then."

"Shoot."

"Why did you pay for the pizza? I left money on the table by the door."

"It's a pizza."

"Exactly. Just a pizza. I can buy it as easy as you."

"It was a nice thing to do."

"Like Belle's visit was a nice thing?"

Reese saw the moment the inane jab hit the mark. "What are you trying to say?"

"You tell me." She shot the response right back, their aimless parry and thrust taking on a sharper edge.

"I think it's great Belle came over. Great that you had a nice afternoon talking and laughing and having a grand old time. And you couldn't be bothered to call me or text me once. Hell, if I hadn't come to the school on Wednesday, would I have even heard from you after dinner with my family?"

Reese glanced down at her plate. "That's some pizza." She picked up her slice, turning it around. "They put truth serum in the cheese?"

Hoyt slammed back his chair, grabbing his plate and tossing it into the sink. The ceramic made a hard thud but nothing broke, even as the sound echoed off the kitchen walls. "This isn't a joke."

"No," Reese agreed. "It's not."

"Then why don't you just say to me what you want to say?"

"I could ask you that same question. Why are you here?"

"Because I wanted to check in on you."

Reese was on her feet now, unwilling to have him stomp around her kitchen like a two-year-old who couldn't put words to his irritation. "And vacuum my floors and buy me dinner? That was your plan on the drive over here?"

"No, I—" He broke off, the same frustration that

rode that proverbial toddler's face filling his own. "I wanted to see you. And then I find out Belle's over here laughing and having a good time and you couldn't be bothered to let me know how you are."

"Is that how we're playing things now? Checking in with each other?" She moved up closer into his space. "We're not dating, remember? And we're not a couple."

"We're having a baby."

"Right. From a wild night of passion and a bad condom. Hardly the stuff of love and romance and commitment."

Reese had no idea where the emotion came from, but what had started as a gentle line of teasing, brought on by the curiosity of having him in her kitchen on a Friday night, had become something else entirely.

Catharsis?

Or just that truth serum she'd teased him was on the pizza?

Because she and Hoyt Reynolds didn't have a relationship. But they now had a bond that would tie them together for life. A tie that meant they needed to sit down and begin to figure out what that all meant.

"When in the last week and a half have I not shown you my commitment? Hell, I even asked you to marry me. That wasn't for show, yet you brushed it off without even considering it." Hoyt shoved his hands in his jeans pockets, the move highlighting his triceps. Reese fought to keep herself focused on his question and off that tantalizing line of strength.

Consider it?

She hadn't thought of much else. How could he possibly think she hadn't spent painstaking hours thinking about marrying him? Hours where making that choice seemed like the answer to all her problems. Only to then adamantly fight herself not to take the easy route and give in, to accept life with a man who didn't love her, just to care for their child.

"I have considered it, Hoyt."

"Could have fooled me."

"Look. This has happened fast and neither of us has had a lot of time to process the implications. Is it so wrong that I'm trying to protect myself?"

Hoyt stared at her from the counter, those tempting muscles drawing her attention despite her best efforts. Did he know how comforting it was to look over and see all that raw strength and ready commitment to do the right thing? To know that he wasn't prepared to abandon her to deal with the consequences of their night together alone? To know that he'd give up his future happiness just to care for his child and give that baby a name?

It meant more than she could ever say and was the very reason she couldn't take him up on the offer. Couldn't consign her child's father to a loveless marriage.

Or live her life knowing love wasn't the first reason— or a reason at all—that he'd proposed to her.

Reese nearly said it. Nearly allowed that truth, so sour on her tongue, to spill out in a torrent of words and emotions and feelings she couldn't hold back any longer. She'd nearly given in, so tired of trying to hold it all together, when all she really wanted was someone to hold her close and promise her that she was making the right decisions. That their child had a bright and happy future.

And that she did, too.

"Hoyt. I—"

The words died in her throat as gunshots erupted outside the kitchen, the window behind Hoyt's head shattering into a million pieces.

Chapter 12

Hoyt dived for Reese, dragging her into his arms before pushing them both to the floor. Every bit of military training kicked in and he cradled her close, forming a shield with his body, all the while keeping his back to the window. Nudging them closer to the corner of the kitchen, he dragged the table with him so that they had cover over their heads, but only the sound of the table legs moving across her tile floor and their heavy breaths interrupted the silence.

"Hoyt. Are you okay?" Reese's hands were on his back, feeling around before moving up to grip the sides of his head. "Are you hurt?"

"Shh. I'm fine. I'm not hit." He kept his arms firmly around her, crooning lightly as the shock of the moment gave way to a rush of adrenaline. "It's okay."

Hoyt saw it the moment that adrenaline crested,

a wave of emotion in its wake. Hot tears coated his T-shirt as she pressed her face against his chest. Her voice was muffled, but he understood her clearly enough. "I thought something happened to you. I don't know how it didn't. You were right there. In front of the window as it just…exploded!"

They sat there like that, the two of them huddled under the table, as he gave her a moment to ride the wave and get it all out. The shock. The fear. And the overwhelming disbelief that someone had shot at them.

His military training ran deep and the urge to get outside and scan the area for the threat was strong, even as he knew whoever was responsible had hightailed it out of there. Which also meant he needed to call Belle and get the police out to see what they could find.

But again, Hoyt sensed in that moment Reese needed him more. So he pulled her close, ignoring the awkward spread of his legs beneath the small space and just kept rubbing large circles over her back as she cried it out.

And let those tears fuel his anger as it spread, sharp and deep, clearing away any lingering reasons to doubt his concerns over the past few days. Anger that spiked when he took in the bullet lodged in the cabinet nearest the sink.

Who was doing this?

Why had someone targeted her?

And what could they possibly hope to gain?

She was a high school teacher. A kind, decent, generous, hardworking schoolteacher who wouldn't hurt a fly and, best as he could tell, kept to herself.

Was this some lingering vendetta against her father?

That thought brought a host of others, including the raw panic that one of drug gangs that had counted some of Russ Grantham's victims as their own might have decided to come after Russ's family.

But would they do it this way?

He was no expert on gang warfare and he'd certainly run his concerns past Belle. Hell, he'd go to the makeshift FBI office the Feds had set up in the Pass if that would help. But would a drug cartel really toy with a victim like this? Spiders? Bullets through windows? It seemed unnecessary and petty somehow. Like a person unable to truly decide if they were in or out on committing a crime. Not the work of a drug kingpin and his minions.

Reese lifted her head, her hazel eyes liquid with tears. "Are you sure you're okay?"

"I'm fine. I promise. Are you okay?"

"I just don't understand this. Nothing about it makes any sense."

He couldn't argue with her, so he simply nodded his head and pulled her close once more. And vowed they'd get to the bottom of it all.

Arden clutched Reese's hand as they sat in her living room, both of them watching the intermittent flash of lights as various members of the MPPD crisscrossed her front yard looking for clues. Arden and Reese had pulled back the filmy curtains to see what was going on but Reese almost wished they'd left them closed, unable to fully see the various police department members seeking clues to a shooter.

Although the initial shock had worn off, Reese still couldn't believe what had happened, or why anyone would shoot at her home. Worse, she still shuddered to think how close a bullet had come to striking Hoyt as he stood there like an easy mark in front of the window.

How had the shooter missed him?

Was it intentional? Or were they a bad shot? Or had Hoyt simply gotten lucky as the bullet missed its intended target? Her.

"I'm sorry you had to come out here for this."

Arden shifted her attention off the activity through the front window and turned fully to look at her. "What are you possibly sorry about?"

"This." Reese waved a hand toward the window. "All of this. Whatever *this* actually is."

"Well it's certainly not your fault and I won't have you apologizing for it." Arden waited a moment, then pressed on. "You're part of us now, Reese. We're here for you. I hope you understand that."

Her conversation with Belle earlier that day—had it really been only a few hours ago?—still lingered. Belle had offered the same sort of support and unconditional acceptance. Even Hoyt's offer of marriage, if not overtly offering love, did suggest a huge measure of care.

Which made her reaction to it all so hard to understand. Didn't she want support through this? The answer was a resounding yes, if not for herself, definitely for her child. So why was she struggling so hard to accept what were clearly genuine, heartfelt sentiments?

"I appreciate your kindness but none of you signed up for this. Hoyt didn't and his family certainly didn't."

Arden shifted once more, tucking a leg up beneath her as she got comfortable on her side of the couch. "I want to make sure I have this straight, so let me feed it back to you. Some crazy person has decided to target you and instead of feeling like you can turn to people who would do anything to help you, the thought has lodged that you should somehow be dealing with this alone?"

"I'm not—"

"Nope." Arden shook her head. "Not finished yet. Are you under some misguided idea that the only reason we're helping you is because of the baby?"

"Well, yeah. Of course."

"Now you're just making me mad."

Whether it was Arden's normally levelheaded nature or the yoga she actively practiced that seemed to keep her on an even keel, Reese was pretty sure in all the years she'd known the woman she'd never actually seen her mad.

She could never say that again.

"What sort of boneheaded, idiotic *friend* would think that the only reason I cared about her was because of a baby?"

"It's not a big leap." As arguments went, hers was terribly weak, but Reese couldn't quite let it go. "I mean, why would you put yourself in danger? And especially not after—"

It only took a heartbeat, maybe less, before Arden leaped. "After what? After your father's crimes? After he killed someone on Reynolds land? Say it, Reese, because the rest of us are sick in the heart of saying it for you."

"Whoa, Arden. What's going on in here?" Hoyt's question rolled over them both, a cross between the tone she imagined he used with skittish horses and the commands he gave his ranch hands when he wanted answers.

"Nothing." Arden shook her head and shoved off the couch.

"Arden, I—" Reese broke off as Arden rushed from the room. The fear that had wrapped itself around her midsection since the shots through the window faded in the face of her friend's anger, replaced with a sinking hurt she had no idea how to handle.

Why couldn't Arden see her point? The Reynolds family wouldn't be a part of any of this if she and Hoyt hadn't had their wild night back in June. No baby, no commitment.

No commitment, no putting them in danger.

"I haven't seen her that mad in a while." Hoyt's gaze was still on the door where Arden had slipped out to the front yard. "She'll get over it."

"How can you be that nonchalant?"

"She's been my sister for twenty-eight years. I've seen her mad before."

"I haven't. It was—" Reese stilled, her own short-sighted comments still ringing in her ears. "Not it, *I*. I was ungrateful."

"You're also shaken up. I think you can give yourself a bit of a pass here."

"Maybe. Or maybe I need to get my emotions under control and try to think of who might be doing this." She heard the bitterness in her own voice and mentally chafed at any hint of victimization. She'd been targeted for some unfathomable reason—just as Hoyt had tried pointing out since the spider—but that didn't mean she was a victim. Or helpless. Nor did it mean she'd leave things as they were with Arden.

But for the moment, she'd work on bucking up and revel in the innate strength and support that was as much a part of Hoyt Reynolds as his green eyes or wide shoulders.

That gaze went sharp, a hard emerald glittering back at her in the soft glow of her living room lights. "Did you think of something?"

"No, not yet." She sighed. "But it does feel less and less like student pranks."

"I know."

Something lay beneath Hoyt's ready agreement. "You have any ideas?"

"Nothing specific or tangible, but something I do want to run by Belle."

Reese waited, but when he didn't finish the thought, she pressed on. "And?"

"It's just a line I want her to tug."

"Then you can certainly tug it for me."

"It's probably wildly off base."

She already knew he was a man who kept his thoughts to himself, but this was ridiculous. "Out with it."

"Reese—"

"Nope. I want to hear this. Not only can I handle it, but I can't consider what's happening to me or keep an eye out for someone aiming to do me harm if you don't share what you're thinking."

While she saw his clear hesitation, the subtle shifting from foot to foot making his discomfort more than obvious, she saw something else.

The moment her argument hit its mark.

"I want Belle to check on the latest with the drug cartels. Maybe some kingpin's got some lingering anger or embarrassment over your father's actions and wants to use you to even the scales."

Reese dropped onto the couch, the sheer impact of the idea swamping her.

Could she actually be the target of a drug lord?

It seemed far-fetched in the extreme, but then again, she'd have said a lot of things seemed fanciful and ridiculous. Finding out her father had turned into a serial killer who hunted drug runners sat squarely at the top of the list.

And then a whole other idea struck, hitting her square in the chest.

"My mother. I have to get to my mother. What if they've targeted her, too?"

Blood still pounded through her veins in a heavy, bumpy rhythm as she pulled into her garage. She still saw visions of the police lights flying past her on the route back into Midnight Pass, expecting one of them to pull her over and find the shotgun she'd stowed in the trunk.

But no one had stopped her at all. Instead, they'd raced for Reese Grantham's house, just like she'd planned.

Taking those shots had been harder than she'd expected, but cathartic, too. Freeing.

Powerful.

And not for the first time did she imagine what Jamie's father had discovered once he began taking down those drug dealers. She'd always heard that revenge was sweet, but she'd use a different term.

Revenge was liberating.

All the small, petty grievances of her life seemed to fade as she held that shotgun. Her ex's abandonment, both physical and emotional. The lingering toll of remembering how Jamie had died. Even the stress of raising children all alone seemed distant, somehow, as she held that gun.

She turned off the engine and hit the garage door. She'd deal with the gun later. For now, it could remain in her trunk, buried under a blanket. She had been careful to take out the bullets, just as Paul had taught her, and wondered even now as they rattled at the bottom of her purse if she should find a way to get rid of them. She'd been careful to take the casings as well, picking them up where they'd scattered around her feet. It hardly made sense to drop them in the trash, but where would she get rid of them?

She hadn't murdered anyone and this was Texas, after all. Who would notice a few shell casings from a good, old-fashioned scaring at the bottom of a garbage can?

The picture forming in her mind of places around town vanished as the distinctive ringtone echoed from her purse. Dragging out the phone, she braced herself for the conversation to come.

She didn't even get out a hello before Paul's voice was barking through the line. "Loretta. You have to come back over here. Ben's sick and Charlie's not too far behind, if the bellyache he's whining about is any indication."

"Paul. It's your night with the boys. They looked forward to seeing you all week."

"I'm not taking them sick like this. I have work in the morning and I can't be up all night dealing with this."

Like she could be up all night, either.

But something about Charlie's little face as she'd dropped them off and Ben's stoic features as he'd trudged up to Paul's door, his little brother's hand in his, filled her mind's eye.

A different sort of power.

Not like holding the gun at all, but something softer. Quieter. And even more powerful.

"I'll be right over."

Loretta ended the call, hit the button for the garage door and restarted the ignition.

It was time to go get her babies.

"Mom!" Reese pounded on her mother's front door, trying the doorknob at the same time, relieved and somewhat mollified to find it locked. "Mom!"

A light flashed on from the back of the house, vaguely visible through the small side windows on either side of the front door. She heard the vague echo of footsteps and backed up to stand beside Hoyt.

He'd insisted on coming with her and what had seemed like a great idea at the time suddenly turned sour as memories of her last conversation with her mother filled her mind's eye.

Right. A good man. Such a good man he got you pregnant.

Although Reese had shared with Arden the conversation she'd had with her mother, Hoyt still didn't know about her visit and it was a damned difficult time to try and explain it all. Instead, she reached for his hand, grateful for the ready support when his responding grip was firm and tight. "I'm sorry if she's a bit off."

He squeezed her hand lightly. "It's fine."

The door swung open and without Serena saying a word, Reese knew things were not fine.

Not at all.

"Mom." She rushed forward anyway, still so relieved her mother hadn't been harmed. Pulling her close, Reese was shocked by how stiff and formal her mother was, her arms still at her sides as Reese tried to hold her close.

"You brought him along."

If Hoyt was at all fazed by Serena's stiff frame, stringy hair or cold greeting, it wasn't obvious as he nodded his head. "Ma'am."

"Let's get inside." Reese stepped back but before she could reach for the door, Hoyt had it firmly in hand, closing out the heat and the sounds of the August night. The steady hum of the TV from the back of the house replaced the light whirling music of the cicadas and the frigid air-conditioning quickly overrode the August heat.

"We need to talk to you."

"Didn't you and I talk enough the other day, Reesie?"

"It's about something else."

Reese didn't miss the subtle curiosity that sparked briefly in her mother's eyes, but it was quickly replaced with the blank stare and pursed lips she'd worn since opening the door. "Fine, come on back."

Although she and Hoyt had discussed strategy on the way over—she wanted to blurt out their suspicions and Hoyt was aiming to be a bit more subtle—they did agree that her mother needed some sense of what was going on and what they suspected. Even if Hoyt's guess was wildly off base, she needed her mother's vigilance, for Serena to pay attention to her own personal safety.

The woman who walked in front of her down the hallway barely looked able to stand, let alone observe the world around her.

One step at a time, Grantham, Reese chided herself. First, she needed her mother to understand what was going on. Then they'd worry about her mental state.

The family room looked as dull and lifeless as it had the other day but Reese ignored it as she took a seat on the couch opposite her mother's chair. Hoyt took the spot next to her, seeming oblivious to the dank, lifeless air. Although she wanted to reach for his hand, that easy strength going a long way toward buoying hers, Reese kept her hands in her lap. No need to incent her mother's ire or draw her off the reason for their visit: Serena's safety.

"Mom, we need to talk to you about something. But first, I wanted to know if anything strange has happened."

"You mean besides my unwed daughter marching in here telling me she's pregnant?"

So much for not fueling her mother's ire. Resolved, Reese pressed on and held back the heavy sigh that wanted to escape. "That's not what I meant. Has anyone strange been by knocking at the door or has anyone been nosing around the house?"

"Of course not."

"And you haven't felt uncomfortable at all?"

"I've been plenty uncomfortable knowing my daughter's been playing the town whore with you." Serena shot a trembling finger at Hoyt before she reached over and picked up her pack of cigarettes. Unlike the other day, this pack was full and it was the work of moments for her mother to have one out and lit, smoke drifting up into the air.

With impressive speed, Hoyt was off the couch and hovering over her mother. He had the cigarette out of her mouth and crushed in the nearby ashtray, his movements firm but never threatening, in a matter of seconds. He swiped the pack as he stepped away, shoving them into his pocket as he resumed his seat on the couch. "The smoke's bad for the baby. Not to mention you."

"Well, I never—"

Hoyt flashed a cold dark smile. "You can have them back when we leave. In the meantime, I need you to listen to your daughter."

Reese wasn't sure if she should stand up and cheer or burst into tears that Hoyt had so neatly pinned her mother down. The lifeless gaze Serena had used to stare at the world had vanished, replaced with sparks and fire Reese hadn't seen in years.

Since before Jamie was sick.

"You're got some nerve, Mr. Reynolds. First you knock up my daughter and now you move around my home as if you own the place."

Hoyt's smile never wavered. "Your daughter clearly has far more patience than I do so I'll say this once. Reese isn't a whore or some knocked-up victim. She's a beautiful, competent woman who's going to be the mother of my child. I'll kindly ask you to remember that if you hope to have any sort of relationship with your grandchild."

Her mother seemed ready to argue before the bluster seemed to go out of her, like a balloon losing all its air. "Why are you here?"

"Mom. You need to listen to us and take this seriously. Hoyt and I were shot at tonight."

If she hadn't seen it with her own eyes, Reese wouldn't have believed the change in her mother's demeanor. As fast as she'd deflated, things seemed to change just as quickly. Serena sat up straighter, her focus fully on Reese as she reached forward, her slender roughened hands gripping Reese's fully. "Tell me what's going on."

Reese and Hoyt took turns, each sharing what they knew and suspected about the events of the past week. The spider and the review of footage at the school. The shots that night as they sat in the kitchen. And Hoyt's very real fears that Russ's actions had come back to haunt them in the form of a violent vendetta.

The frailty Serena had carried since Russ's death the previous April faded with each syllable, the clear danger to her daughter and future grandchild seeming to give her strength.

"What does Belle think?" Serena asked. "Russ might have kept things from me at the end, but I was a cop's wife. I know how this stuff works. The gang warfare and the violence criminals can perpetrate if they want to get back at someone. I'm not doubting your words, Reesie, but a spider seems tame for that crowd. The bullets," Serena nodded. "Not so much."

"I know, Mom. But it also means we don't think it's a bunch of kids pranking around."

"No," her mother agreed. "I don't see it, either."

"And you haven't felt anything off, Mrs. Grantham?" Hoyt asked, the earlier subtle enmity between the two of them vanished now that they fought a common enemy.

"I haven't left the house much since my husband's death, but I also don't sleep much. I'd have known if someone was lurking around my property."

Reese didn't doubt it, but she'd have said the same

if questioned even a few days before. Even up until tonight, she hadn't felt anything odd as she and Hoyt had come into the kitchen and set out plates for pizza. But if it wasn't dumb, ill-advised kids and it wasn't lifetime criminals, who could it be?

Because whatever was going on, it was obviously escalating. And Reese couldn't help but feel she sat directly in the crosshairs.

Chapter 13

Hoyt tightened Stink's reins as they neared the southern end of Reynolds property, pulling up next to Ace and Tate, who both sat high on their mounts. August had gotten even hotter, so that it felt like the devil himself had opened the gates of hell and was fanning the flames. Everyone was miserable and damned tired.

But Hoyt knew that his own personal brand of acting like a royal bastard had reached unprecedented heights.

Hell, half the reason he was out riding Stink instead of helping Ace and Tate with the cattle grazing on this section of the ranch was because they'd already exchanged a nasty string of words. As a result, he'd headed off to check on some of the longhorns they had grazing on the opposite end of the property just to spend some time in his own head.

It had been a week and a half since the gunshots.

Eleven days without any clues or any further aggression. While he was more than glad that nothing else had happened, the strange tightrope of emotion that had him constantly vigilant and rarely resting had begun to take its toll. Add on Reese starting back at school this coming Monday and he was out of his mind that something was going to happen to her and the baby.

All of which had resulted in a witch's brew of emotion that sat like sludge in his gut.

"How does the herd look?" Hoyt opted for casual, curious to see if his brothers would toss his earlier bad mood back at him. Other than the raised eyebrow routine from Ace, neither brother mentioned it.

"The calves are coming along well. That one we've been keeping an eye on is getting stronger and stronger, so I think the little guy'll make it." Ace scratched at a small spot above his ear. "Doc Torres said he's heartier than we might have thought."

Hoyt's gaze drifted to Tate's, even as both men kept their faces impassive. Their silent exchange might confirm the earlier storm had passed, but it opened a new line of questions over Ace's assessment. In fact, if Hoyt weren't careful, he'd start a new storm if he poked this situation too hard.

He and Tate both knew it took a lot of worry for the herd for Ace to spend time with his ex. The fact that veterinarian Dr. Veronica Torres had been back in the Pass for over a year and Ace had seen her fewer than three times, usually passing off visits with the large-animal vet to Hoyt or Tate, hadn't been lost on any of them.

"When was Doc Torres here?" Hoyt asked.

"Earlier." Ace shrugged, before pointing toward the calf in question. "Little guy over there. He's finding his way, even if he's not quite ready to leave his mother's side."

Tate's usual good humor could smooth out pretty much any situation, but even Tate steered clear of any further questions about the very delectable Veronica Torres. Ace had always claimed his relationship with Veronica was water under the bridge, but Hoyt had never fully believed it. Although they'd never discussed it, he suspected Tate and Arden felt the same. Ace's steady ability to find an excuse to be gone when Veronica came out to the ranch only proved it.

But that was a discussion for another day.

Today, Hoyt bore the brunt of Tate's attention.

"How's Reese holding up?"

"Fine," Hoyt said. "Better than fine, actually. School starts on Monday and she's anxious to get back."

While the dog days of August hadn't done anything to keep moods light and breezy, the end of summer came around like clockwork every year. He was used to it and normally, other than an extra shower each day, it didn't faze him.

It was Reese who had changed things. Reese and all the things that remained unsaid between the two of them. And the danger he feared would strike before he could find a way to say those things he needed to say.

All of which was ridiculous. It wasn't like he was some love-struck teenager who needed to declare himself to the woman of his dreams.

"There haven't been any further incidents. That has to be a good sign," Tate said, conviction not quite lining his tone.

"No, there haven't. Nor has there been any explanation for the ones that have happened."

Realistically, he should be grateful for that fact. Reese was healthy and happy, excited for the new school year to begin. Their visit the past week to the doctor had confirmed the baby was doing well and developing on schedule—evidenced by the small hand he saw waving back at him on the ultrasound—and her classroom was set up and ready for her students. She was happy—thriving, even.

But even knowing that and experiencing the awestruck joy at seeing his child on the screen, Hoyt couldn't quite conceal his fear that danger still lurked. The Midnight Pass PD had officially ruled the shots into her home the work of a prankster, but Belle had ensured the department maintained a close eye on Reese's neighborhood. But even they had their limits. The police department was only so large, and without a real case or clues to follow, there wasn't much they could do.

He understood that. Rationally and logically, the police couldn't sit around and wait for something to happen. They'd taken the gunshots seriously, scouring Reese's property and setting up a watch for over a week at her house and at her mother's to see if anyone even remotely suspicious came by. All that effort failed to produce even a single individual who garnered heightened suspicion.

Which Reese had seemingly taken to mean the problem had vanished. Hell, yesterday he'd arrived over there for dinner to find the woman weeding her front shrubbery. With headphones in her ears, no less. He'd pleaded with her to see reason, only to get a lecture—a damn lecture!—to lighten up and relax a bit.

Although his family had borne the brunt of his ire lately, he hadn't been able to keep his thoughts to himself and managed to pick a pretty solid fight with Reese as well. All of which was somewhat swinging in his favor until he'd made the boneheaded move of suggesting she take a leave of absence from teaching for a while.

Tate's voice broke into Hoyt's thoughts once more, nary a hint of humor tinging his words. "Are you going to let us in on whatever it is going on in that stubborn head of yours or do we have to send you back to the house?"

"I'm fine."

"You're not, but let's put that aside for a minute," Ace added, a solid show of force with Tate. "When are you going to confide in us and talk about what the hell's going on instead of throwing up this wall of bs?"

"It's nothing I can't handle."

"You sure about that, little brother?" Ace didn't let up. "Because you've moved past grumpy, frustrating and surly and headed straight for Asshat Ville."

"And while you may be a surly jerk, you rarely wear the asshat," Tate said, those usual edges of good humor tinging his words.

"The woman is maddening. She was outside last night when I got there. Weeding!"

Ace and Tate shot each other a side-eye and if Hoyt didn't already feel bad about the morning's blow up, he'd have laid into both of them. As it was, he was still about ready to swing Stink around and head back for the stables.

Until Ace spoke up. "Is it at all possible you have feelings for this woman?"

"Of course I have damn feelings for her! She's having my child. And damn it all, she's Reese." Hoyt stopped, chest heaving as something hard and heavy settled just beneath his breastbone.

Feelings?

Woman of his dreams?

And something that went deeper than a night of passion that still haunted his thoughts, even though nearly three months had passed.

Three months where he had barely looked at another woman, let alone thought about one. Where the child who'd resulted from that night grew within its mother's womb, cradled and nestled against the world. Where his life had changed more than any other time, including after his father's betrayal.

The past three months had changed him, irrevocably and completely, and he hadn't understood a bit of it.

Only now he did.

"I've got to go."

Hoyt had barely swung Stink around when Tate's faux whisper reached him, loud and clear. "It's about time that stubborn ass figured out which end was up."

Reese drove down the long, smooth macadamized entrance to Reynolds Station, heading for the ranch house becoming visible in the distance. The day was hot but she couldn't blame her restlessness on the late summer temperatures, especially as air blew cool and fresh from her dashboard. Nor could she blame it on her pregnancy, which seemed to have turned a corner over the past few days. She hadn't had a single bout of morning sickness and some of the afternoon exhaustion that had been a constant battle the past few months seemed to have evaporated, too.

She was restless because of Hoyt Reynolds, Midnight

Pass's hottest cowboy and the current object of her affection, vexation and, in those quiet moments when she was very, very honest with herself, every ounce of attraction she possessed.

Oh, how she wanted the man.

Even yesterday, when he'd made her so mad she could have chewed her lesson planner, she'd wanted him. Tall and rangy, he'd stood in her kitchen, lecturing her on safety and being aware of her surroundings, and all she could think about was dragging the hem of his faded blue T-shirt up over those flat and well-ridged abs and having her way with him.

On the kitchen floor. Or up against the washing machine. Or sprawled across the middle of her bed, putting all that space to good use.

That's what she'd wanted.

Instead, she'd borne up under his endless lecturing of safety and self-care and awareness of her surroundings to the point she wanted to scream. Or chew on that lesson planner that even now sat open and unfilled on her table.

Her kitchen window had long been fixed, Hoyt and his brothers seeing to the job themselves. He'd also insisted on a new alarm system that had been a bit of an adjustment, as she now had to dutifully punch in a code every time she came and went.

A big part of her wanted to believe that these changes were for her benefit. And then she'd go and contradict herself, recognizing that they were simply for the baby. Which, of course, she wanted. Nothing was more important than the safety of her child. Hoyt wanted that too, and she could hardly fault him for both his concern and his desire to protect his unborn child.

But was it so wrong to think that he wanted all these changes for her, too?

Reese shook it off as she drove farther down the driveway. All of this horrible maudlin sad-sack-itis that she couldn't seem to shake had grown tedious. She was sick to death of her own company and was counting down the days to school starting, just to have a few hours each day to get out of her own head. Which was when a new thought had taken root, sprouted, grown limbs and leaves pretty much all at once.

What she *really* wanted was to have sex with him.

All the pregnancy books said the hormones were normal and that having a healthy sex drive while pregnant was even a perk of the situation. She and Hoyt were still both single, unattached adults. And damn it, she wanted him. What was so wrong about that?

What's so wrong about it is that you want more than sex.

Reese pulled her car in next to Arden's and ignored that sly little voice that had kept her steady company since her wild night of abandon with Hoyt.

"And you know what," she whispered back to it, a sort of fierce desperation pinging off her car windshield as she spoke into the air, "it doesn't matter what my heart wants. My body wants him and I'm going to enjoy it. Every single second of it."

What she hadn't quite counted on, Reese realized as she stepped out of the car and stared up at the Reynolds ranch house, was how she was going to play all of this in front of his family. A point that only became way sharper when Arden stepped out the front door and waved at her, a big smile on her face.

Reese met her halfway, pulling her friend into a tight hug. "Hope you don't mind I just dropped by."

Arden pulled back, gave her a dark stare. "I've given you a bit of breathing room and worked really hard to get over our little tiff in your living room. Don't make me go back to being mad and pissy."

Reese smiled and wrapped an arm around Arden's waist. "Okay. You win. Thanks for the warm welcome."

Arden squeezed back. "That's more like it."

"Look. About the other week. I owe you an apology. A rather large one."

"Oh, come on." Arden waved a hand in the air. "Don't be silly. It was a moment in time and it's over."

Reese waited while Arden opened the door and followed her into the house. "I do owe you an apology and I should've come over before now. But every time I tried to find the words, they seemed hollow and empty and, well, stupid. Thank you for caring about me? Thank you for wanting to make sure I was okay?"

Arden laid a hand over her arm as they walked into the kitchen. "You're here. That's all that matters."

It was so simple and easy and quintessential Arden.

And it went a long way toward easing the knots in her stomach.

"This is no excuse, and I don't want to make it seem like one, but I'm getting used to this. Depending on people. It's a bit new for me."

Reese didn't want to make excuses. She was responsible for her own actions and always had been. That had been one of the hardest things about her brother's addiction. She knew he couldn't help it and fully understood that his addiction *was* an illness. But she'd also struggled to understand how he could seemingly dismiss the love of his family and his own personal care.

It was because of that that she had developed her own sense of responsibility. And Arden did deserve a full apology.

"So thank you. I appreciate the care and concern and even more than that, knowing that you have my back."

Arden pulled her close, her pretty blue eyes welling with tears. "Of course I have your back. We all do."

Reese held on tight, the ready support and easy acceptance of her apology meaning everything to her. More than that, it reinforced all she'd mulled over in her mind for the past week and a half.

Hoyt didn't seem to think she was taking the things that had happened seriously enough, but she was. And she did feel that they were more than harmless pranks. But what was she supposed to do about it? Sit and hide in her home like a scared hermit?

She'd be damned if she was going to live that way.

While she had taken a personal stand not to live in fear, that hadn't stopped her from worrying about it every free moment she had. What was really going on? And who could possibly have a vendetta against her?

Although the drug-lord angle had to be considered, she simply couldn't bring herself to go down that path. If a criminal wanted her dead because of her father's actions, wouldn't they have simply taken action? It had almost become scary how easily that thought drifted through her mind, but with the acknowledgment came power. And with that power came an ability to focus and watch her surroundings through clear eyes.

No one strange had been to her home or even appeared to be lurking outside of it. She'd seen no cars that she didn't know, nor had security at the school turned up anything untoward. And further, now that her mother knew to watch out and keep track of her environment, Serena hadn't seen anything, either.

Were they really going to sit around in fear that some drug lord was plotting their demise?

No way.

While she'd firmly taken that scenario off the table, it unfortunately meant something else was on it. Something nameless and faceless and completely unknown to her.

How did you face a threat like that?

How did you question that someone had it out for you when you didn't even know what you had done?

And how did you live with the knowledge that somebody wanted to do you harm and not try to live your life to the fullest?

That's why she was here. Why she wanted to make up with Arden and find a way past the emotional landmines Hoyt seemed to unearth every time she looked at him or thought of him or spent even the shortest time in his company.

It was why she wanted to *live*.

A point that hit home five minutes later when Hoyt and his brothers came through the door. Although Tate and Ace were good-looking men—both of whom drew their fair share of sighs when they walked into a room—for her money, neither held a candle to Hoyt. Long and lean, his strong form and broad shoulders drew her gaze as easily as he tugged at her heart.

He was quiet and stoic, both of which only added to his sense of mystery and unapproachability. Traits she'd have used to describe him before getting to know him over the past few weeks. But underneath it all was someone she'd enjoyed getting to know. He didn't say much, but it didn't mean he wasn't paying attention. Nor did it mean he didn't have an opinion.

What it did mean was that in those moments when she got him to open up, she got a sense she was seeing a side to him that few others ever got to. It was intimate and gratifying and humbling that he'd share with her.

And it had taken her from infatuated and interested straight into love.

Heartbreaking, stupid, crazy love.

"Hey, Reese." Hoyt had no idea why the greeting came out sounding so hollow, but now that he'd started he knew he needed to see it through. "You feeling okay today?"

"I'm good."

Only she didn't look good. She looked a little shell-shocked. "Are you sure?"

"Fine. Really, I'm fine."

"She looks great," Arden jumped in. "In fact, I'd say she's starting to get that pretty, pregnant glow about her."

Hoyt wasn't sure about a glow, because Reese looked like she always did to him. Beautiful.

Hell, the woman had glowed since forever.

He still remembered what she looked like when they were younger. Those long coltish legs and slim hips. He could still envision her the summer after he came back from school. He had gone away to college, finishing up his last two years at UT after doing two years at the local community college.

In the time he had been gone, little had changed in the Pass. It was why—maybe, Hoyt thought, it was exactly why—she had nearly bowled him over the day he saw her in town.

He'd been about to head home from the feed store when Arden texted him to pick up a few more things at the market. He was walking in as Reese was walking out, those endless miles of legs peeking out from beneath sexy little jean shorts.

Looking back on it, he didn't think they'd said more than a hello. But he'd always remembered that moment. There was something a little wild about her, which had struck him at the time, at odds with what he knew of her. Because Reese Grantham had the exact opposite reputation.

She wasn't wild. Nor was she prone to even raising her voice, let alone wild streaks of willful behavior. Everyone in town knew that Russ and Serena Grantham's daughter was a good girl. But in that moment, Hoyt had seen something else. It was a little flicker, nothing more.

But as he thought back on it, he had to believe that in that moment, he saw her. Really saw her. That hint of the wild that lurked beneath her skin. That same little hint of wild that had drawn him to her that crazy night at Border Line. That little hint of wild that had had her asking him to stay.

And the answering tug of his own wild when he'd said yes.

Chapter 14

For years, Hoyt had considered and reconsidered the fact that he lived and worked with his family. He never saw it as a burden, but he could admit that most grown men didn't live under the same roof as their two older brothers and younger sister.

More, most found a way to move on with their lives, build a home of their own and start a family. He'd hit thirty and done none of those things so far. Yet every time he considered leaving he dismissed the thought, acknowledging to himself that not only was it easy to live in the ranch house, but that he actually liked his siblings.

Love, sure. That was part of the deal. But like was a whole different ball of wax and he counted himself immeasurably lucky that he was as much friends with his brothers and sister as they were blood.

Besides, he'd always reasoned with himself, when

he did start a family, there was more than enough acreage to build his own home right here on Reynolds Station land. The fuss and bother of doing it before then seemed like a waste.

Until today.

Three pairs of eyes—four, when he added Belle's arrival just before dinner—sized him and Reese up, watching the two of them like lab mice in a cage.

Were they blushing? Showing signs of attraction? Were they too lethargic or too animated? Were their pheromones leaping into the air between them, infusing the entire room with some sort of exacting, lust-filled anxiety?

They were the weirdest thoughts, made only weirder by the fact that he'd looked at Reese so many damned times his vision was likely crossing. And as for those imagined pheromones, there was nothing imaginary about it. The woman's essence filled the room, light and airy and driving him crazy.

The only thing that made any of it bearable was that Reese seemed to feel it too. He caught her eye more than once, and while he had the overwhelming urge to apologize for his nosy family, there was also that underlying feeling of being comrades in arms.

Was this what parenting would be like?

The two of them, paired up when their child inevitably had a streak of rebellion spill out or a tantrum well up in that special way only kids could truly manage. What about when they fought with one of their siblings? What would happen then?

His hand bobbled so hard Hoyt nearly dropped his fork.

Siblings? Co-parenting? Children? As in multiple babies.

No, he amended to himself.

As in a family with Reese.

"Would you pass the potatoes, please?" he asked Ace, attempting to cover up the clumsy move with the fork.

His brother did as asked, but Hoyt didn't miss the smile that crinkled his older brother's eyes. Or the large helping of potatoes already on his plate that he added to with the additions from the bowl.

"So, Reese," Belle started in. "School starts on Monday. Do you know who you're getting for your class yet?"

"I know most of the kids. I have a few trouble-makers, but nobody I can't handle. Besides, the few that do act out usually stand down once I explain the real meaning behind *The Scarlet Letter*."

"I remember those days," Tate said with a smile. "I had no idea that *A* meant something so interesting."

"As I recall, you were rather fascinated with *Moby Dick* as well," Belle said, elbowing him in the ribs.

"Which was nothing like I expected," Tate said. "Who knew a book about a whale could be so boring?"

Reese reached for her water glass. "I taught that one year and swore to myself, never again. That's when I got my own personal rule for teaching. If I can't get through the book, I'm not making twenty fifteen-year-olds read it, either."

The conversation spun out about remembered classes in school and a funny story Belle had from a traffic stop that afternoon and even a few discussions about ranch business. If he weren't so wound up and stuck in his own head, those visions of multiple children still keeping him company, Hoyt might've enjoyed himself. Instead, all he could think about was Reese and him and this imagined future that had suddenly settled over him like a warm blanket.

"Do you still get excited for the first day of school?"

Reese nodded at Ace. "I do. It's not the same feeling as when we were students, but there is still a lot of excitement. It always feels like a fresh start. Like a new opportunity stretched out before you to make a difference."

"You don't get bored teaching the same books every year?" Ace asked.

"Not really. I change it up and I have gotten into a rhythm with things I enjoy teaching. But the kids give me a new perspective every year so that even if I feel I know the book, every time they bring something new to it."

"It's sort of like the herd each year. The new calves. I always feel like it should be the same, but it never is." Hoyt wasn't sure where the comment came from, but now that it was out he realized it was true. Each season was different and not just because the family worked to refine and better the processes each year, whether it was their efforts to be both more green and more organic or testing new methods of herd rotation or alternative types of feed. That was the business.

But each season, the herd was different and that was ranching. New calves changed the dynamic. Their protective mothers responded in kind, managing their young and adjusting to each animal's place in the herd. And all who worked Reynolds Station had to change and adjust along with them.

Clearly, his family hadn't expected that sort of response from him, as they all stared at him from around the table.

"Come on. Ace? Tate? Don't you feel it, too? Every time we go through calving season, it's like something new to be hopeful about."

Ace nodded, that teasing glance Hoyt had seen earlier nowhere in evidence. "Yeah, I guess it's true, little brother. New life brings new possibilities. Always."

Reese looked around the sitting room of Hoyt's bedroom, and wondered how she'd gotten here. Oh, sure, she'd driven over to the ranch determined to have her way with him. An intention that had somehow gotten waylaid by an apology to Arden that had somehow turned into dinner. Dinner had turned into dessert. The dessert had turned into family movie night, with a spirited watching of the latest superhero movie to come out on DVD.

And now they were upstairs. In Hoyt's bedroom.

To be fair, it seemed to be more of an apartment. With the exception of not having a kitchen, he had a large space that was obviously his home within the ranch, including a sitting area that boasted a predictably large television and a big comfy sectional set just off the entrance. His room was visible through another door, and she could see a large king-size bed covered in a rich green comforter.

Did that mean she was in his bedroom? With his family downstairs?

"I should probably get going."

Hoyt stood at the opposite end of the sectional, the TV remote in hand but the TV still off. "I thought you wanted to talk."

"I did. I mean, I do. But it's late. I should be going."

"What if I asked you not to?"

The heat and need that had been a constant presence in her life for nearly three months practically shouted at her to say yes, she'd stay. The heart she was trying desperately to ignore was already screaming that not only would she like to stay, but that she'd like a permanent invitation to forever.

But the practical, determined woman who rarely did anything out of character tried diligently to ignore them both and do the right thing.

Yet, even with that determination, she couldn't hold back the truth. "I'd like to. But it's complicated and we both know that."

"Is it? Because I'm standing here, looking at you, and suddenly it doesn't feel very complicated at all. In fact—" Hoyt edged closer around the couch "—it feels rather simple."

"Nothing about our situation is simple."

"No?" He closed those last few feet and came to a stop in front of her. "What's not simple?"

"Us. The baby. The fact that we're not even supposed to be together." Oh, it hurt to say those words. But they had to be said. No matter what was between them, she wouldn't settle for anything less than the truth.

"Not supposed to be together?"

"Well, yeah. We're together because of a broken condom. We had one night together, that's all. You know, the whole two consenting adults routine."

"I'm still not following. Want to try a little harder?"

"Come on, Hoyt. Don't be dense. We're not in a relationship. We barely knew each other. Let's not confuse things."

"Don't know each other? I find that hard to believe, especially because I have told you more over the past three weeks than I've told anybody besides the three other people that live in this house."

He moved in close, the warmth of his body going a long way toward taking her defenses down another notch.

"And another thing."

"What's that?"

"I want you. *You*, Reese Grantham. And it has nothing to do about the baby, even though I want him or her very much."

Everything she wanted in the world seemed to exist in that moment. Taking heart from that simple thought, she took the last step that separated them and reached up, entwining her arms around Hoyt's neck. "If I'm being honest, this is the reason I came over this afternoon."

A sexy smile played at the corners of his mouth. "I knew it. You're here to have your way with me."

"I guess I am."

"Lucky me."

"No," Reese said, suddenly breathless as she lifted up on tiptoes and pressed her lips against his. On a light whisper, she added, "Lucky me."

Her words seemed to spur them both into action, her whisper fading into the air as Hoyt's mouth opened under hers. Fierce need drove them both, the air raw and electric around them. Their mouths fused together, tongues crashing against one another in a carnal play for dominance and pleasure.

Her hands were wild on his body, clawing at the T-shirt that hung loosely over the top of his jeans before dragging it up and over the hard length of his torso, chest and shoulders. And then she had him, his warm flesh beneath her palms and his body pressing closer and closer to her as his arms tightened around her waist. One large palm settled against her ass, pulling her tight against him so that the firm lines of his erection pressed urgently against her stomach.

Although she'd have gladly settled for the couch, she was momentarily disoriented when Hoyt shifted direction, his strong arms sweeping her up so that she was no longer vertical.

"Hoyt!"

"I've been waiting for this for months. We'll save the couch for later."

"Later?"

He pressed a hard kiss on her lips as he walked determinedly toward the bedroom. "I need some room to work now."

"Is that a promise?"

"I like to think so."

The gentle way he laid her onto the bed was at odds with the urgent frenzy that had gripped them both in the sitting room, but the hard body that followed her down, covering her with his delicious weight, quickly suggested otherwise. Before she could catch her breath, his hands were everywhere, roaming the length of her body and quickly divesting her of her shorts and T-shirt. Her bra followed next and she nearly cried out when his mouth came down over one nipple, the fullness of her breast achy beneath his mouth.

Vaguely, a memory of something she'd read in one of her daily pregnancy emails about breast sensitivity filled her thoughts before Hoyt shifted just so, his tongue tracing the edge of her nipple, and she cried out at the shot of pleasure that whipped through her body like wildfire. How was it possible to feel like this?

She'd have almost called her body a traitor, but the needs coursing through her were so bold and wanton and the sensations so sharp and pleasurable, she didn't dare. Instead, she decided to live up to the promise she'd made to herself only moments before.

Lucky me, she thought.

And prepared to ride the storm.

He wanted her. Was there anything more simple than that? Or more powerful?

That night in June that had haunted him for nearly three months was finally replaced with the reality of Reese. In his arms, her flesh warm and exposed beneath his hands. Beneath his gaze. Just for him.

Hoyt traced her with his fingertips, even as the urgency to join their bodies pushed him toward more. Her skin was so soft, he marveled, as he ran his index finger over her cheek across the fullness of her lips and down over her neck. He continued on with the exploration, over her chest, admittedly turned on by the generous fullness of her breasts. While he'd had no complaints back in June, her pregnancy had rounded her out in the most beautiful of ways.

"What are you looking at?" she asked softly.

"You. And the beautiful evidence of your pregnancy."

"Oh. You mean pregnancy boobs?"

He laughed at that despite himself. "I was actually thinking of them as the lush, ample hills of your bosom. But whatever works."

"I've had friends who called this the side benefit but I think it was really their husband's side benefit."

Hoyt saw it the moment her comment registered, the light teasing that sparkled from her eyes fading. Before she could think too hard about their situation, he pressed on. "Who needs sides?"

He captured her lips, determined to erase any anxiety or concern that there was something missing from their relationship. He wanted that sparkle back, damn it.

He wanted *her*.

Hoyt knew the moment he was successful. Her tentative response to his kisses changed, her body growing restless beneath his as her lips grew bolder. A soft moan escaped the back of her throat and he pressed on, kissing her as his hands explored the rest of her body.

The curves of her breasts gave way to her still flat stomach. Although the evidence of her pregnancy wasn't quite there, he could feel a softness that hadn't been there in June. The reality of why slammed into him with all the power of a semi.

His child was cradled there. Nestled inside Reese's body, growing every day.

His child.

Shifting his position, he moved down the bed so that he could rest his head over her stomach. With his lips, he pressed a kiss to its planes and then laid his head to the side so that he could listen. Although there was nothing to hear yet because the baby was still too small, he knew with undeniable certainty there was a heartbeat beneath his ear.

Reese threaded her fingers through his hair, clearly sensing his intention, her hand resting lightly on the back of his head.

They'd made a child.

He'd understood that in every way possible and had spent the past three weeks not only coming to grips with it but growing more and more excited at all that was to come. Yet, until this moment, he hadn't truly understood what it all meant.

Hadn't truly pictured the reality of the baby.

His child wasn't something that existed in the future. His child was here. Now. A living entity between them.

The urgency and intensity that pushed them to that moment faded slightly. His feelings were no less intense, nor was the pounding of his heart anywhere close to calm, even as time seemed to shift around them. Like the quiet within a storm or the stillness just before an earthquake. Only instead of destruction, he saw hope and life.

"What?" Reese's voice was a soft whisper.

"I can't hear a heartbeat yet, but I know it's there."

"I know."

Hoyt pressed one more kiss to her stomach before shifting once again to spread out fully next to her. He lay on his side with his head propped on his hand, his elbow giving him leverage to look down at her. "There's something between us, Reese. Don't you feel it?"

"There's a baby between us."

"It's more than that and you know it."

Her mouth, still swollen from his kisses, settled into a firm line. "Is it? Can you honestly say we'd be here right now if it weren't for the baby?"

Hoyt didn't have an answer for her, but he knew that there was no other place he'd rather be.

Maybe it was time to tell her that. Whether it was reassurance or simply the need to tell her how he felt,

he had no idea. But it was time to put to words all he'd
held back.

"I wanted to call you, you know. After that night."

"You did?" While she quickly hid it, Hoyt didn't miss
the mix of confusion and hope that lit up her eyes, turning them a deep brownish-green in the dim light that
spilled into his bedroom from the living room.

"I did. Only every time I had the phone in my hand
I realized I didn't know what to say. Things happened
so fast, and I didn't want you to think I was only calling for a repeat performance."

"You could've just told me that."

"Would you have believed me? I'm a guy, and it's not
like we were going out. I didn't want you to think—"
He stopped, unwilling to continue down the path that
sounded far too much like excuses. "I didn't call. And
that's on me. But please don't take that to mean I don't
care. And whatever you do, please don't take it to mean
that I don't want you."

"As long as we're sharing secrets, I have one for you.
I wanted you to call, too. And I came close to calling
you myself a few times. But I didn't want to seem like
I was chasing you or was unable to handle a one-night
stand."

"That wasn't a one-night stand, Reese. Not to me."

She did smile with that. "I hate to burst your bubble,
cowboy, but until this very moment it technically was
a one-night stand."

"Then how come I haven't seen it that way?"

And he hadn't. While he didn't run rampant around
the county, he did have experience with lone evenings
between consenting adults. He knew what they looked

like and fully understood how they served a single purpose: to scratch an itch.

His night with Reese hadn't fit that description. Nowhere near it, as a matter of fact.

"I don't do that very often. I'm not real sure of the rules, except for one."

"What rule is that?" he asked.

"You don't go chasing after the guy after it's all done."

Something unexpected settled deep in his chest. On one hand, it was humbling to know that she had wanted to see him again as much as he had wanted to see her. And on the other, it made him realize what a complete and absolute ass he had been.

"Those are the rules, you say?"

"Of course they are. Men don't do what they don't want to do, Hoyt. If you'd wanted to call, you would have."

He practically felt her shutting down, pulling away from him, despite the closeness of their bodies. The reality was he had wanted to call, only he'd made that stubborn, idiotic choice to remain standoffish and aloof. And because of it, he'd left her thinking that she was unwanted and that their night together hadn't meant anything to him.

"Not calling is on me. But so is making it up to you."

"Making what up to me?"

"Convincing you that I want you. And that I have wanted you for the past three months."

Since he was a man of action, he set out to do just that.

Still elevated up on his elbow, he used his free hand to once again trace the lines of her face. She was so beautiful, but it was more than that. More than her soft skin with those high cheekbones set off by those deep hazel eyes. It was the strength he saw, embedded in that gaze. It was the experiences she'd had, carved in the very fiber of her being. A woman who had sustained terrible loss, yet who still pushed forward, believing in the future. A future for herself, for her unborn child and for the students she taught every day.

There was strength there—strength that went well beyond the physical. And it humbled him.

Bending his head, he pressed his lips to hers, willing her to understand all that he felt and thought and believed.

Other than his family, he shared little of himself with anyone. Yet, he'd opened up to her. She knew his thoughts. She knew what mattered to him.

And she carried his future.

There'd be time to say all of that, to both reassure and promise that he wanted to build something with her, but for now it was up to him to show her.

Deepening the kiss, he returned his hands to her lush curves. All that was still unsaid between them moved to the background as their need for each other took over. There would be time for words later—he vowed that to himself—but for now it was enough to be together.

The insistent throb of desire came in marked waves, battering his body with the desperate need to join with her. With seeking fingers, he settled himself at the entrance to her body, even more turned on by the hot wetness he found. She was ready for him in the age-old beauty Mother Nature had created. Willing a calmness within himself he didn't feel, he continued to focus on her. And slipped first one finger and then another into those tight welcoming folds.

The hitch of her breath and the restless movement of her legs against his told Hoyt all he needed to know. He kept up the gentle yet insistent movements, pushing her higher and higher with his fingers and the steady pressure of his palm. His mouth was relentless on hers, his tongue mimicking the actions of his fingers as he swallowed one delicious moan after another.

He knew the moment her pleasure crested, desire and need arcing between them like electricity. And felt himself fall a little farther into the abyss when she pulled him close, her lips pressed to his.

"Now, Hoyt. I need you. Now."

With sudden realization, he stretched across her toward the night stand, his hand closing over a condom when a low throaty giggle met his ear. "Isn't it a bit late for that?"

Something dark and dangerous swirled in his stomach. He'd never in his life been with a woman without the barrier of a condom and her offer tempted him beyond belief. "I don't know…" He fumbled, struggling for the right words. "I mean, I'm clean and I haven't been with anyone since we were together and—"

He stilled at the amusement that rode her features, such a wild departure from the seriousness that had filled the space between them only minutes before. "My doctor's given me a clean bill of health, too. And since there's no risk of pregnancy, maybe we can dispense with the formalities, if you know what I mean."

"Dispense with—"

His lust addled brain struggled to keep up with her when her long fingers wrapped around his erection.

Once again, that silky, seductive whisper filled his ear. "If you get my meaning."

He got her meaning and more, especially when her fingers tightened, the deliberate pressure of her palm driving a wave of sensation rocketing through his already over-sensitized body. While he'd been focused on her pleasure, he knew his own ability to resist her was on a very tight leash. A few more strokes like that one and he'd be gone.

Lost.

And there was no way he was going there without her.

Moving overtop of her body, he allowed her to guide him home, overwhelmed by the feel of her as they joined. Heat enveloped him, exposing a wildness inside of him that was so elemental Hoyt had no idea it had even been there.

"Let go, cowboy." That whisper once more. "Please."

It was the *please* that said everything and like a dam cracking wide open, he began to move inside of her. With long, sure strokes, he filled her again and again, marveling at how easily she kept pace. And with the sure knowledge she'd take all he had to give and more, he lost himself to her, riding them both through the pleasure that seemed custom-made for the two of them.

Riding them into the heart of the storm, assured of a safe landing on the other side.

Chapter 15

Loretta huddled behind the back wall of the Reynolds Station stables, taking stock of her surroundings. The structure was large and sturdy and she was surprised to see just how big it was up close. A stable this size meant they had a heck of a lot of horses. It also meant a lot of destruction once the flames started lapping at all that wood.

She wanted this.

She knew she wanted it, but she had to ignore the heavy pounding in her throat as she gingerly held the loaded backpack in her hands.

She had no issue with the Reynolds family, but they'd been getting too chummy with Reese Grantham of late and it was time she sent another message. Targeting Reese's house hadn't worked out so far, so maybe going bigger was just what she needed to get the woman's attention. Just what she needed to make Reese Grantham see the error of her ways.

If the Reynolds family was collateral damage, then so be it.

That was Hoyt Reynolds's own damn fault for all the time he'd been spending with the ice queen.

His daily visits to her house hadn't slowed, the two of them getting together every night to have dinner and who knew what else. She hadn't been able to stake out the house every day but she usually managed a drive by in the evening after she put Ben and Charlie down. It was a risk to leave the kids, but she only lived a few miles away and the time out allowed her to keep tabs on the woman's evenings.

All of which seemed occupied with Hoyt Reynolds.

Tonight had been a departure, that was for sure. But it had given her the time she needed to put a new plan in place.

She'd been playing around with the Molotov cocktail idea for a while. Plenty of movies used them and it was a relatively simple concept. She'd originally thought to place one in Reese's shed, but decided to go bigger when it became obvious Reese was spending the night at Casa Reynolds.

Add on the fact that Paul had the boys tonight and she had a chance to make her move.

The pack had grown heavy after trudging for at least a mile and a half over Reynolds property from the Farm to Market road that lined the northern end of their land, but it had been worth it. Her car was stowed behind a copse of trees that didn't make it readily visible to passersby and the road was sparsely used at that.

She tried to slip in a back door and was surprised to find it locked. It was a layer of security she hadn't expected and she quickly set about trying to pick the lock. Although she wasn't an ace at working with locks, she knew enough and had prepared herself for a few obstacles. This was a working ranch, after all. It wasn't likely they kept all their goods out in the open for anyone to breeze into.

It was also why she'd been careful about checking for cameras. A few had been posted at the entrance to the ranch as well as strategically around the property, but the spot she'd chosen to enter the land had been empty of digital eyes.

Just like Russ Grantham.

His actions had reinforced her idea of coming to the ranch to cause confusion and fear. He'd used the property and had gone undetected. Or would have gone undetected if that bitch Belle Granger hadn't taken him down. But he sure as hell hadn't been caught because of cameras.

How would you even begin to police acreage so vast it made up its own zip code?

You didn't, Loretta thought with grim satisfaction. That's what made it all so damn perfect.

The lock sprang free under her probing bobby pin and she turned the knob, pushing into the stable. She stood just inside the door and gave her eyes time to adjust. The moon was big and high tonight, likely the biggest flaw in her plan to go undetected, but she'd taken her shot and she was going to see this through.

The gentle breathing of the horses reached her first, before the movements of a few closest to her, registering her presence. A light whicker echoed from the nearest stall before the horse added a heavier whinny to his greeting.

"Shh, sweetheart. Hush now." She kept her voice light, but the damn braying didn't let up. Determined not to let the thought of all these animals trapped get to her, she moved forward, selecting the spot for her little surprise.

The extensive wood framing was perfect for what she'd planned. Add on the hay in each stall, and she had all the fuel she needed for a raging fire. Setting down her backpack, she set up her cocktail and went to work adding some accelerant to the ground and nearby wood beams that provided structural support to the roof.

That endless whinnying continued, with more and more of the horses growing curious to her presence, adding their voices to the mix. She stayed where she was, swinging arcs of fuel as she walked backward toward the door, not daring to go any farther into the barn for fear of additional cameras she hadn't seen yet.

This would have to do.

Emptying the last of the grill fuel with a hard squeeze of the can, she stuffed it back into her pack and took the last few steps to the door. She made quick work of the wipes she'd brought with her, thoroughly cleaning her hands against any possible lighter fluid that had gotten on her skin. Satisfied she'd removed any and all traces, she shoved the used wet wipes into her pocket, her hand closing around the matches.

The last thing she did before closing the door behind her was light the match and toss it into the neat trail of fluid she'd laid down behind her.

* * *

Reese lay with her head pillowed against Hoyt's chest, the feeling unfamiliar yet welcome. They'd spent the night together the first time they'd had sex, but other than that evening and a few nights with her college boyfriend, she'd spent relatively few times in her life actually sleeping with a man.

Or if not sleeping, she corrected herself, spending the night together in the same bed.

They'd made love once more before both falling asleep around midnight, but now here she was, wide awake and thinking at full speed at—she glanced over him toward the bedside clock—2:00 a.m.

Few thoughts were welcome or productive at 2:00 a.m.

She should know, because she'd seen her fair share of that ungodly hour throughout her life, worrying over her family or their actions.

The night had been a revelation, especially the news that he wanted to call her…after. While she believed him—Hoyt had no reason to lie—it seemed like such a waste on both their parts. There was a genuine attraction there, so why hadn't either of them acted on it?

Did it even matter anymore?

They were together now, even if they had, by some odd, unspoken agreement, decided not to speak about the future.

Yet, that future had seemed starkly real when he laid his head against her stomach, listening for their child's heartbeat.

Oh, she'd done her level best to hide it, but that moment had nearly undone her. The feel of his large body against hers and the weight of his head cradled against her belly and the sight of him listening to their child…

Well, what was a pregnant woman expected to withstand?

If her ovaries hadn't already been occupied by emitting hormones for her growing child, they'd likely have exploded at the tender gesture.

As it was, she'd barely held back the tightness in her throat that had threatened a heap of tears.

Suddenly restless, Reese disengaged herself, careful not to wake Hoyt. He groaned slightly, then rolled onto his stomach, oblivious to the world. She'd take the time—just a few seconds, really—to look at him. That familiar stretch of jaw, now covered in a day's growth of beard, made her want to reach out and touch him but she held back, not wanting to wake him. The thick muscles of his back, now relaxed in sleep, were still rather impressive as he sprawled across the mattress. And even his feet, peeking from under the edge of the sheet, drew her attention.

The man was just *big*.

Every time she tried to find a different descriptor, she kept coming back to that one. Big and raw and masculine and—oh, goodness, she needed to get some distance. Needed to find a way to keep her heart from swelling in her chest and her mind from envisioning a future.

Wasn't that the real crux of it?

What they shared now was heady and passionate and of the moment. What she was really looking for was forever. As much as she wanted to believe they would find their way there, the obstacles that lay before them seemed much too high.

Not to mention the fact that the man hadn't talked about forever. Oh, he'd talked of marriage, but the sort that was a chore or something you did out of a sense of responsibility.

Not out of love.

Suddenly unable to stare at him a moment longer she grabbed his T-shirt and slipped into it, walking to the window to stare out into the night. Although the ranch house was large, Hoyt's wing was in the back, facing the stables. Moonlight washed over the corral and farther beyond she saw the large brand for Reynolds Station that sat perched above the horse stables.

Had there ever been a time in her life when she didn't recognize that image? The large *R* with the *S* entwined below it, wrapped up in a thick iron circle.

She'd asked her father once what the word *station* meant. He'd been confused, thinking she meant a TV station, until she explained her question. Everyone in the Pass knew the three large ranching families but both Vasquez and Crown had used more familiar words to name their ranches. Vasquez and Sons Estate and Crown Ranch were familiar and easy to understand.

Russ had laughed when he finally understood her meaning and explained that station was an Australian term used to describe a ranch or a farm.

"Why not just call it a ranch?" Reese wanted to know.

"I don't know, sweetie. Maybe you should ask Arden next time you see her in school."

"I guess so." Reese chewed her lip a moment, considering the news. "I mean, are they from Australia?"

"I don't think so." Russ rubbed his forehead in thought as he made the last turn into town. "I think they're fifth-generation Texans, like us."

"So before that?"

Russ laughed again. "I'm sorry, sweetie, I just don't know. If it would help, next time I see Mrs. Reynolds, I'll make a point to ask her."

"Thanks, Daddy."

It was funny, she thought; even then, the Reynolds family had fascinated her. She remembered how she used to watch Ace Reynolds walk through town, a dreamy teenager in cowboy boots and jeans that fit him to a tee. Tate had been a little closer to her in age but he'd only ever had eyes for Belle and most of the girls had always respected that, including her. But it was Hoyt she'd really watched, anyway.

Even when they were in school, nary a farm in sight, he was a cowboy through and through. He'd worn boots as long as she'd known him, only changing into sneakers for gym. Although he'd been a year ahead of her, they'd shared a double period of English and composition when she was in ninth grade and he in tenth. He'd done every one of his papers on ranching or the history of the American cowboy.

With her mind already drifting, floating from those random memories to more recent ones, her gaze continued to roam around the backyard. The empty paddock looked calm and settled, almost as if it lay in wait for tomorrow's activity. In addition to being a working cattle ranch, she knew the Reynolds family had a reputation for training horses. Undoubtedly, the paddock got plenty of use when training season was in high gear. Just that evening at dinner, Hoyt and Tate had both mentioned another delivery of rescued mustangs from an organization they'd obviously worked with before. Both men had sounded excited about the new arrivals.

Would her child learn to ride a horse?

Even as she thought the question, Reese knew the answer was undoubtedly a yes. Although few families in the Pass had homes or property like Reynolds Station, many had land and it wasn't unusual for the kids in town to take up horseback riding. They also had an active 4-H club at the high school and an equestrian team renowned throughout the state.

So, yeah, her child would probably learn to ride.

Images of a small child seated on a horse, firmly in Hoyt's lap, filled her mind. She nearly visualized the whole scene, the night-darkened sky before her fading, when something near the stable drew her attention.

Movement?

Reese edged closer to the window, peering out into the darkness. Although the moon was high, the stable was huge and threw off a large shadow on the end nearest the paddock. That's where she'd seen movement and she leaned closer, willing something to happen again.

Nothing wavered in the stillness and she almost stepped away, admonishing herself for seeing ghosts, when the motion came once more, along with the clear swing of a side door to the stable and a person running hell for leather from the stable and on behind the paddock.

"Hoyt." She didn't scream, but he responded, up instantly at the heavy command in her voice.

"What is it?"

"Outside." She waved him over, unwilling to pull

her gaze off the stable for too long. "Something at the stable. A person."

He was beside her in an instant, the sleepy warmth of his body enveloping her as he leaned in behind her to stare out the window.

It was only the work of a moment to see a huge ball of flame burst out of the stable, blowing out the front doors and knocking off the Reynolds brand where it sat high on the edifice.

"Call 9-1-1!" Hoyt screamed the words as he dragged on his jeans and boots. By the time he noticed his T-shirt was gone, Reese already had it off over her head and in his hands before he could consider getting another one.

"Go. I'll call and get everyone up."

He glanced back at her once more, where she had already jammed herself into her shorts and T-shirt from earlier, her phone in hand as she made the necessary calls.

Hoyt charged from the house, the sounds of everybody waking evident around him. He vaguely registered Reese screaming for everyone to wake up but was out the door before he could hear any further response. Flames engulfed the stable, shooting into the sky and lighting up the night.

He could feel the heat as he pounded closer and closer to the stables but his only focus was getting to the horses.

Stink.

Stink had to be okay.

The thought played over and over in his mind as he rushed toward the stable door. It was only as heat engulfed him in a raging wave that he realized it was much too hot to go inside in only his T-shirt. Forcing as deep a breath as he could with the rancid smoke filling the air, Hoyt focused on all he'd learned in his former life.

Assess.

Identify.

Act.

That training had saved his life on more than one occasion and, if he had his way, would save Stink's life now.

Racing back toward a large hose they kept near the paddock for ease in filling water buckets, Hoyt turned it on and doused himself as fast as possible. As luck would have it, a stable blanket still lay folded over the paddock fence, and he grabbed it, soaking it as quickly as he could.

Knowing there was no longer any time to wait, he dragged the dripping blanket, hoping it was wet enough, and raced toward the stables, wrapping it around himself as he went. Head covered, he went in low, flipping the locks on stall doors as he went. The horses were already screaming, their high-pitched cries full of fear at the reality of what burned around them. Hooves thundered behind him as each door burst open, and Hoyt kept his focus on lock after lock as he worked his way down the length of the stable.

The fire burned around him, filling his lungs and batting at the thin armor he'd placed around his shoulders and head. He knew he didn't have much time, the sound of cracking wood filling the air along with the raging whoosh of the fire, but he had to get to Stink.

The second to last lock flipped open, leaving Tate's horse, Tot, free to run. And then he was at Stink's stall door. Dragging on the lock, he took a moment to look in the eyes of his horse. His comrade and his friend.

And prayed he'd gotten there in time.

Unlike the other horses, Stink remained silent. Hoyt saw the fear that flickered deep in those brown eyes, lit up by the flames that burned around them, but Stink stayed calm, remaining by his side.

Hoyt moved quickly along the same path he'd come, his horse at his side, focused on the door.

Focused on escape.

That loud cracking echoed again, filling the air around him as everything seemed to get hotter. The cracking sound intensified and it was only as he and Stink cleared the middle of the stable that the roof collapsed behind them.

Hoyt pushed on harder, determined to get out now that he'd freed all the horses. Determined to get back to Reese.

Images of her filled his mind's eye. Her. The child she carried. And the desperate need that now filled him to return to her.

More of that violent cracking filled the air and Hoyt leaped for the exit of the building, Stink racing out just before him.

It was only as he neared the door, the fresh night air greeting him along with the shouts of his brothers, that he felt the heavy tug behind him. Something slammed into his back, knocking him to the ground as heat seemed to cover him fully.

He pushed to his knees, desperate to crawl to the exit, when another heavy weight fell on him. Reese's face in the distance was the last thing he saw before the world went black.

* * *

Reese screamed as she watched several boards of wood from the barn fall on top of Hoyt. Ace and Tate were several yards in front of her and both leaped into action, racing toward the burning barn and their brother. She heard sirens in the distance, but they seemed muted and vague as the sound of fire filled the air.

Who knew fire could be so loud as it consumed every single thing in its path?

The ranch hands had already come out of the bunkhouse, several swarming around to calm the horses while several others had joined Tate and Ace as they pulled Hoyt from the increasing debris filling the stable yard. It was only when a shout went up that everyone moved even more quickly.

"It's collapsing!"

Belle and Arden each reached for her, pulling her away from the fiery tableau that spread out before her. Reese felt the shout creeping up her throat—instinctively knew she'd yelled Hoyt's name—but heard nothing as the building collapsed in an inferno.

Reese desperately sought for signs of Hoyt and his brothers, but saw nothing in the wild light that filled the space before her eyes.

"Reese! Come on! You have to get back!" Belle screamed the words at her, her eyes filled with terror. It was that panic—one she understood intimately—that had Reese moving. Belle was as scared for Tate as she was for Hoyt and it did them no good to become added fodder for the blaze.

She huddled with Belle and Arden on the far side of the paddock, searching for any sign of the men carrying Hoyt from the fire. Sirens pierced the air, red and blue lights evident in the distance, as two firetrucks screamed down the driveway, followed closely by the paramedics. But it was the three faces they all cared about so much—Ace and Tate, carrying their brother between them—that had her, Belle and Arden racing forward.

Reese got to them first, reaching for Hoyt, who hung limp between his brothers. Each had one of his arms around their necks, holding him up even as he stood unconscious between them.

"Hoyt!" She moved up, her hands reaching for his soot-covered neck, seeking a pulse. She struggled for the briefest moment, her own pulse beating like a gong beneath her skin, but hung on, her index and middle fingers gently probing the skin of his neck.

She finally found one, soft and thready, but steady, and let out a cry. "He's alive."

Ace was gentle when he reached for her, moving her out of the way. "The crossbeam over the entrance fell on him. I don't know if we should be moving him like this but we had to try."

Working in unison, he and Tate laid Hoyt out, gently pillowing his head on a blanket Arden had brought from the house. Reese was already on the ground, kneeling beside him when the paramedics rushed up. "Ma'am. Excuse us, ma'am."

Tate's arms were already around her, pulling her away, giving the medics room to work.

As she watched them lay a plastic mask over Hoyt's face, Reese sent up a silent prayer as the tears poured in hot streams down her face.

Don't let him die.

* * *

"You stubborn ass." Tate growled the words from across the room as Hoyt struggled to a sitting position.

The scent of antiseptic and that distinctive odor of hospital filled his nose, but it was significantly better than the lingering smoke that seemed to cling to him like stink on manure.

"Where's Reese?" Hoyt swallowed around the wheezy notes and reached for the glass of water beside his bed. Damn, he felt terrible. His entire back hurt, with much the same pain he'd felt the time he'd been thrown from a horse onto dry hard-packed summer ground.

He'd survived that and he'd surely survive this, but damn it all, he felt like hell.

"Down the hall with Arden. Doctor's checking her out as a precaution. Would you sit the hell still? We've only been here an hour."

He was on his feet before he could stop himself, the machines he was attached to going off in a clanging whirl. "What happened to her?"

Tate was by his side in an instant, holding him in place and easing him back to a seated position. "Whoa, little brother. Nothing's wrong with her." Tate moved into his line of sight, his gaze sharp and deliberate as he forced eye contact. "She's fine. Do you hear me?"

The disorientation that had kept him company each time he'd opened his eyes still lingered, but faded with the steady gaze of his brother. "Why is she being checked out?"

"Precaution only. She was across the yard from the fire but the doctor wanted to check out any possible smoke inhalation. He also wanted her obstetrician to check her out and the woman arrived a little while ago. I'd tell you if it was more serious."

Hoyt trusted his family implicitly and took comfort from Tate's words. That clawing, raging need to get to Reese hadn't faded fully, but it did recede as he knew Arden was with her.

"What happened out there?" Tate dropped to the bed next to him, his heavy sigh summing up his concern perfectly.

"Reese saw it. She's the reason we got the horses out in time."

"Saw it?"

Hoyt struggled to erase the cobwebs that seemed determined to clog up his memories, working backward through the events to get a clear picture. "She stayed the night. And I guess she couldn't sleep because one minute I'm dead to the world and the next she's waking me up, telling me something's happening at the barn."

"Someone did this deliberately?"

"Must be." Hoyt tried to piece it together, before it all came back in a wild rush. "She woke me up and said there was something out there. And no sooner did I get to the window then I saw the barn flare up like the Fourth of July."

"And you ran into it like the freaking conquering army."

Tate didn't get mad often. Even when he was angry, he wasn't really all the way mad. Hoyt knew his brother—and knew his moods as well as his own—and it was only when he heard the careful cadence and low-voiced words that he knew Tate had gone well past pissed off and straight into a barely leashed temper.

"What else could I do? Stink was in there. So was Tot and all the rest of the horses. They depend on us."

Tate leaped up, whirling on him like a man demented. "I depend on you, you stupid ass! You! Not my horse. My freaking brother.

"Damn fool—" Tate paced the room like a man possessed. "And you ran straight into the damn thing, the freaking length of a football field, full up and on fire."

"I know how big the stable is."

"Could have fooled me, you dumb bastard."

Tate continued pacing, each step fierce and deliberate. His normal good humor and easygoing nature were nowhere to be found. If anything, Hoyt realized, his brother was only getting madder.

Recognizing he had to get the situation under control, Hoyt said the only thing he could. "I couldn't leave Stink. At least not without trying."

It was the exact right thing to say and finally forced Tate to make eye contact. "You really are a freaking idiot."

"The pain in my chest with every breath I take is doing a damn fine job of reminding me of that."

"Damn it, man." Tate dropped down next to him. "You're my brother. You. The one I love beyond reason." He nodded toward Ace. "Along with that ugly mug over there."

Tate was gentle as he pulled him close and Hoyt wasn't about to argue. This was his brother and while he may have been the one to give a scare, he'd also had the thought, racing out of that building, that he'd never see Tate again. "I love you, too."

"Remember that, dumbass." Tate wrapped an arm

around Hoyt's shoulder. "You. Not my horse, who I also love in a way that borders on the unnatural, but you."

"Belle know?"

"That I love you?"

Hoyt shoved him back, even though he was weaker than a day-old colt. "I meant the horse."

"Yeah." Tate laughed, their impasse at an end. "For reasons I can't quite fathom, she seems to find it endearing."

Chapter 16

Reese fussed around the edge of Hoyt's bed, well aware it made him nuts and unable to help herself.

Five days.

It had been five endless days of inquisition and fear and absolute turmoil at the ranch and they were no closer to finding the culprit than when it had all started.

None of it had been for lack of trying.

Belle was going on nearly sixty hours of minimal sleep, along with half the Midnight Pass PD. They'd ultimately turned over the investigation to the county fire marshal, but it hadn't stopped them from doing all they could to find the culprit. From what Belle had muttered before laying her head down on the kitchen table the night before, they'd been through endless traffic footage from in and around town, along with scouring all feeds on the ranch, and had yet to turn up anything workable.

Reese had been questioned endlessly on whom she'd seen running from the stables, but other than the glimpse she'd spotted of the perpetrator running from the back end of the stable and out behind the paddock, she had little else to offer.

It was maddening.

And the fact that she had a grouchy, unbearable patient wasn't helping.

"I'm fine, damn it."

"The doctor said you need more rest. You had a barn fall on you, Hoyt Reynolds. A damn freaking barn." Reese looked down to see her hands spread akimbo on her hips and couldn't quite hide how silly she felt.

Hoyt must have seen it, too, because she saw the first hint of a smile through the grumpy frown he'd been sporting since Thursday.

"It was only a portion of the barn."

"Do you think this is funny?"

"Not particularly. But watching you standing there like an avenging angel certainly gets my motor running."

If she looked silly standing there with her hands on her hips, Reese knew she must look even stranger goggling at him with wide eyes. "Are you coming on to me?"

"Well, you are standing there, your breasts heaving in a very attractive manner."

"My breasts are not—" She looked down at herself—her heaving self—before crossing her arms over her chest. "This is not funny. You're hurt."

"I'm feeling better by the minute, baby. And besides, I rested enough. I feel fine."

"Then stand up without holding anything for support, walk across the room, turn around and come back to me."

The damn man was out of bed before she could blink and he followed her instructions so fast she barely had time to register when he dived for her on the return trip, capturing her in his arms and pinning her onto the bed. "See?"

She did see. Or, more to the point, she felt. Felt all those strong rangy muscles pulling her close. She felt his need, hard and insistent against her. And most of all, she felt that answering response coiling below inside of her.

"I hardly think this is the time or the place."

"Ooh," he said and smiled. "I just got the stern teacher voice. You realize you're only getting yourself in deeper and deeper here."

"That is not my stern teacher voice."

"What are you waiting for then? Lay it on me."

Reese couldn't help it. Despite all that was going on and all that was still not figured out, she couldn't hold back the laughter. Nor could she hold back just how good it felt to lie there with him, wrapped up in each other, teasing and laughing and simply enjoying the moment.

"You're incorrigible."

"And now you're using SAT words." Hoyt slapped his forehead before falling back on his side next to her. "You unman me, woman."

"Is this some weird lingering teenage boy fantasy? Something like you're too hot for your teacher?"

He rolled over, propping himself up next to her, a wolfish grin that was about as far from boyish as you could get covering his face. "I'm more than happy to play that game if you want to."

"This is a new side to you." She poked him in the chest. "I have to say, I kind of like it."

"You haven't seen anything yet."

And then he proceeded to prove it to her, running his lips across her jawline and up toward the shell of her ear. With a light breath, he blew along the same path he licked with his tongue, sending a series of shivers skating down her spine.

Reese was still worried about his health, but couldn't quite muster up the words to ask him to stop. Then he reached for her, pulling her so that she sat astride his body, and she decided he was a better judge of how he felt than she was.

Opting to put that thinking to the test, she tugged her tank top up over her head, tossing it to the floor. Her bra followed as she made quick work of the clasp. When nothing but desire remained in his eyes at her movements, she reached for the hem of his T-shirt, pulling on the cotton and gently disengaging him from the sleeves before drawing it over his head.

"So far, so good."

"You don't know what good is."

Reese shivered at the promise in his words, but couldn't resist tossing them right back at him. "No, my sexy cowboy. *You* don't know what good is."

Emboldened by the heat she saw deep in his gaze, she used the moment to her advantage. Trailing a line of kisses down over the lines of his chest, she lingered over each nipple before carving a delicious path over the thick muscles that corded his stomach. When each tightened in turn beneath her lips, she knew she'd gained the upper hand. But it was that last stretch, after she passed the barrier of his fly button, when Reese knew she'd truly won.

Hoyt's stomach contracted on a sharp inhale of breath as she reached beneath his boxers and took him firmly in hand. He fit fully into her palm, hard and ready for her, but she was determined to torture him a bit longer.

Maintaining a steady pressure with her hands, she bent and took him fully into her mouth, molding her lips to his hard length. His low moans were like music, a resounding chorus of life and desire and pleasure that filled her with a special sort of happiness.

She'd been so worried for him and so convinced that he'd come to harm because of her. It was gratifying to know that not only was he well, but that she could give him pleasure like this. Pleasure that erased the pain of what had come before.

"Reese." Her name came out on a low guttural growl.

Ignoring the urgency, she pressed on, continuing the slow torture of her tongue against his flesh.

"Reese." He added an insistent tug against her shoulders, effectively ending the torture she so willingly gave. "We'll do this together."

"Have I missed something?" she teased. "Because it feels like we're together."

Before she could say anything else, he had her flipped over on her back, his broad frame covering her. With no question as to his destination, he filled her in one long thrust, drawing a scream from her as her body responded to the sensual intrusion.

She'd had no idea her orgasm was so close, but she came hard in a matter of thrusts as their bodies joined and rejoined. Before she could even catch her breath, another wave built, even higher than the first, her body going bowstring tight as she built toward another orgasm.

With no other recourse and nowhere else she'd rather be, Reese held on to his shoulders and welcomed him home. And as the pleasure wove in and over and around both of them, she knew the truth.

She loved him.

With everything she was and everything she'd ever be.

Although it was hard to argue with an afternoon of lovemaking, Hoyt felt his sour mood return as evening gave way to night.

Reese went back to school tomorrow.

He knew he couldn't hold her back. On one hand, he didn't want to. She was a grown woman and she'd more than proven herself capable of living her life. It wasn't his place to suggest otherwise. But damn it, how was he supposed to look at her and not want to wrap her up in his arms and keep her safe?

Especially when a faceless threat still lurked in the shadows.

"I think that dish is dry," Arden said, interrupting his thoughts.

Hoyt looked up from where he been steadily polishing a dinner plate and saw that his sister was right. "Sorry. Just a little distracted."

"I think you're entitled. And to be fair, I think we've all been a little distracted over the past few days."

"Understatement of the century."

She took the plate from his hand and gestured him

toward the kitchen table. "Let's sit down for a few minutes."

He had a unique relationship with each of his siblings. With Ace, it was very much big brother, a smattering of idolizing his oldest sibling and, even to this day, a solid bit of hero worship. With Tate, it was typical older brother–little brother stuff that veered easily from friendship to fisticuffs and back to friendship again.

With Arden...

Well, with Arden, the sands always shifted. But no matter how much they changed, he always knew she would lead him to solid ground. His baby sister was not only the most mature of all of them but saw with startling clarity what the rest of them resisted like a plague of locusts.

"Want to tell me what's going on?" she asked.

"You mean besides, as Reese put it, having a barn fall on me?"

Arden winced. "That's not funny."

"Reese didn't say it like it was funny. In fact, she seemed rather pissed about it."

"Well," she sighed. "Okay then."

He let his gaze drift around the kitchen. The peach colored walls, the feel of the Texas pine beneath his fingers as he drummed on the tabletop and the thick bench seat he sat on, hewn and sanded down by his grandfather's own hand: all of it was as familiar to Hoyt as his own face.

It should have brought comfort.

But all he seemed to find were shadows lurking in every corner.

"Reese goes back to school tomorrow."

"I know. I also know Belle has put extra patrols on

and the security office at the school is well aware of the need to look out for her."

"It's a risk."

"Do you honestly think it's a risk? Reese informed everyone she needed to, all the way up to the superintendent. No one has asked her to sit out the semester."

They hadn't, and even Hoyt thought that was strange. "And why is that? A local teacher, with her father's recent history, who has been the victim of several attacks, and no one even bats an eye?"

"The way Reese told it, both the assistant principal and the PTA went to bat for her."

It still bugged him, but if the Parent–Teacher Association was willing to bring her back, he could hardly complain. Even as the what-ifs rattled around his brain endlessly.

What if they'd missed something? What if the threat was redirected at her? What if someone got to her before he could stop them?

"They're supposed to be looking out for the students," he finally said, the argument sounding weak to his ears.

"I'd say it's looking out for the students when they ensure that one of the best teachers in the state is kept on, as well as watched out for."

"Come on, Arden. Why are you taking their side? Aren't you worried about this?"

"Worried? I'm worried every day. But that doesn't mean I can stop living my life. Doesn't mean any of us can. What sort of example would Reese set for those kids if she turned tail and ran?"

Hoyt wanted to agree with her—wanted to see her teaching as a higher calling—but every time he got close to accepting the idea of Reese being gone every day, something inside him curled up in fear. Bone-deep, gut-curling fear.

Arden reached out and laid a hand over his forearm. He eyed her slender fingers and steady palm, the gesture so like his mother's that it hurt. "Is something else going on here?"

"What's that supposed to mean? I'm worried about her. I'm worried about all of us."

"That's not what I asked."

While he knew she'd get them to firm footing eventually, at the moment, his sister's changing moods were rather like quicksand. "Out with it."

"It wasn't Reese's house that was attacked. It was ours."

"I know."

"Maybe this doesn't have anything to do with her. Maybe this has something to do with us."

While he'd certainly considered it—heck, they'd even all had a family meeting on it—Hoyt still found it odd that the incidents would begin at Reese's and then move over to Reynolds Station. "Belle has been tugging at that line, too. Hell, Arden, so have all of us."

"And nothing's clicked."

"Not a single damn thing."

"Then let me go back to the question you didn't answer."

He knew what was coming. He'd been a part of this family too long not to. "When am I going to admit that I'm in love with Reese?"

Arden rubbed a hand over his arm. "That's the one."

"Hell if I know."

* * *

Reese sat in the back of the Midnight Pass High School auditorium, pleased and relieved and more than a little touched by the wall of support that flanked both sides of her on a row of uncomfortable metal folding chairs. Hoyt sat next to her, with Ace and Arden on his left and Belle and Tate on Reese's right. Belle had even worn her police uniform, a visible sign of the law and order she worked so hard to keep.

When they'd first suggested they were all joining her for the first PTA meeting of the year, she'd tried to convince them to stay home. Yet, here she was with her phalanx of cowboys, a cop and a yoga instructor to boot.

An ass-kicking yoga instructor, Reese added to herself.

She'd been back at school a little over a week now and other than the stress of crafting interesting lesson plans that had the power to mow through teenage hormones and getting to know her new students, there hadn't been any further danger. While she knew she should have been happy about that, a strange sense of hovering high in the air without a net had taken root and wouldn't quite leave her.

Nor had the same sensation seemingly left the Reynolds family.

Everyone was living on high alert, waiting for something to happen.

At this point, she was spending more time at their house than her own. But on the nights she did choose to stay in her own place, Hoyt insisted on staying with her. Their lovemaking had continued, unabated, and she kept wondering when that would all go away, too.

And then she'd admonish herself to enjoy the moment and push it all to the back of her mind.

Which then made room for thoughts of whomever had set fire to the barn and had likely left her a hairy spider on her porch and a bullet hole through her kitchen.

Vicious cycle, she mentally sighed to herself before returning to listen to the PTA president's droning voice. A voice she ought to pay more attention to since it was the woman and her board who'd smoothed the way for her to start the school year.

Once the fire happened in the Reynolds barn, she knew she had to alert the school to what was going on. While she needed her teaching contract, she also needed to feel that her students were safe and secure. Where she'd anticipated a difficult conversation, she'd been amazed to find an old acquaintance in her corner.

Loretta Green. No, Reese corrected herself. She was Loretta Chapel now.

Who would have thought?

She'd never gotten the idea that Jamie's high school girlfriend liked her, if she paid any attention to her at all. But it had been Loretta who'd defended her to the PTA and stressed her value to the school. This support, just like that from the Reynolds family who flanked her even now, had been as unexpected as it was welcome.

Of course, who knew how long it would last when the PTA also discovered her pregnancy, but one step at a time, Arden kept reassuring her.

The discussions of funding, school board projects and student scholarships moved along rather quickly and before she knew it, Reese and her entourage were standing at the coffee table enjoying a bit of Southern hospitality after the meeting.

"I can't say the meeting was all that riveting, but there is cake."

Belle patted Tate's back before dipping her fork into a slice of pound cake. "Why do you think I always volunteer each month for this assignment?"

"That's what you do over here?" Tate asked.

"You bet."

"I feel so swindled." Tate pulled his fiancée close. "But now that I know your secrets I may have to tag along. These meetings are open to the public. And I am a good, honest, upstanding taxpayer, as you all know."

Despite the congenial air, Hoyt had remained quiet, saying no to the cake and sipping on his disposable cup of coffee. She moved closer to him, careful not to make too big a personal display that others might notice as too intimate. "You doing okay over here?"

"I'll be better when we get out of here."

Panic fluttered through her, putting the nerves that had settled throughout the evening back on edge. "Did you see something?"

"No. But this place doesn't sit right with me."

Reese thought back over the evening and struggled to understand what was bothering him. There hadn't been any contentious moments. Nor had there been anyone out of place or unexpected attending the meeting.

"I hate to break it to you, but this was about as run-of-the-mill and boring as these meetings get."

"Do you have to stay much longer?"

She waited a beat, looking deep into his green eyes. Not a single hint of humor or ease reflected back at her. "Let me just say a few goodbyes and we can get out here."

She nearly made it over to Jake, determined to thank her assistant principal once again, when Loretta found her.

"Reese. It's been so long."

Loretta pulled her close for a hug and Reese hung on, touched by the warm greeting. "It has been. How old are your boys now?"

"Ten and eight. Ben and Charlie."

Reese saw the pride and delight as Loretta said her sons' names and marveled at the fact that she'd be doing the same in a matter of months.

"How is your mother doing?"

"She's doing well. It's nice to see her start to have something to look forward to."

"Oh?" Loretta's eyebrows lifted, clearly excited by fresh gossip. "What is she excited about?"

"Um. Um, well, she's been thinking about selling the house," Reese improvised, the fib tripping off her tongue. "Already got word she may have a buyer."

Damn, what was wrong with her?

She'd nearly spilled the beans about her pregnancy to a board member of the PTA. Was she trying to get fired? Add on that now she had to try to explain to her mother why the Midnight Pass grapevine was suddenly expecting her house to go up for sale, and she was doing a fine job over cake and coffee. When Hoyt glowered at her from the corner, she figured it was her cue to wrap it up. "Listen, I hate to run, but it's going to be an early morning tomorrow. It has been so nice to see you."

"You, too, Reese."

Fully aware her evening was at an end, Reese made eye contact with Jake and gave him a quick wave and nod before following Hoyt and his family out the door.

And for no reason at all, she felt a strange chill run the length of her spine.

* * *

It's been too long.

The words rumbled over and over in her mind as Loretta did her level best to tuck Charlie into bed. He'd been a demon for the sitter—at least according to the sitter—and now she was stuck peeling him off the ceiling because the idiot girl had given in and allowed him an advance dive into the candy she'd bought on sale and hidden for Halloween.

Charlie had found it.

He always found it. If it was candy, soda or cookies, the child had a nose like a bloodhound. Too bad that same sense of discovery didn't work on broccoli, carrots or anything else green, yellow or orange.

"Mommy?"

"What, sweetie?" She brushed his hair off his forehead with her index finger, pleased to see his eyelids getting droopy.

"What's love?"

"Love? It's how I feel about you."

"No." Charlie shook his small head. "Love-love. Like grown-ups have."

Loretta was curious what had prompted the question and didn't have to wait long as Ben hissed from the single bed on the opposite side of the room, "You're not supposed to ask that, Charlie."

Her interest grew sharper as it was obvious something had started the line of questions. "What's this about?"

"Nothing," Ben said before rolling over on his side to face the wall.

"No. It's not nothing," Loretta probed. "What's with this question?"

Special Ops Cowboy

"Daddy has a girlfriend." Charlie came out with it first, despite Ben's protest to shut up from the other bed.

Loretta fought the heavy rage that seemed to build from the very center of her being. Forcing a calm she didn't feel, she opted to leverage the more chatty of her two children. "When did this happen?"

"Last time we were there," Charlie said, eager to share the details he had now that he knew the cat was out of the bag.

"Did you meet Dad's new girlfriend?"

"Uh-huh." Charlie nodded his head. "Her name is Casey."

"She's nice," Ben said, chiming in. "She's twenty-six."

Loretta had no idea how her children knew that or why the very thought bothered her so much. She'd been young once. Not that long ago, in fact. She even still remembered what it felt like to be young and hopeful and looking toward the future. "Good for her."

"Daddy told us not to tell you," Charlie said.

"Well, that's just silly," Loretta reassured him. "You can tell me anything."

"Anything?" Ben asked.

Loretta got up, crossed over to Ben's bed, taking a seat beside him. "Of course you can. I'm your mom. You can always talk to me."

"Okay. I love you."

"I love you, too," came winging back from the other side of the room.

Loretta kissed Ben first, then crossed to Charlie's bed, pressing her lips to his forehead. She'd done very little in her life that she was proud of, but without question she was proud of her boys.

What would it have been like if Jamie waited for her down the hall? Or even better, sat in the room with her, tucking the boys in? If these were his sons and the four of them were a family.

If things had been different.

An image of Reese Grantham standing close with Hoyt Reynolds, their heads bent toward each other in intimate conversation, filled her mind's eye.

Jamie never got a future, but Reese sure seemed to. One that had her obviously ingratiating herself with the Reynolds family while she screwed Hoyt Reynolds every chance she got.

Oh, she'd been kind enough tonight, playing to her position on the board and being all nicey-nicey after the meeting. But it was fake. The ice queen didn't do nice.

And what was that weird thing about Reese's mother? She kept her ear to the ground and she hadn't heard a damn word about anyone wanting to buy the home of a former serial killer.

No way.

Which meant Reese had slipped and her mother was looking forward to something else.

A wedding?

Regardless of what it was, Reese had lied. Straight to her face. And Loretta would do well to keep that in mind.

Chapter 17

Reese placed a hand over the bulging closure to her shorts and knew she had to give in to the inevitable. On a small sigh, she pushed back from her kitchen table and hunted up a safety pin in her utility drawer. It wasn't the best solution, but it would have to do until she could get a few new items.

Her pregnancy might not be evident to others, but it was more than evident to her. Flowy blouses had served her well so far at work and she figured if anyone noticed she'd gained weight they'd think she'd gone on a few too many ice-cream benders over the summer months. But soon, everyone would know ice cream had nothing to do with it.

And then she'd no longer be able to hide the truth.

It had been three weeks since school started. There hadn't been any further incidents, nor had Belle and her team found any clues. Which was more than a little disconcerting as the heat of August gave way to an even hotter spell in September, but what could any of them do?

And while it might be disconcerting, life had to go on, Reese thought as she took her seat again and returned to the stack of essays that needed grading. As each day passed, she'd gotten herself back into a rhythm.

Even if the beat was different from anything she'd ever experienced.

Was she living with Hoyt? Was he living with her? Since they spent every night together, either at her place or over at the ranch, it was hard to convince herself differently, but they also hadn't declared what they were doing with each other, either.

In fact, both of them seemed determined not to put a name on what was between them.

While it flew in the face of everything she wanted for herself, another part of her was unwilling to upset the status quo. Because the status quo meant Hoyt was a part of her life. If she started unsettling things, he might go away, and then where would she be?

Even if she was miserable where she was.

Her mother had broached the subject a few times but hadn't pressed too hard. Although Serena was still struggling with the loss of Reese's father, as Reese had hoped, the news of the baby had her mother looking more toward the future than the past. She'd even gotten a laugh from Serena when she'd heard about the slip to Loretta at the PTA meeting. Oddly, the story seemed to have put a notion in her mother's head and just the prior weekend Serena had mentioned maybe looking for a new house.

Yes sirree, they were definitely moving to a new beat.

The sound of the front door opening and closing sent a shot of excitement through her and Reese imagined the tall, rangy cowboy that was about to come down her hallway and around the corner into her kitchen.

She wasn't disappointed.

The jeans that seemed custom-made for his hips and long legs molded to his frame. A faded old T-shirt with the Reynolds Station brand over the chest would, she already knew, be soft to the touch. And, in a surprising departure, she saw a pair of flip-flops on his feet.

"Arden getting to you?"

"Hmm?" he asked as he set dinner—a loaded pizza—down on the counter.

"I'm not sure I've ever seen your bare feet outside of bed."

"These?" Hoyt stared down at his feet and flopped the heel a few times. "A necessary evil."

"Why's that?"

"Because my boots are covered in a sizeable layer of cow dung I haven't had a chance to wash off. My sister banned them from the house and, seeing as how I now have half a stable, they're in there waiting for a good cleaning."

"I know you own more than one pair of boots."

"My other pair are currently covered in rattlesnake venom and are even now lathered in a homemade solution Arden has insisted I use to clean them off."

"Snakes?"

He was reaching for plates in the cabinet but turned at her question. "Well, yeah."

"You deal with snake venom often enough to have a cleaning solution?"

"Of course we do."

The sweet images of her child running wild and free over Reynolds land came to a crashing halt. "How often do you deal with snakes attempting to feast on your boots?"

"Reese. This is south Texas. Don't tell me you've never dealt with a snake before."

"Yes. With a shotgun and a dead-eyed aim. Not attempting to sink its teeth into my shoes."

"I'm sorry if it bothers you but it's fairly routine."

"Don't the horses get upset?"

"Stink usually senses them well before I do."

She shook her head, not sure if she was horrified or impressed that his horse had more sense and awareness than he did. Daft man.

"What are you working on?" He set their two plates opposite where she had her papers laid out before his hand snaked out and grabbed one of the essays on top. His eyebrows rose higher and higher as he read the title. "Slut Shaming in Puritan Times."

Reese added napkins to their place settings from a small wicker basket in the center of the table. "We kicked off the year with a bang. *The Scarlet Letter*'s up first and the kids seemed awed I used those exact words."

"Times sure have changed. Did old Mrs. Rovner even know the word *slut*?"

"Our English teacher was far more sly than we gave her credit for."

"And how would you know that?" Hoyt asked around a big bite of his pizza.

"She was an adult. As kids, we can't imagine that they know more, especially anything having to do with sex. And then you hit an age when you realize they knew it all a whole lot longer than you did."

"Seems like you've made a study of this."

"How can't I? I'm going to be that big sly surprise when the kids find out I'm pregnant."

The words tumbled out, one after another, all the fear and concern that had dogged her since the day she discovered she was pregnant spilling out.

Hoyt laid down his pizza, his green gaze penetrating. "What's this about?"

"The reality of what's about to happen. My pants barely fit. I'm gaining weight. And it's only a matter of a few more weeks where gauzy blouses aren't going to cover me any longer."

"So you tell them. Talk to your boss and tell him what's going on. You're pregnant, not contagious. They certainly can't fire you."

"No, but they don't have to be happy about having an unwed pregnant teacher on staff. The PTA went to bat for me after the events in August. I can't see this ingratiating me in their eyes, especially after they put their necks on the line."

"So what do you want to do about it? Marriage is still on the table. In fact, I don't recall ever taking it off."

On the table?

Just like a box of pizza or the papers she was grading?

On. The. Table.

"What's that supposed to mean?"

Seemingly oblivious to the quiet tenor of her voice, Hoyt pressed on. "It means the same thing it meant a month ago. Let's get married. Our child will have my name and so will you."

"Oh, my heart's aflutter. How romantic, Hoyt."

"What do you want from me? You're the one sitting here saying it's some sort of crime to be an unwed pregnant woman. I don't fully understand why, but I have the solution to this problem you seem to think is so huge. Let's get married."

Reese fought against the rising tide of panic that swelled through her midsection like a tsunami. Didn't she want the status quo? Wasn't she all about not rocking the boat and changing the dynamic between them?

More, those swirling dreams that haunted her in the middle of the night—the ones where she and Hoyt made a family—were right here, just in reach.

Didn't she want that?

Hell and damnation, wasn't the man giving her exactly what she'd asked for?

When a resounding, miserable *no* echoed through her mind, Reese knew the truth. Yes, she wanted to marry him. And yes, she wanted her child to have his name.

But she couldn't do it without love. Great, sweeping, forever kind of love.

It's what she wanted—all she'd ever wanted, really—and she'd be damned if she was going to settle for less.

"I think it's time to take it off the table."

Hoyt knew he'd messed up, but almost eighteen hours later, he still couldn't figure out exactly where he'd gone wrong. It had all gone off the rails when he'd mentioned marriage, but hell if he could figure out why. Wasn't that what she wanted?

Marriage fixed her problem.

And damn it all, it was what *he* wanted. Why had that gotten lost in all this?

I think it's time to take it off the table.

What was that even supposed to mean?

Although he'd left her to finish grading papers in the kitchen and set himself up in the living room to watch a ball game, he refused to leave her alone for the night. They might not like each other very much right now but he wasn't leaving her to fend for herself.

Which had made cleaning his boots the perfect antidote to a sleepless night and aimless day. His boots were caked and smelly and he attacked them with a wire brush over a heap of newspaper, satisfied to have something to take his anger out on. The past few weeks had been full of long tiring days as they all did double duty, keeping up with all the normal work of the ranch while trying to get the stables rebuilt as fast as possible.

He'd initially resisted the idea of bringing in hired hands—it invited too many strangers onto the property—but finally had to give in when the extra work had gotten overwhelming for everyone. Belle's promise to background-check the contractor they'd found, along with the construction company's reputation for fully vetting their employees, had finally put his mind at ease.

And it meant he had a halfway functional barn, the frame up, the roof even now over his head and about half the stalls rebuilt.

Ace had taken the fire as an opportunity to upgrade and institute state-of-the art cameras and computers, an updated feeding system and a new way to manage the locks and security. They couldn't ensure there'd never be another disaster, but the fire had hit far too close for comfort and they were going to do everything in their power to protect their animals.

Even now, the thought of Stink locked in his stall filled him with a cold, bone-wrenching fear that ate at him in his quiet moments.

Or at least the quiet moments that didn't involve him doing his level best to figure out Reese Grantham.

"Those boots look pretty good. But they might not if you keep scrubbing them that way."

Hoyt looked up from where he attacked his boot, pleasantly surprised to see Belle. "You look pretty as a picture. But I don't usually see you at three in the afternoon. Playing hooky?"

"Sort of. I got an afternoon off and decided I'd like to enjoy it at home. What will officially be home in two more months." She did a little twirl and Hoyt smiled in spite of his bad mood.

Two months.

His brother would be a married man and Hoyt would gain a new sister.

Things had moved fast, but that was after they'd moved incredibly slow. Like a ten-year glacier that finally came unmoored back in April.

Since then, he'd gotten his brother back. The happy-go-lucky persona Tate had projected all these years had actually become happy. No longer a facade. Tate had a new lease on life. It was an amazing testament to his love for Belle and the reality of finding true and lasting happiness.

"Arden said you were in here in the laundry room with that delightfully smelly footware and I figured it was a good time to poke my nose in where it doesn't belong."

Hoyt avoided a sigh and settled in, seeing as how Belle was about to give her new sister status a test-drive.

He dropped a lone, now-clean boot on the ground next to the other one, prepared to listen.

"Arden said you looked upset when you came home."

"She thinks anyone not in touch with their chakras or their twelfth eye or their personal Zen state has a problem."

"Usually I'd agree with her, but I saw Reese this morning, too, when I made my rounds at the school. She looked pretty miserable, too."

Okay, Reynolds, settle in. This wasn't just a test-drive, but a race around the whole damn track.

"We had words last night. It's fine. It'll blow over."

"You proposed to her?"

Hoyt did look up then, his patience at an end. "She told you that?"

"Not at first. I had to drag it out of her. To be fair, the woman's gone without her morning caffeine for over three months. It was a weak moment."

Some small part of him knew Belle was trying to lighten the mood, but he was hard-pressed to find any measure of understanding.

And what was wrong with Reese?

It wasn't bad enough she'd rejected his offer of marriage, but now she was running her mouth to everyone else? He already felt like a rejected fool, and now his family knew about it. Who else had she told?

Even as he thought it, Hoyt knew that was unfair. Whatever the two of them might have, it wasn't about gossip or innuendo or exposing one another's privacy.

But damn, he wasn't ready to have this conversation. Especially not with a well-meaning Belle who was looking at him like some poor, abandoned kitten mewling on the side of the road.

"Look. I—" He broke off at the hard shake of her head.

"I'm sorry. My phone's been buzzing like a hive of angry bees. You mind if I answer this?"

"Sure. Fine."

He'd nearly turned away when he saw her frown as she read the face of her phone. But it was a few moments later when the bottom absolutely dropped out from beneath him.

"Yes, this is Detective Granger…What happened at the high school?…Is the building on lockdown?…I'll be right there."

Aimless words filled Reese's mind as she sat tied to her desk chair. Words like *why* and *how* and *this is impossible* screamed through her mind, even as she remained silent. More purposeful words followed. Three, actually.

I love Hoyt.

While she wished she had screamed them over and over when she'd had the chance, Reese still remained silent. Silent and wary as twenty-five pairs of eyes stared solemnly back at her from their desks, their attention swinging from her to the woman who stood in front of the whiteboard, a gun in hand.

No one dared to move.

A few kids cried silently at their desks, but all had taken their seats when the announcement had gone out to shelter in place.

And it had been Reese herself who'd let in the enemy. She'd assumed Loretta Chapel needed a place to hide and had let the woman in, barring the door behind her.

How could she have known Loretta was the one everyone was hiding from?

"Loretta." Reese kept her voice calm, trying again to initiate the woman in conversation. "Please let the children go. They've done nothing."

Loretta didn't move. She just kept staring at the windows covered by drawn shades, occasionally muttering to herself.

Reese assumed there was movement outside. The police and the FBI and SWAT had to be out there. Preparing. Watching. Doing *something* useful.

But for the past half hour, all she knew was the horror of what lived inside. Here. In her classroom.

This was meant to be a safe place. A haven for learning and camaraderie and youth. People built their futures here. They found who they were going to be here.

They didn't have to sit staring at a deranged woman with a gun pointed at their heads.

"Loretta. Please talk to me. Tell me what this is about. You're a mother of two beautiful boys. You're on the PTA. Surely you can tell me what's wrong?"

Reese wasn't sure if it was the mention of Loretta's children or the fact that she'd attempted conversation every few minutes, but it finally seemed to work. Loretta turned dull eyes toward her, even as the gun never wavered in her hand. "You really don't know?"

"No," Reese sputtered, taken aback by the question. *Know what?* "What should I know?"

"Typical." A harsh laugh accompanied the assessment but that was all Reese got.

Buoyed by the fact she'd gotten anything, she pushed once more. "Loretta. Please. Let the kids go."

Loretta stared at the class and Reese had the eerie

sense that Loretta was looking through them. "What kids?"

"The ones. Here. The children in my class." Although she knew fifteen-year-olds chaffed at being called children, Reese kept pressing the point, willing something to break through whatever shield of madness had gripped the woman.

"I remember this room. When we were all here. When Jamie and I used to sit back there and hold hands before homeroom."

Jamie?

Reese struggled to keep up, her panic for her students at odds with the mention of her brother. What did Jamie have to do with this?

"I know you dated my brother. I didn't know this was your classroom."

"Here. The cafeteria. The auditorium. The football field. All of them bring back so many memories of how he and I used to be." Something sparked beneath the dull. "Before."

"I know."

That spark leaped to flame instantly, Reese's words the obvious accelerant. "Of course you know. You've always known but you've ignored it! Damn priss of the century, the little perfect ice queen who was never willing to dirty your hands or accept that your brother had a problem."

Protests leaped to her lips but Reese held them back. Whatever twisted assessment Loretta had arrived at relative to Reese's relationship with Jamie wasn't steeped in anything but the woman's mad musings.

So she held back.

And struggled to find a way to get them all out of there.

* * *

Hoyt paced the Midnight Pass High School parking lot, as close to the police barriers as he could get, and wondered how it had come to this. A gun in the school? An active shooter, although no one had yet been reported wounded. Every child and teacher accounted for except one class.

Reese and her students.

Belle had assured him repeatedly that they had eyes on the place and were even now getting sharpshooters positioned in the ceiling. It should have provided comfort, but it didn't. Nor did it give any rhyme, reason or clue why a member of the PTA was holding Reese and her students hostage.

Belle waved him over, a listening device in hand. "Reese has her talking. You're well trained and even though you have a vested interest in this, we need all the help we can get."

"Of course."

"I want your take on this." Belle waved the earpiece. "Anything you can think of or might know. Anything Reese might have mentioned. We need it all."

Hoyt shoved in the offered earpiece and felt the tears welling as he heard Reese's voice. Clear and sweet, it was the voice of the woman he loved.

And now, she was the hostage of some deranged shooter.

"Loretta. Please talk to me. Tell me what this is about. You're a mother of two beautiful boys. You're on the PTA. Surely you can tell me what's wrong?"

"You really don't know?" Hoyt heard the emptiness in the other woman's voice and it cratered through him

like a ramrod to the chest. He couldn't see her but that only made what he heard that much more devastating.

The absence of hope.

"No. What should I know?"

"Typical."

The laugh was high and tinny to his ears, but Hoyt drowned it out as something else Reese had said tried to take root in his mind. When the thought didn't come, he keyed back into the exchange, desperate for some glimmer of hope that Reese could pull the woman out of this untenable path.

"I remember this room. When we were all here. When Jamie and I used to sit back there and hold hands before homeroom."

"I know you dated my brother. I didn't know this was your classroom."

"Here. The cafeteria. The auditorium. The football field. All of them bring back so many memories of how he and I used to be. Before."

"I know."

"Of course you know. You've always known..."

Hoyt struggled to bring it into focus. *What* was so important?

The PTA?

Loretta dating Reese's brother, Jamie?

The fact that they went to school together?

Hoyt dismissed them all one by one. Belle and the assembled team knew all of that already.

But what—

"Her kids!" Hoyt reached for Belle, gripping her fingers. "Loretta has kids. Two boys. You need to use them. Use the kids."

"Use the kids how? The cops have them back at the station with a social worker."

Once more, his training kicked in. He'd assessed and identified. Now it was time to act.

"We need to break through, and her kids are the only way. Put them on the PA."

Reese stared at the clock and knew they were losing precious time. Loretta hadn't said much more to her in the past twenty minutes, nor had she given any indication she was even mentally present, despite Reese's repeated attempts to engage her in further conversation.

Maybe it was for the best.

The more time that went by, the more time SWAT had to get into position.

But shouldn't they have been in position already? If there was a shot to take, wouldn't they have taken it?

"Loretta Chapel."

The sudden blast of the loudspeaker pulled all of them upright. Everyone's gazes snapped to attention, twenty-five students waiting for whatever would come next in the discussion between two adults.

"Loretta. Maybe they want to make a deal." Reese kept her voice calm, forcing a bit of hope into the words. "I know you want these children to get out of here safely. That's what they want, too."

The loudspeaker echoed again, suddenly a new presence filling the room. "We'd like to talk to you. Miss Grantham has an intercom on her wall, to the left of the door. You can speak back to us from there."

Loretta made no move to acknowledge the initiation, nor did she move from her place by the window, the gun never wavering from where it aimed at Reese.

"Mommy?" A child's voice warbled through the intercom, the first sound to truly get Loretta's attention. "Mommy, it's Ben."

Reese wanted to say something but she waited, willing that small little voice to be the tool that would finally break through.

"Are you there?"

Before Ben could say anything else, another small voice came in. "Why are there all these police around?"

"Shh, Charlie," Ben admonished. "We have to help."

"The police help," Charlie said, his little boy voice matter-of-fact.

Reese saw it, the moment the veneer of bravado and boldness cracked wide open, revealing a wellspring of pain and hurt that had clearly accompanied Loretta for far too long. The woman stood and walked toward Reese, lowering the gun as she moved closer. "Take this. Please."

Reese hesitated for the briefest moment, hardly daring to hope, before she took the offered piece, both of them wordless.

And then she watched Loretta walk to the unit mounted on the wall, depressing the button to speak to her children.

"Ben. Charlie. Are you still there?"

"Hi, Mommy!" Twin shouts greeted her as hard racking sobs convulsed her shoulders.

All that had happened seemed to fade. The weeks of terror and the near loss of life, human and equine in the Reynolds stable and the raw, achy fear that had filled her today as Loretta took over her classroom.

It would all still be there.

But in this moment, someone Reese knew was hurting. Someone who she might still be able to help, unlike her father, who hadn't asked for help before it was too late.

Determined, she cracked open the shotgun, removing every bullet and stowing them in her desk drawer. She crossed to the row of desks and her still unmoving students and handed the gun to Rob Consuelos in the front row. His love of hunting was well known and she directed him to lock the gun in her back cabinet.

And then she went to stand beside Loretta.

Her hand on the speaker, she let her voice ring out, determined to be the light for this woman who clearly lived in such darkness.

"This is Reese Grantham. I'm with Loretta Chapel and twenty-five of my students. We are all safe. Mrs. Chapel is unarmed. When you're ready, I can open the classroom door. Please let my students come out first."

A set of instructions came winging back over the intercom, and with calm, steady movements, her students filed out one by one, hands up as they were told.

"Thank you, Robbie." Reese saw he'd done as instructed, handing her the cabinet key before he filed out behind his class.

It was only after they were gone and she was alone with Loretta that Reese pulled her close. Anger and fear still worked through her system like heavy sludge, but she fought to get past it. Somewhere in that swirling morass, Reese fought to find the small light that kept telling her someone else's child wasn't going to pay the same price she was for a parent's loss of self. "It's going to be okay."

Loretta shook her head. "I don't think that it is."

"Your boys still have a mother. You can work on everything else."

Belle walked into the room first, followed by several agents and SWAT team members covered head to toe in gear. Loretta went to them willingly, the anger that had carried her into the school and through the classroom evaporating like mist. In its place, Reese saw fear and resignation, but she also saw resolve.

And as Belle and the team escorted the woman out, Reese hoped desperately that she could find peace.

Hoyt kept edging closer to the front entrance of the school, desperate to race through the barriers to get to Reese. He'd heard her voice, calm and competent, asking the officers to come in and he'd never been more proud.

He'd also never been more relieved and more ready to get down on his knees and beg than in that moment.

Belle came into view through the glass front doors, along with the officers who'd followed her in. Loretta Chapel was between them, her hands behind her back as she was escorted out of the building.

Someone from child services had already taken Loretta's boys off campus and were even now arranging for them to spend time with their grandparents. Hoyt wanted to ask after them, but things had happened so fast. He knew Belle would have the details and he was committed to seeing that they both had help through the coming months and years.

But for now, all he wanted was Reese.

And then he saw her, that tall, slim form, the coltish gait and the thick swirl of dark hair that framed her face before falling down her back.

His Reese.

His love.

She'd barely cleared the door when he was there, pulling her close, desperate for the feel of her in his arms. He held her against his chest, his arms tight around her, hers equally tight around his waist.

"I thought I'd lost you."

"I know." She whispered it, nodding her head against his neck as they both stood there and simply held on.

"Why'd she do it?"

"I think it was about Jamie—" Reese started, before stopping. "Just like I think that's why my father acted, but who really knows? I only hope she can get help. That her boys can get help."

Light.

Reese Grantham was goodness and light and air and every breath that filled his lungs. He knew it—had always known it—but listening to her defend a woman who had nearly killed her only proved it.

She saw the good in others. Even more important, she believed it was there.

A light breeze wafted around them, still redolent with heat but just strong enough to suggest that fall was coming. She was alive and unharmed and took the time to savor the warmth that wrapped around them both.

"You're sure you're okay?"

"I'm fine. No." She laughed, dropping an arm to press against her stomach. "We're fine. You won't believe this, but I even felt the baby flutter just now as I was walking out to you."

"The baby moved?" Hoyt pulled back, his hands

going to her stomach, covering the one she'd placed there. "Just now?"

"Yes. It was the lightest touch, but I can only hope it's the first of many." She pressed a kiss to his lips. "The first of many greetings he or she gives to their father."

Hoyt pulled her close, unable to do anything but hold her and reassure himself that she was okay and that the baby was still nestled safe in her womb. "It's a welcome to our future. For all three of us."

"Our future?"

"Marriage is back on the table, Ms. Grantham, whether you like it or not."

"Oh, Hoyt, you and those romantic words." She wrapped her arms around his neck. "I love every single one of them."

"And I love you. It took me too long to say it, but know I mean those words and all they imply. I love you and I want a future with you. I want a commitment with you. I want a life with you."

"Most one-night stands don't end in marriage proposals."

He nearly interrupted her before she laid a finger over his lips. "Please. Let me finish."

He nodded as she continued on.

"That's what I kept telling myself. That this couldn't be real or that there couldn't be anything between us because of how we started. But I was wrong."

Hoyt knew she was wrong because he'd traveled that twisty path himself, confused when he kept coming up with the answer that he loved her, but unable to see quite how they'd gotten there.

Only they had gotten there. Together.

"Is there any hope our child won't be even more stubborn than us?" she asked, her smile broad.

"I suspect our combined genes can't produce anything else."

"Oh, I can think of something," Reese said, as she linked their arms and directed them toward the parking lot.

"What's that?"

"A few more to round out our undoubtedly stubborn brood."

"More children is definitely on the table, too, my love."

"I guess it's a good thing we got a head start." She pressed her smiling lips against his and Hoyt's curved in response.

He couldn't agree more.

It was a very good idea.

* * * * *

Don't miss Tate and Belle's story—
The Cowboy's Deadly Mission,
*the first book in Addison Fox's thrilling
Midnight Pass, Texas, miniseries—*
available now from Harlequin Romantic Suspense!